Bad Characters

Books by Jean Stafford

Boston Adventure
The Mountain Lion
Children Are Bored on Sunday
The Catherine Wheel
Elephi, the Cat with a High I.Q.
The Interior Castle (collection)
Bad Characters

Bad Characters

Jean Stafford

Farrar, Straus & Company, New York

In memory of Joe
with all my heart

Author's Note

I do not look on all the characters in these stories as bad;
some of them do have wicked hearts, but as many of them
are victims. Emily Vanderpool, who narrates the title
story and who acknowledges that she has a bad character,
is someone I knew well as a child; indeed, I often occupied her skin and, looking back, I think that while
she was notional and stubborn and a trial to her kin,
her talent for iniquity was feeble—she wanted to be a
road-agent but she hadn't a chance. Her troubles
stemmed from the low company she kept, but she did

not seek these parties out: they found her. It is a wide-spread human experience. The strenuous young man in "A Reasonable Facsimile" is not bad, he is merely poisonous and the sociologist in "Caveat Emptor" is, by reason of his calling, awful and to be avoided at all cost but he isn't bad. The personification of rectitude, Judge Bay, who appears in several of the stories, and Landlady Placer in "In the Zoo" go on my black list which is headed by the name of Frau Professor Galt in the short novel, "A Winter's Tale."

Except for "Caveat Emptor," which appeared in *Mademoiselle*, "The Captain's Gift" in *The Sewanee Review*, and "A Winter's Tale" in *New Short Novels* (Ballantine Books), all of these stories originally came out in *The New Yorker*.

Jean Stafford

Contents

Bad Characters

Bad Characters

Up until I learned my lesson in a very bitter way, I never had more than one friend at a time, and my friendships, though ardent, were short. When they ended and I was sent packing in unforgetting indignation, it was always my fault; I would swear vilely in front of a girl I knew to be pious and prim (by the time I was eight, the most grandiloquent gangster could have added nothing to my vocabulary—I had an awful tongue), or I would call a Tenderfoot Scout a sissy or make fun of athletics to the daughter of the high-school coach. These outbursts came without plan; I would simply one day, in the middle of a game of Russian bank or a hike or a conversation, be possessed with a passion to be by myself, and my lips instantly and without warning would accommodate me. My friend was never more surprised than I was when this irrevocable slander, this terrible, talented invective, came boiling out of my mouth.

Afterward, when I had got the solitude I had wanted, I was dismayed, for I did not like it. Then I would sadly finish the game of cards as if someone were still across the table from me; I would sit down on the mesa and through a glaze of tears would watch my friend departing with outraged strides; mournfully, I would talk to myself. Because I had already alienated everyone I knew, I then had nowhere to turn, so a famine set in and I would have no companion but Muff, the cat, who loathed all human beings except, significantly, me—truly. She bit and scratched the hands that fed her, she arched her back like a Halloween cat if someone kindly tried to pet her, she hissed, laid her ears flat to her skull, growled, fluffed up her tail into a great bush and flailed it like a bullwhack. But she purred for me, she patted me with her paws, keeping her claws in their velvet scabbards. She was not only an ill-natured cat, she was also badly dressed. She was a calico, and the distribution of her colors was a mess; she looked as if she had been left out in the rain and her paint had run. She had a Roman nose as the result of some early injury, her tail was skinny, she had a perfectly venomous look in her eye. My family said—my family discriminated against me—that I was much closer kin to Muff than I was to any of them. To tease me into a tantrum, my brother

Jack and my sister Stella often called me Kitty instead of Emily. Little Tess did not dare, because she knew I'd chloroform her if she did. Jack, the meanest boy I have ever known in my life, called me Polecat and talked about my mania for fish, which, it so happened, I despised. The name would have been far more appropriate for *him*, since he trapped skunks up in the foothills—we lived in Adams, Colorado—and quite often, because he was careless and foolhardy, his clothes had to be buried, and even when that was done, he sometimes was sent home from school on the complaint of girls sitting next to him.

Along about Christmastime when I was eleven, I was making a snowman with Virgil Meade in his backyard, and all of a sudden, just as we had got around to the right arm, I had to be alone. So I called him a son of a sea cook, said it was common knowledge that his mother had bedbugs and that his father, a dentist and the deputy marshal, was a bootlegger on the side. For a moment, Virgil was too aghast to speak—a little earlier we had agreed to marry someday and become millionaires—and then, with a bellow of fury, he knocked me down and washed my face in snow. I saw stars, and black balls bounced before my eyes. When finally he let me up, we were both crying, and he hollered that if I didn't get off his property that instant, his father would arrest me and send me to Canon City. I trudged slowly home, half frozen, critically sick at heart. So it was old Muff again for me for quite some time. Old Muff, that is, until I met Lottie Jump, although "met" is a euphemism for the way I first encountered her.

I saw Lottie for the first time one afternoon in our own kitchen, stealing a chocolate cake. Stella and Jack had not come home from school yet—not having my difficult disposition, they were popular, and they were at their friends' houses, pulling taffy, I suppose, making popcorn balls, playing casino, having fun—and my mother had taken Tess with her to visit a friend in one of the T.B. sanitariums. I was alone in the house, and making a funny-looking Christmas card, although I had no one to send it to. When I heard someone in the kitchen, I thought it was Mother home early, and I went out to ask her why the green pine tree I had pasted on a square of red paper looked as if it were falling down. And there, instead of Mother and my baby sister, was this pale, conspicuous child in the act of lifting the glass cover from the devil's-food my mother had taken out of the oven an hour before and set on the plant shelf by the window. The child had her back to me, and when she heard my footfall, she wheeled with an amazing look of fear and hatred on her pinched and pasty face. Simultaneously, she put the cover over the cake again, and then she stood motionless as if she were under a spell.

I was scared, for I was not sure what was happening, and anyhow it gives you a turn to find a stranger in the kitchen in the middle of the afternoon, even if the stranger is only a skinny child in a moldy coat and sopping-wet basketball shoes. Between us there was a lengthy silence, but there was a great deal of noise in the room: the alarm clock ticked smugly; the teakettle simmered patiently on the back of the stove; Muff, cross at having been waked up, thumped her tail against the side of the terrarium in the window where she had been sleeping—contrary to orders—among the geraniums This went on, it seemed to me, for hours and hours while that tall, sickly girl and I confronted each other. When, after a long time, she did open her mouth, it was to tell a prodigious lie. "I came to see if you'd like to play with me," she said. I think she sighed and stole a sidelong and regretful glance at the cake.

Beggars cannot be choosers, and I had been missing Virgil so sorely, as well as all those other dear friends forever lost to me, that in spite of her flagrance (she had never clapped eyes on me before, she had had no way of knowing there was a creature of my age in the house—she had come in like a hobo to steal my mother's cake), I was flattered and consoled. I asked her name and, learning it, believed my ears no better than my eyes: Lottie Jump. What on earth! What on earth— you surely will agree with me—and yet when I told her mine, Emily Vanderpool, she laughed until she coughed and gasped. "Beg pardon," she said. "Names like them always hit my funny bone. There was this towhead boy in school named Delbert Saxonfield." I saw no connec- tion and I was insulted (what's so funny about Vander- pool, I'd like to know), but Lottie Jump was, techni- cally, my guest and I *was* lonesome, so I asked her, since she had spoken of playing with me, if she knew how to play Andy-I-Over. She said "Naw." It turned out that she did not know how to play any games at all; she couldn't do anything and didn't want to do anything; her only recreation and her only gift was, and always had been, stealing. But this I did not know at the time.

As it happened, it was too cold and snowy to play outdoors that day anyhow, and after I had run through my list of indoor games and Lottie had shaken her head at all of them (when I spoke of Parcheesi, she went "Ugh!" and pretended to be sick), she suggested that we look through my mother's bureau drawers. This did not strike me as strange at all, for it was one of my favorite things to do, and I led the way to Mother's bedroom without a moment's hesitation. I loved the smell of the lavender she kept in gauze bags among her chamois gloves and linen handkerchiefs and filmy scarves; there was a pink fascinator knitted of something as fine as spider's thread, and it made me go quite soft—I wasn't soft as a rule, I was as hard as nails and I gave my mother a rough time—to think of her wearing it around her head as she waltzed on the ice in the bygone days. We examined stockings, nightgowns, camisoles, strings of beads, and mosaic pins, keepsake buttons from dresses worn on memorial occasions, tortoiseshell combs, and a transformation made from Aunt Joey's hair when she had racily had it bobbed. Lottie admired particularly a blue cloisonné perfume flask with ferns and peacocks on it. "Hey," she said, "this sure is cute. I like thing-daddies like this here." But very abruptly she got bored and said, "Let's talk instead. In the front room." I agreed, a little perplexed this time, because I had been about to show her a remarkable powder box that played *The Blue Danube*. We went into the parlor, where Lottie looked at her image in the pier glass for quite a while and with great absorption, as if she had never seen herself before. Then she moved over to the window seat and knelt on it, looking out at the front walk. She kept her hands in the pockets of her thin dark-red coat; once she took out one of her dirty paws to rub her nose for a minute and I saw a bulge in that pocket, like a bunch of jackstones. I know now that it wasn't jackstones, it was my mother's perfume flask; I thought at the time her hands were cold and that that was why she kept them put away, for I had noticed that she had no mittens.

Lottie did most of the talking, and while she talked, she never once looked at me but kept her eyes fixed on the approach to our house. She told me that her family had come to Adams a month before from Muskogee, Oklahoma, where her father, before he got tuberculosis, had been a brakeman on the Frisco. Now they lived down by Arapahoe Creek, on the west side of town, in one of the cottages of a wretched settlement made up of people so poor and so sick—for in nearly every ramshackle house someone was coughing himself to death—that each time I went past I blushed with guilt because my shoes were sound and my coat was warm and I was well. I wished that Lottie had not told me where she lived, but she was not aware of any pathos in her family's situation, and, indeed, it was with a certain boastfulness that she told me her mother was the short-order cook at the Comanche Café (she pronounced this word in one syllable), which I knew was the dirtiest, darkest, smelliest place in town, patronized by coal miners who never washed their faces and sometimes had such dangerous fights after drinking dago red that the sheriff had to come. Laughing, Lottie told me that her mother was half Indian, and, laughing even harder, she said that her brother didn't have any brains and had never been to school. She herself was eleven years old, but she was only in the third grade, because teachers had always had it in for her—making her go to the blackboard and all like that when she was tired. She hated school—she went to Ashton, on North Hill, and that was

why I had never seen her, for I went to Carlyle Hill—
and she especially hated the teacher, Miss Cudahy, who
had a head shaped like a pine cone and who had killed
several people with her ruler. Lottie loved the movies
("Not them Western ones or the ones with apes in," she
said. "Ones about hugging and kissing. I love it when
they die in that big old soft bed with the curtains up
top, and he comes in and says 'Don't leave me, Mar-
guerite de la Mar' "), and she loved to ride in cars. She
loved Mr. Goodbars, and if there was one thing she
despised worse than another it was tapioca. ("Pa calls it
fish eyes. He calls floating island horse spit. He's a big
piece of cheese. I hate him.") She did not like cats (Muff
was now sitting on the mantelpiece, glaring like an
owl); she kind of liked snakes—except cottonmouths
and rattlers—because she found them kind of funny;
she had once seen a goat eat a tin can. She said that one
of these days she would take me downtown—it was a
slowpoke town, she said, a one-horse burg (I had never
heard such gaudy, cynical talk and was trying to memorize it all)—if I would get some money for the trolley
fare; she hated to walk, and I ought to be proud that she
had walked all the way from Arapahoe Creek today for
the sole solitary purpose of seeing me.

Seeing our freshly baked dessert in the window was a
more likely story, but I did not care, for I was deeply
impressed by this bold, sassy girl from Oklahoma and
greatly admired the poise with which she aired her
prejudices. Lottie Jump was certainly nothing to look
at. She was tall and made of skin and bones; she was
evilly ugly, and her clothes were a disgrace, not just ill-
fitting and old and ragged but dirty, unmentionably so;
clearly she did not wash much or brush her teeth, which

were notched like a saw, and small and brown (it crossed my mind that perhaps she chewed tobacco); her long, lank hair looked as if it might have nits. But she had personality. She made me think of one of those self-contained dogs whose home is where his handout is and who travels alone but, if it suits him to, will become the leader of a pack. She was aloof, never looking at me, but amiable in the way she kept calling me "kid." I liked her enormously, and presently I told her so.

At this, she turned around and smiled at me. Her smile was the smile of a jack-o'-lantern—high, wide, and handsome. When it was over, no trace of it remained. "Well, that's keen, kid, and I like you, too," she said in her downright Muskogee accent. She gave me a long, appraising look. Her eyes were the color of mud. "Listen, kid, how much do you like me?"

"I like you loads, Lottie," I said. "Better than anybody else, and I'm not kidding."

"You want to be pals?"

"Do I!" I cried. So *there,* Virgil Meade, you big fat hootnanny, I thought.

"All right, kid, we'll be pals." And she held out her hand for me to shake. I had to go and get it, for she did not alter her position on the window seat. It was a dry, cold hand, and the grip was severe, with more a feeling of bones in it than friendliness.

Lottie turned and scanned our path and scanned the sidewalk beyond, and then she said, in a lower voice, "Do you know how to lift?"

"Lift?" I wondered if she meant to lift *her.* I was sure I could do it, since she was so skinny, but I couldn't imagine why she would want me to.

"Shoplift, I mean. Like in the five-and-dime."

I did not know the term, and Lottie scowled at my stupidity.

"*Steal*, for crying in the beer!" she said impatiently. This she said so loudly that Muff jumped down from the mantel and left the room in contempt.

I was thrilled to death and shocked to pieces. "Stealing is a sin," I said. "You get put in jail for it."

"Ish ka bibble! I should worry if it's a sin or not," said Lottie, with a shrug. "And they'll never put a smart old whatsis like *me* in jail. It's fun, stealing is— it's a picnic. I'll teach you if you want to learn, kid." Shamelessly she winked at me and grinned again. (That grin! She could have taken it off her face and put it on the table.) And she added, "If you don't, we can't be pals, because lifting is the only kind of playing I like. I hate those dumb games like Statues. Kick-the-Can— phooey!"

I was torn between agitation (I went to Sunday school and knew already about morality; Judge Bay, a crabby old man who loved to punish sinners, was a friend of my father's and once had given Jack a lecture on the criminal mind when he came to call and found Jack looking up an answer in his arithmetic book) and excitement over the daring invitation to misconduct myself in so perilous a way. My life, on reflection, looked deadly prim; all I'd ever done to vary the monotony of it was to swear. I knew that Lottie Jump meant what she said—that I could have her friendship only on her terms (plainly, she had gone it alone for a long time and could go it alone for the rest of her life)— and although I trembled like an aspen and my heart went pitapat, I said, "I want to be pals with you, Lottie."

"All right, Vanderpool," said Lottie, and got off the window seat. "I wouldn't go braggin' about it if I was you. I wouldn't go telling my ma and pa and the next-door neighbor that you and Lottie Jump are going down to the five-and-dime next Saturday aft and lift us some nice rings and garters and things like that. I mean it, kid." And she drew the back of her forefinger across her throat and made a dire face.

"I won't. I promise I won't. My *gosh*, why would I?"

"That's the ticket," said Lottie, with a grin. "I'll meet you at the trolley shelter at two o'clock. You have the money. For both down and up. I ain't going to climb up that ornery hill after I've had my fun."

"Yes, Lottie," I said. Where was I going to get twenty cents? I was going to have to start stealing before she even taught me how. Lottie was facing the center of the room, but she had eyes in the back of her head, and she whirled around back to the window; my mother and Tess were turning in our front path.

"Back way," I whispered, and in a moment Lottie was gone; the swinging door that usually squeaked did not make a sound as she vanished through it. I listened and I never heard the back door open and close. Nor did I hear her, in a split second, lift the glass cover and remove that cake designed to feed six people.

I was restless and snappish between Wednesday afternoon and Saturday. When Mother found the cake was gone, she scolded me for not keeping my ears cocked.

She assumed, naturally, that a tramp had taken it, for she knew I hadn't eaten it; I never ate anything if I could help it (except for raw potatoes, which I loved) and had been known as a problem feeder from the beginning of my life. At first it occurred to me to have a tantrum and bring her around to my point of view: my tantrums scared the living daylights out of her because my veins stood out and I turned blue and couldn't get my breath. But I rejected this for a more sensible plan. I said, "It just so happens I didn't hear anything. But if I had, I suppose you wish I had gone out in the kitchen and let the robber cut me up into a million little tiny pieces with his sword. You wouldn't even bury me. You'd just put me on the dump. *I* know who's wanted in this family and who isn't." Tears of sorrow, not of anger, came in powerful tides and I groped blindly to the bedroom I shared with Stella, where I lay on my bed and shook with big, silent *weltschmerzlich* sobs. Mother followed me immediately, and so did Tess, and both of them comforted me and told me how much they loved me. I said they didn't; they said they did. Presently, I got a headache, as I always did when I cried, so I got to have an aspirin and a cold cloth on my head, and when Jack and Stella came home, they had to be quiet. I heard Jack say, "Emily Vanderpool is the biggest polecat in the U.S.A. Whyn't she go in the kitchen and say, 'Hands up'? He woulda lit out." And Mother said, "Sh-h-h! You don't want your sister to be sick, do you?" Muff, not realizing that Lottie had replaced her, came in and curled up at my thigh, purring lustily; I found myself glad that she had left the room before Lottie Jump made her proposition to me, and in gratitude I stroked her unattractive head.

Other things happened. Mother discovered the loss of her perfume flask and talked about nothing else at meals for two whole days. Luckily, it did not occur to her that it had been stolen—she simply thought she had mislaid it—but her monomania got on my father's nerves and he lashed out at her and at the rest of us. And because I was the cause of it all and my conscience was after me with red-hot pokers, I finally *had* to have a tantrum. I slammed my fork down in the middle of supper on the second day and yelled, "If you don't stop fighting, I'm going to kill myself. Yammer, yammer, nag, nag!" And I put my fingers in my ears and squeezed my eyes tight shut and screamed so the whole county could hear, "Shut *up!*" And then I lost my breath and began to turn blue. Daddy hastily apologized to everyone, and Mother said she was sorry for carrying on so about a trinket that had nothing but sentimental value—she was just vexed with herself for being careless, that was all, and she wasn't going to say another word about it.

I never heard so many references to stealing and cake, and even to Oklahoma (ordinarily no one mentioned Oklahoma once in a month of Sundays) and the ten-cent store as I did throughout those next days. I myself once made a ghastly slip and said something to Stella about "the five-and-dime." "The five-and-*dime!*" she exclaimed. "Where'd you get *that* kind of talk? Do you by any chance have reference to the *ten-cent store?*"

The worst of all was Friday night—the very night before I was to meet Lottie Jump—when Judge Bay came to play two-handed pinochle with Daddy. The Judge, a giant in intimidating haberdashery—for some reason, the white piping on his vest bespoke, for me,

handcuffs and prison bars—and with an aura of disapproval for almost everything on earth except what
pertained directly to himself, was telling Daddy, before
they began their game, about the infamous vandalism
that had been going on among the college students. "I
have reason to believe that there are girls in this gang as
well as boys," he said. "They ransack vacant houses and
take everything. In one house on Pleasant Street, up
there by the Catholic Church, there wasn't anything to
take, so they took the kitchen sink. Wasn't a question of
taking everything *but*—they took the kitchen sink."

"What ever would they want with a kitchen sink?"
asked my mother.

"Mischief," replied the Judge. "If we ever catch them
and if they come within my jurisdiction, I can tell you I
will give them no quarter. A thief, in my opinion, is the
lowest of the low."

Mother told about the chocolate cake. By now, the
fiction was so factual in my mind that each time I
thought of it I saw a funny-paper bum in baggy pants
held up by rope, a hat with holes through which tufts of
hair stuck up, shoes from which his toes protruded, a
disreputable stubble on his face; he came up beneath
the open window where the devil's food was cooling and
he stole it and hotfooted it for the woods, where his
companion was frying a small fish in a beat-up skillet. It
never crossed my mind any longer that Lottie Jump
had hooked that delicious cake.

Judge Bay was properly impressed. "If you will steal a
chocolate cake, if you will steal a kitchen sink, you will
steal diamonds and money. The small child who pilfers
a penny from his mother's pocketbook has started down
a path that may lead him to holding up a bank."

It was a good thing I had no homework that night, for I could not possibly have concentrated. We were all sent to our rooms, because the pinochle players had to have absolute quiet. I spent the evening doing cross-stitch. I was making a bureau runner for a Christmas present; as in the case of the Christmas card, I had no one to give it to, but now I decided to give it to Lottie Jump's mother. Stella was reading *Black Beauty,* crying. It was an interminable evening. Stella went to bed first; I saw to that, because I didn't want her lying there awake listening to me talking in my sleep. Besides, I didn't want her to see me tearing open the cardboard box—the one in the shape of a church, which held my Christmas Sunday-school offering. Over the door of the church was this shaming legend: "My mite for the poor widow." When Stella had begun to grind her teeth in her first deep sleep, I took twenty cents away from the poor widow, whoever she was (the owner of the kitchen sink, no doubt), for the trolley fare, and secreted it and the remaining three pennies in the pocket of my middy. I wrapped the money well in a handkerchief and buttoned the pocket and hung my skirt over the middy. And then I tore the paper church into bits—the heavens opened and Judge Bay came toward me with a double-barrelled shotgun—and hid the bits under a pile of pajamas. I did not sleep one wink. Except that I must have, because of the stupendous nightmares that kept wrenching the flesh off my skeleton and caused me to come close to perishing of thirst; once I fell out of bed and hit my head on Stella's ice skates. I would have waked her up and given her a piece of my mind for leaving them in such a lousy place, but then I remembered: I wanted *no* commotion of any kind.

I couldn't eat breakfast and I couldn't eat lunch. Old Johnny-on-the-spot Jack kept saying, *"Poor* Polecat. Polecat wants her fish for dinner."* Mother made an abortive attempt to take my temperature. And when all that hullabaloo subsided, I was nearly in the soup because Mother asked me to mind Tess while she went to the sanitarium to see Mrs. Rogers, who, all of a sudden, was too sick to have anyone but grownups near her. Stella couldn't stay with the baby, because she had to go to ballet, and Jack couldn't, because he had to go up to the mesa and empty his traps. ("No, they *can't* wait. You want my skins to rot in this hot-one-day-cold-the-next weather?") I was arguing and whining when the telephone rang. Mother went to answer it and came back with a look of great sadness; Mrs. Rogers, she had learned, had had another hemorrhage. So Mother would not be going to the sanitarium after all and I needn't stay with Tess.

By the time I left the house, I was as cross as a bear. I felt awful about the widow's mite and I felt awful for being mean about staying with Tess, for Mrs. Rogers was a kind old lady, in a cozy blue hug-me-tight and an old-fangled boudoir cap, dying here all alone; she was a friend of Grandma's and had lived just down the street from her in Missouri, and all in the world Mrs. Rogers wanted to do was go back home and lie down in her own big bedroom in her own big, high-ceilinged house and have Grandma and other members of the Eastern Star come in from time to time to say hello. But they wouldn't let her go home; they were going to kill or cure her. I could not help feeling that my hardness of heart and evil of intention had had a good deal to do with her new crisis; right at the very same minute I had been saying "Does that old Mrs. Methusclah *always* have to spoil my fun?" the poor wasted thing was probably coughing up her blood and saying to the nurse, "Tell Emily Vanderpool not to mind me, she can run and play."

I had a bad character, I know that, but my badness never gave me half the enjoyment Jack and Stella thought it did. A good deal of the time I wanted to eat lye. I was certainly having no fun now, thinking of Mrs. Rogers and of depriving that poor widow of bread and milk; what if this penniless woman without a husband had a dog to feed, too? Or a baby? And besides, I didn't want to go downtown to steal anything from the ten-cent store; I didn't want to see Lottie Jump again—not really, for I knew in my bones that that girl was trouble with a capital "T." And still, in our short meeting she had mesmerized me; I would think about her style of talking and the expert way she had made off with the perfume flask and the cake (how had she carried the cake through the streets without being noticed?) and be bowled over, for the part of me that did not love God was a black-hearted villain. And apart from these considerations, I had some sort of idea that if I did not keep my appointment with Lottie Jump, she would somehow get revenge; she had seemed a girl of purpose. So, revolted and fascinated, brave and lily-livered, I plodded along through the snow in my flopping galoshes up toward the Chautauqua, where the trolley stop was. On my way, I passed Virgil Meade's house; there was not just a snowman, there was a whole snow family in the back yard, and Virgil himself was throwing a stick for his dog. I was delighted to see that he was alone.

Lottie, who was sitting on a bench in the shelter eating a Mr. Goodbar, looked the same as she had the other time except that she was wearing an amazing hat. I think I had expected her to have a black handkerchief over the lower part of her face or to be wearing a Jesse James waistcoat. But I had never thought of a hat. It was felt; it was the color of cooked meat; it had some flowers appliquéd on the front of it; it had no brim, but rose straight up to a very considerable height, like a monument. It sat so low on her forehead and it was so tight that it looked, in a way, like part of her.

"How's every little thing, bub?" she said, licking her candy wrapper.

"Fine, Lottie," I said, freshly awed.

A silence fell. I drank some water from the drinking fountain, sat down, fastened my galoshes, and unfastened them again.

"My mother's teeth grow wrong way to," said Lottie, and showed me what she meant: the lower teeth were in front of the upper ones. "That so-called trolley car takes its own sweet time. This town is blah."

To save the honor of my home town, the trolley came scraping and groaning up the hill just then, its bell clanging with an idiotic frenzy, and ground to a stop. Its broad, proud cowcatcher was filled with dirty snow, in the middle of which rested a tomato can, put there, probably, by somebody who was bored to death and couldn't think of anything else to do—I did a lot of

pointless things like that on lonesome Saturday afternoons. It was the custom of this trolley car, a rather
mysterious one, to pause at the shelter for five minutes
while the conductor, who was either Mr. Jansen or Mr.
Peck, depending on whether it was the A.M. run or the
P.M., got out and stretched and smoked and spit. Sometimes the passengers got out, too, acting like sightseers
whose destination was this sturdy stucco gazebo instead
of, as it really was, the Piggly Wiggly or the Nelson Dry.
You expected them to take snapshots of the drinking
fountain or of the Chautauqua meeting house up on
the hill. And when they all got back in the car, you
expected them to exchange intelligent observations on
the aborigines and the ruins they had seen.

Today there were no passengers, and as soon as Mr.
Peck got out and began staring at the mountains as if
he had never seen them before while he made himself a
cigarette, Lottie, in her tall hat (was it something like
the Inspector's hat in the Katzenjammer Kids?), got into
the car, motioning me to follow. I put our nickels in
the empty box and joined her on the very last double
seat. It was only then that she mapped out the plan for
the afternoon, in a low but still insouciant voice. The
hat—she did not apologize for it, she simply referred to
it as "my hat"—was to be the repository of whatever we
stole. In the future, it would be advisable for me to have
one like it. (How? Surely it was unique. The flowers, I
saw on closer examination, were tulips, but they were
blue, and a very unsettling shade of blue.) I was to
engage a clerk on one side of the counter, asking her the
price of, let's say, a tube of Daggett & Ramsdell vanishing cream, while Lottie would lift a round comb or a
barrette or a hair net or whatever on the other side.

Then, at a signal, I would decide against the vanishing cream and would move on to the next counter that she indicated. The signal was interesting; it was to be the raising of her hat from the rear—"like I've got the itch and gotta scratch," she said. I was relieved that I was to have no part in the actual stealing, and I was touched that Lottie, who was going to do all the work, said we would "go halvers" on the take. She asked me if there was anything in particular I wanted—she herself had nothing special in mind and was going to shop around first—and I said I would like some rubber gloves. This request was entirely spontaneous; I had never before in my life thought of rubber gloves in one way or another, but a psychologist—or Judge Bay—might have said that this was most significant and that I was planning at that moment to go on from petty larceny to bigger game, armed with a weapon on which I wished to leave no fingerprints.

On the way downtown, quite a few people got on the trolley, and they all gave us such peculiar looks that I was chickenhearted until I realized it must be Lottie's hat they were looking at. No wonder. I kept looking at it myself out of the corner of my eye; it was like a watermelon standing on end. No, it was like a tremendous test tube. On this trip—a slow one, for the trolley pottered through that part of town in a desultory, neighborly way, even going into areas where no one lived—Lottie told me some of the things she had stolen in Muskogee and here in Adams. They included a white satin prayer book (think of it!), Mr. Goodbars by the thousands (she had probably never paid for a Mr. Goodbar in her life), a dinner ring valued at two dollars, a strawberry emery, several cans of corn, some shoelaces, a set of poker chips, countless pencils, four spark plugs ("Pa had this old car, see, and it was broke, so we took 'er to get fixed; I'll build me a radio with 'em sometime —you know? Listen in on them ear muffs to Tulsa?"), a Boy Scout knife, and a Girl Scout folding cup. She made a regular practice of going through the pockets of the coats in the cloakroom every day at recess, but she had never found anything there worth a red cent and was about to give that up. Once, she had taken a gold pencil from a teacher's desk and had got caught—she was sure that this was one of the reasons she was only in the third grade. Of this unjust experience, she said, "The old hoot owl! If I was drivin' in a car on a lonesome stretch and she was settin' beside me, I'd wait till we got to a pile of gravel and then I'd stop and say, 'Git out, Miss Priss.' She'd git out, all right."

Since Lottie was so frank, I was emboldened at last to ask her what she had done with the cake. She faced me with her grin; this grin, in combination with the hat, gave me a surprise from which I have never recovered. "I ate it up," she said. "I went in your garage and sat on your daddy's old tires and ate it. It was pretty good."

There were two ten-cent stores side by side in our town, Kresge's and Woolworth's, and as we walked down the main street toward them, Lottie played with a Yo-Yo. Since the street was thronged with Christmas shoppers and farmers in for Saturday, this was no ordinary accomplishment; all in all, Lottie Jump was someone to be reckoned with. I cannot say that I was proud to be seen with her; the fact is that I hoped I would not meet anyone I knew, and I thanked my lucky stars that Jack was up in the hills with his dead skunks, because if he had seen her with that lid and that Yo-Yo, I would never have heard the last of it. But in another way I *was* proud to be with her; in a smaller hemisphere, in one that included only her and me, I was swaggering—I felt like Somebody, marching along beside this lofty Somebody from Oklahoma who was going to hold up the dime store.

There is nothing like Woolworth's at Christmastime. It smells of peanut brittle and terrible chocolate candy, Djer-Kiss talcum powder and Ben Hur Perfume—smells sourly of tinsel and waxily of artificial poinsettias. The crowds are made up largely of children and women, with here and there a deliberative old man; the women are buying ribbons and wrappings and Christmas cards, and the children are buying asbestos pot holders for their mothers and, for their fathers, suède bookmarks with a burnt-in design that says "A good book is a good friend" or "Souvenir from the Garden of the Gods." It is very noisy. The salesgirls are forever ringing their bells and asking the floorwalker to bring them change for a five; babies in go-carts are screaming as parcels fall on their heads; the women, waving rolls of red tissue paper, try to attract the attention of the harried girl behind the counter. ("Miss! All I want is this one batch of the red. Can't I just give you the dime?" And the girl, beside herself, mottled with vexation, cries back, "Has to be rung up, Moddom, that's the rule.") There is pandemonium at the toy counter, where things are being tested by the customers—wound up, set off, tooted, pounded, made to say "Maaaah-Maaaah!" There is very little gaiety in the scene and, in fact, those baffled old men look as if they were walking over their own dead bodies, but there is an atmosphere of carnival, nevertheless, and as soon as Lottie and I entered the doors of Woolworth's golden-and-vermilion bedlam, I grew giddy and hot—not pleasantly so. The feeling, indeed, was distinctly disagreeable, like the beginning of a stomach upset.

Lottie gave me a nudge and said softly, "Go look at the envelopes. I want some rubber bands."

This counter was relatively uncrowded (the seasonal stationery supplies—the Christmas cards and wrapping paper and stickers—were at a separate counter), and I went around to examine some very beautiful letter paper; it was pale pink and it had a border of roses all around it. The clerk here was a cheerful middle-aged woman wearing an apron, and she was giving all her attention to a seedy old man who could not make up his mind between mucilage and paste. "Take your time, Dad," she said. "Compared to the rest of the girls, I'm on my vacation." The old man, holding a tube in one hand and a bottle in the other, looked at her vaguely and said, "I want it for stamps. Sometimes I write a letter and stamp it and then don't mail it and steam the stamp off. Must have ninety cents' worth of stamps like that." The woman laughed. "I know what you mean," she said. "I get mad and write a letter and then I tear it up." The old man gave her a condescending look and said, "That so? But I don't suppose yours are of a political nature." He bent his gaze again to the choice of adhesives.

This first undertaking was duck soup for Lottie. I did not even have to exchange a word with the woman; I saw Miss Fagin lift up *that hat* and give me the high sign, and we moved away, she down one aisle and I down the other, now and again catching a glimpse of each other through the throngs. We met at the foot of the second counter, where notions were sold.

"Fun, huh?" said Lottie, and I nodded, although I felt wholly dreary. "I want some crochet hooks," she said. "Price the rickrack."

This time the clerk was adding up her receipts and did not even look at me or at a woman who was angrily and in vain trying to buy a paper of pins. Out went Lottie's scrawny hand, up went her domed chimney. In this way for some time she bagged sitting birds: a tea strainer (there was no one at all at that counter), a box of Mrs. Carpenter's All Purpose Nails, the rubber gloves I had said I wanted, and four packages of mixed seeds. Now you have some idea of the size of Lottie Jump's hat.

I was nervous, not from being her accomplice but from being in this crowd on an empty stomach, and I was getting tired—we had been in the store for at least an hour—and the whole enterprise seemed pointless. There wasn't a thing in her hat I wanted—not even the rubber gloves. But in exact proportion as my spirits descended, Lottie's rose; clearly she had only been target-practicing and now she was moving in for the kill.

We met beside the books of paper dolls, for reconnaissance. "I'm gonna get me a pair of pearl beads," said Lottie. "You go fuss with the hairpins, hear?"

Luck, combined with her skill, would have stayed with Lottie, and her hat would have been a cornucopia by the end of the afternoon if, at the very moment her hand went out for the string of beads, that idiosyncrasy of mine had not struck me full force. I had never known it to come with so few preliminaries; probably this was so because I was oppressed by all the masses of bodies poking and pushing me, and all the open mouths breathing in my face. Anyhow, right then, at the crucial time, I *had to be alone*.

I stood staring down at the bone hairpins for a moment, and when the girl behind the counter said, "What kind does Mother want, hon? What color is Mother's hair?" I looked past her and across at Lottie and I said, "Your brother isn't the only one in your family that doesn't have any brains." The clerk, astonished, turned to look where I was looking and caught Lottie in the act of lifting up her hat to put the pearls inside. She had unwisely chosen a long strand and was having a little trouble; I had the nasty thought that it looked as if her brains were leaking out.

The clerk, not able to deal with this emergency herself, frantically punched her bell and cried, "Floorwalker! Mr. Bellamy! I've caught a thief!"

Momentarily there was a violent hush—then such a clamor as you have never heard. Bells rang, babies howled, crockery crashed to the floor as people stumbled in their rush to the arena.

Mr. Bellamy, nineteen years old but broad of shoulder and jaw, was instantly standing beside Lottie, holding her arm with one hand while with the other he removed her hat to reveal to the overjoyed audience that incredible array of merchandise. Her hair all wild, her face a mask of innocent bewilderment, Lottie Jump, the scurvy thing, pretended to be deaf and dumb. She pointed at the rubber gloves and then she pointed at me, and Mr. Bellamy, able at last to prove his mettle, said "Aha!" and, still holding Lottie, moved around the counter to me and grabbed *my* arm. He gave the hat to the clerk and asked her kindly to accompany him and his redhanded catch to the manager's office.

I don't know where Lottie is now—whether she is on the stage or in jail. If her performance after our arrest meant anything, the first is quite as likely as the second. (I never saw her again, and for all I know she lit out of town that night on a freight train. Or perhaps her whole family decamped as suddenly as they had arrived; ours was a most transient population. You can be sure I made no attempt to find her again, and for months I avoided going anywhere near Arapahoe Creek or North Hill.) She never said a word but kept making signs with her fingers, adlibbing the whole thing. They tested her hearing by shooting off a popgun right in her ear and she never batted an eyelid.

They called up my father, and he came over from the Safeway on the double. I heard very little of what he said because I was crying so hard, but one thing I did hear him say was "Well young lady, I guess you've seen to it that I'll have to part company with my good friend Judge Bay." I tried to defend myself, but it was useless. The manager, Mr. Bellamy, the clerk, and my father patted Lottie on the shoulder, and the clerk said, "Poor,

afflicted child." For being a poor, afflicted child, they
gave her a bag of hard candy, and she gave them the
most fraudulent smile of gratitude, and slobbered a
little, and shuffled out, holding her empty hat in front
of her like a beggar-man. I hate Lottie Jump to this day,
but I have to hand it to her—she was a genius.

The floorwalker would have liked to see me sentenced
to the reform school for life, I am sure, but the manager
said that considering this was my first offense, he would
let my father attend to my punishment. The old-maid
clerk, who looked precisely like Emmy Schmalz, clucked
her tongue and shook her head at me. My father hustled
me out of the office and out of the store and into the car
and home, muttering the entire time; now and again
I'd hear the words "morals" and "nowadays."

What's the use of telling the rest? You know what
happened. Daddy on second thoughts decided not to
hang his head in front of Judge Bay but to make use of
his friendship in this time of need, and he took me to
see the scary old curmudgeon at his house. All I remember of that long declamation, during which the Judge
sat behind his desk never taking his eyes off me, was the
warning "I want you to give this a great deal of thought,
Miss. I want you to search and seek in the innermost
corners of your conscience and root out every bit of badness." Oh, *him!* Why, listen, if I'd rooted out all the
badness in me, there wouldn't have been anything left
of me. My mother cried for days because she had
nurtured an outlaw and was ashamed to show her face
at the neighborhood store; my father was silent, and he
often looked at me. Stella, who was a prig, said, "And
to think you did it at *Christmas*time!" As for Jack—
well, Jack a couple of times did not know how close he

came to seeing glory when I had a butcher knife in my hand. It was Polecat this and Polecat that until I nearly went off my rocker. Tess, of course, didn't know what was going on, and asked so many questions that finally I told her to go to Helen Hunt Jackson in a savage tone of voice.

Good old Muff.

It is not true that you don't learn by experience. At any rate, I did that time. I began immediately to have two or three friends at a time—to be sure, because of the stigma on me, they were by no means the élite of Carlyle Hill Grade—and never again when that terrible need to be alone arose did I let fly. I would say, instead, "I've got a headache. I'll have to go home and take an aspirin," or "Gosh all hemlocks, I forgot—I've got to go to the dentist."

After the scandal died down, I got into the Campfire Girls. It was through pull, of course, since Stella had been a respected member for two years and my mother was a friend of the leader. But it turned out all right. Even Muff did not miss our periods of companionship, because about that time she grew up and started having literally millions of kittens.

The End
of a Career

By those of Angelica Early's friends who were given to
hyperbole, she was called, throughout her life, one of
the most beautiful women in the world's history. And
those of more restraint left history out of their appraisal
but said that Mrs. Early was certainly one of the most
beautiful of living women. She had been, the legend
was, a nymph in her cradle (a doting, bibulous aunt was
fond, over cocktails, of describing the queenly baby's

pretty bed—gilded and swan-shaped, lined with China silk of a blue that matched the infant eyes, and festooned with Mechlin caught into loops with rosettes), and in her silvery coffin she was a goddess. At her funeral, her friends mourned with as much bitterness as sorrow that such a treasure should be consigned to the eyeless and impartial earth; they felt robbed; they felt as if one of the wonders of the world had been demolished by wanton marauders. "It's wrong of God to bury His own masterpiece," said the tipsy aunt, "and if that's blasphemy, I'll take the consequences, for I'm not at all sure I want to go on living in a world that doesn't contain Angelica."

Between her alpha and omega, a span of fifty years, Mrs. Early enjoyed a shimmering international fame that derived almost entirely from the inspired and faultless *esprit de corps* of her flesh and her bones and her blood; never were the features and the colors of a face in such serene and unassailable agreement, never had a skeleton been more singularly honored by the integument it wore. And Angelica, aware of her responsibility to her beholders, dedicated herself to the cultivation of her gift and the maintenance of her role in life with the same chastity and discipline that guide a girl who has been called to the service of God.

Angelica's marriage, entered upon when she was twenty-two and her husband was ten years older, puzzled everyone, for Major Clayton Early was not a connoisseur of the complex civilization that had produced his wife's sterling beauty but was, instead, concerned with low forms of plant life, with primitive societies, and with big game. He was an accomplished huntsman—alarming heads and horns and hides covered the walls of his den, together with enlarged photographs of himself standing with his right foot planted firmly upon the neck of a dead beast—and an uneducated but passionate explorer, and he was away most of the time, shooting cats in Africa or making and recording observations in the miasmas of Matto Grosso and the mephitic verdure of the Malay Peninsula. While he was away, Angelica, too, was away a good deal of the time—on islands, in Europe, upstate, down South—and for only a few months of the year were they simultaneously in residence in a professionally and pompously decorated maisonette that overlooked Central Park. When Major Early was in town, he enjoyed being host to large dinner parties, at which, more often than not, he ran off reels on reels of crepuscular and agitated movies that showed savages eating from communal pots, savages dancing and drumming, savages in council, savages accepting the white man's offerings of chewing gum and mechanical toys; there were, as well, many feet of film devoted to tarantulas, apes, termite mounds, and orchidaceous plants. His commentary was obscure, for his vocabulary was bestrewn with crossword-puzzle words. Those evenings were so awful that no one would have come to them if it had not been for Angelica; the eye could stray from a loathsome witch doctor on the screen and rest in comfort and joy on her.

Some people said that Early was a cynic and some said that he was a fool to leave Angelica unguarded, without children and without responsibility, and they all said it would serve him right if he returned from one of his safaris to find himself replaced. Why did a man so antisocial marry at all, or, if he must marry, why not take as his wife some stalwart and thick-legged woman who

would share his pedantic adventures—a champion skeet
shooter, perhaps, or a descendant of Western pioneers?
But then, on the other hand, why had Angelica married
him? She never spoke of him, never quoted from his
letters—if there were any letters—and if she was asked
where he was currently travelling, she often could not
answer. The speculation upon this vacant alliance
ceased as soon as Early had left town to go and join his
guides, for once he was out of sight, no one could remember much about him beyond a Gallic mustache
and his ponderous jokes as his movies jerked on. Indeed,
so completely was his existence forgotten that matchmakers set to work as if Angelica were a widow.

They did not get far, the matchmakers, because, apart
from her beauty, there was not a good deal to be said
about Angelica. She had some money—her parents had
left her ample provision, and Early's money came from
a reliable soap—but it was not enough to be of interest
to the extremely rich people whose yachts and châteaux
and boxes at the opera she embellished. She dressed
well, but she lacked the exclusive chic, the unique fillip,
that would have caused her style in clothes to be called
sui generis and, as such, to be mentioned by the press.
Angelica was hardly literate; the impressions her girlish
mind had received at Miss Hewitt's classes had been
sketched rather than etched, but she was not stupid and
she had an appealing, if small and intermittent, humor.
She was not wanting in heart and she was quick to com-
miserate and give alms to the halt and the lame and the
poor, and if ugliness had been a disease or a social evil,
she would, counting her blessings, have lent herself to
its extirpation. She wasn't a cat, she wasn't a flirt or a
cheat, wasn't an imbecile, didn't make *gaffes;* neither,

however, alas, was she a wit, or a catalyst, or a trans-
gressor to be scolded and punished and then forgiven
and loved afresh. She was simply and solely a beautiful
woman.

Women, on first confronting Angelica Early, took a
backward step in alarm and instinctively diverted the
attention of their husbands or lovers to something at the
opposite end of the room. But their first impression was
false, for Angelica's beauty was an end in itself and she
was the least predatory of women. The consequence of
this was that she had many women friends, or at any
rate she had many hostesses, for there was no more
splendid and no safer ornament for a dinner table than
Angelica. The appointments of these tables were often
planned round her, the cynosure, and women lunching
together had been known to debate (with their practical
tongues in their cheeks but without malice) whether
Waterford or Venetian glass went better with her and
whether white roses or red were more appropriate in
juxtaposition to her creamy skin and her luminous ash-
blond hair. She was forever in demand; for weeks before
parties and benefit balls hostesses contended for her
presence; her status—next to the host—in protocol was
permanent; little zephyrs of excitement and small calms
of awe followed her entrance into a drawing room. She
was like royalty, she was a public personage, or she was,
as the aunt was to observe at her funeral, like the

masterpiece of a great master. Queens and pictures may not, in the ordinary sense, have friends, but if they live up to their reputations, they will not want for an entourage, and only the cranks and the sightless will be their foes. There were some skeptics in Angelica's circle, but there were no cranks, and in speaking of her, using the superlatives that composed their native tongue, they called her adorable and indispensable, and they said that when she left them, the sun went down.

Men, on first gazing into those fabulous eyes, whose whites had retained the pale, melting blue of infancy, were dizzied, and sometimes they saw stars. But their vertigo passed soon, often immediately, although sometimes not until after a second encounter, planned in palpitations and bouts of fever, had proved flat and inconsequential. For a tête-à-tête with Angelica was marked by immediacy; she did not half disclose a sweet and sad and twilit history, did not make half promises about a future, implied the barest minimum of flattery and none at all of amorousness, and spoke factually, in a pleasant voice, without nuance and within the present tense. Someone had said that she was *sec*—a quality praiseworthy in certain wines but distinctly not delicious in so beautiful a woman. All the same, just as she had many hostesses, so she had many escorts, for her presence at a man's side gave him a feeling of achievement.

Angelica was not, that is, all façade—her eyes themselves testified to the existence of airy apartments and charming gardens behind them—but she was consecrated to her vocation and she had been obliged to pass up much of the miscellany of life that irritates but also brings about the evolution of personality; the unmolested oyster creates no pearl. Her heart might be shivered, she might be inwardly scorched with desire or mangled with jealousy and greed, she might be benumbed by loneliness and doubt, but she was so unswerving in her trusteeship of her perfection that she could not allow anxiety to pleat her immaculate brow or anger to discolor her damask cheeks or tears to deflower her eyes. Perhaps, like an artist, she was not always grateful for this talent of beauty that destiny had imposed upon her without asking leave, but, like the artist, she knew where her duty lay; the languishing and death of her genius would be the languishing and death of herself, and suicide, though it is often understandable, is almost never moral.

The world kindly imagined that Mrs. Early's beauty was deathless and that it lived its charmed life without support. If the world could have seen the contents of her dressing table and her bathroom shelves! If the world could have known the hours devoured by the mututinal ritual! Angelica and her reverent English maid, Dora, were dressed like surgeons in those morning hours, and they worked painstakingly, talking little, under lights whose purpose was to cast on the mirrors an image of ruthless veracity. The slightest alteration in the color of a strand of hair caused Angelica to cancel all engagements for a day or two, during which time a hairdresser was in attendance, treating the lady with dyes and allaying her fears. A Finn daily belabored her with bundles of birch fagots to enliven her circulation; at night she wore mud on her face and creamed gloves on her hands; her hair was treated with olive oil, lemon juice, egg white, and beer; she was massaged, she was vibrated, she was steamed into lassitude and then stung back to life by astringents; she was brushed and creamed and salted and powdered. All this took time, and, more than time, it took undying patience. So what the world did not know but what Angelica and her maid and her curators knew was that the blood that ever so subtly clouded her cheeks with pink and lay pale green in that admirable vein in her throat was kept in motion by a rapid pulse whose author was a fearful heart: If my talent goes, I'm done for, says the artist, and Angelica said, If I lose my looks, I'm lost.

So, even as she attentively lent the exquisite shell of her ear to her dinner partner, who was telling her about his visit to Samothrace or was bidding her examine with him his political views, even as she returned the gaze of a newcomer whose head was over his heels, even as she contributed to the talk about couturiers after the ladies had withdrawn, Angelica was thinking, in panic and obsession, of the innumerable details she was obliged to juggle to sustain the continuity of her performance.

Modern science has provided handsome women—and especially blondes, who are the most vulnerable—with defenses against many of their natural enemies: the sun, coarsening winds, the rude and hostile properties of foreign waters and foreign airs. But there has not yet been devised a way to bring to his knees the archfiend Time, and when Angelica began to age, in her middle forties, she went to bed.

Her reduction of the world to the size of her bedroom was a gradual process, for her wilting and fading was so slow that it was really imperceptible except to her unflinching eyes, and to Dora's, and to those of an adroit plastic surgeon to whose unadvertised sanitarium, tucked away in a rural nook in Normandy, she had retreated each summer since she was forty to be delivered of those infinitesimal lines and spots in her cheeks and her throat that her well-lighted mirror told her were exclamatory and shameful disfigurements. Such was the mystery that shrouded these trips to France that everyone thought she must surely be going abroad to establish a romantic menage, and when she paused in Paris on her return to New York, she was always so resplendent that the guesses seemed to be incontrovertibly confirmed; nothing but some sort of delicious fulfillment could account for her subtlety, her lovely, tremulous, youthful air of secret memories. Some of her friends in idle moments went so far as to clothe this lover with a fleshy vestment and a personality and a nationality, and one of the slowly evolved myths, which was eventually stated as fact, was that he was a soul of simple origin and primal magnetism—someone, indeed, like Lady Chatterley's lover.

Angelica would suddenly appear in Paris at the end of August with no explanation of the summer or of that happy condition of her heart that was all but audible as a carol, and certainly was visible in her shimmering eyes and her glowing skin. She lingered in Paris only long enough to buy her winter wardrobe, to upset the metabolism of the men she met, to be, momentarily, the principal gem in the diadem of the international set, and to promise faithfully that next year she would join houseparties and cruises to Greece, would dance till dawn at *fêtes chempêtres,* and would, between bull-fights, tour the caves of Spain. She did not, of course, keep her promises, and the fact is that she would have disappointed her friends if she had. At these times, on the wing, it was as if she had been inoculated with the distillation of every fair treasure on earth and in Heaven, with the moon and the stars, with the seas and the flowers, and the rainbow and the morning dew. Angelica was no longer *sec,* they said; they said a new dimension had brought her to life. Heretofore she had been a painted ship upon a painted ocean and now she was sailing the crests and the depths, and if her adventurous voyage away from the doldrums had come late in life, it had not come too late; the prime of life, they said, savoring their philosophy and refurbishing their cliché, was a relative season. They loved to speculate on why her lover was unpresentable. Wiseacres proposed, not meaning it, that he was a fugitive from the Ile du Diable; others agreed that if he was not Neanderthal (in one way or another) or so ignobly born that not even democracy could receive him into its generous maw—if he was not any of these things, he must be intransigently married. Or could he perhaps be one of those glittering Eastern rulers who contrived to take an incognito holiday from their riches and their dominions but could not, because of law and tradition, ever introduce Angelica into their courts? Once or twice it was proposed that Angelica was exercising scruples because of her husband, but this seemed unlikely; the man was too dense to see beyond his marriage feasts of Indians and his courtship of birds.

Whoever the lover was and whatever were the terms of their liaison, Angelica was plainly engaged upon a major passion whose momentum each summer was so forcefully recharged that it did not dwindle at all during the rest of the year. Now she began to be known not only as the most beautiful but as one of the most dynamic of women as well, and such was the general enthusiasm for her that she was credited with *mots justes* and insights and ingenious benevolences that perhaps existed only in the infatuated imaginations of her claque. How amazingly Angelica had changed! And how amazingly wrong they all were! For *not* changing had been her lifelong specialty, and she was the same as ever, only more so. Nevertheless, the sort of men who theretofore had cooled after their second meeting with her and had called her pedestrian or impervious or hollow now continued to fever and fruitlessly but breathlessly to pursue her. Often they truly fell in love with her and bitterly hated that anonymous fellow who had found the wellspring of her being.

Inevitably the news of her friends' speculations drifted back to her in hints and slips of the tongue. Angelica's humor had grown no more buxom with the passage of the years, and she was not amused at the enigma she had given birth to by immaculate conception. She took herself seriously. She was a good creature, a moral and polite woman, but she was hindered by unworldliness, and she was ashamed to be living a fiction. She was actually guilt-ridden because her summertime friend was not an Adonis from the Orient or a charming and ignorant workingman but was, instead, Dr. Fleege-Althoff, a monstrous little man, with a flat head on which not one hair grew and with the visage of a thief—a narrow, feral nose, a pair of pale and shifty and omniscient eyes, a mouth that forever faintly smiled at some cryptic, wicked jest. There was no help for it, but she was ashamed all the same that it was pain and humiliation, not bliss and glorification, that kept her occupied during her annual retreat. The fact was that she earned her reputation and her undiminishing applause and kept fresh the myth in which she moved by suffering the surface skin of her face to be planed away by a steel-wire brush, electrically propelled; the drastic pain was sickening and it lasted long, and for days—sometimes weeks—after the operation she was so unsightly that her looking glass, which, morbidly, she could not resist, broke her heart. She lay on a chaise in a darkened bedroom of that quiet, discreet sanitarium, waiting, counting the hours until the scabs that encrusted her flensed skin should disappear. But even when this dreadful mask was gone, she was still hideous, and her eyes and her mouth, alone untouched, seemed to reproach her when she confronted her reflection, as red and shining as if she had been boiled almost to death. Eight weeks later, though, she was as beautiful as she had been at her zenith, and the Doctor, that ugly man, did not fail, in bidding her goodbye, to accord himself only a fraction of the credit and assign the rest to her Heavenly Father. Once, he had made her shiver when, giving her the grin of a gargoyle, he said, "What a face! Flower of the world! Of all my patients, you are the one I do not like to flail." Flail! The word almost made her retch, and she envisioned him lashing her with little metal whips, and smiling.

During the time she was at the sanitarium (a tasteful and pleasant place, but a far cry from the pastoral bower her friends imagined), she communicated with no one except her maid and with the staff, who knew her, as they knew all the other ladies, by an alias. She called herself Mrs. London, and while there was no need to go so far, she said she came from California. It was a long and trying time. Angelica had always read with difficulty and without much pleasure, and she inevitably brought with her the wrong books, in the hope, which she should long since have abandoned, that she might improve her mind; she could not pay attention to Proust, she was baffled by the Russians, and poetry (one year she brought "The Faerie Queene"!) caused her despair. So, for two and a half months, she worked at needlepoint and played a good deal of solitaire and talked to Dora, who was the only confidante she had ever had, and really the only friend. They had few subjects and most of them were solemn—the philosophy of cosmetics, the fleetingness of life. The maid, if she had a life of her own, never revealed it. Sometimes Angelica, unbearably sad that she had been obliged to tread a straight-and-narrow path with not a primrose on it, would sigh and nearly cry and say, "What have I done with my life?" And Dora, assistant guardian of the wonder, would reply, "You have worked hard, Madame.

Being beautiful is no easy matter." This woman was highly paid, but she was a kind woman, too, and she meant what she said.

It was Angelica's hands that at last, inexorably, began to tell the time. It seemed to her that their transfiguration came overnight, but of course what came overnight was her realization that the veins had grown too vivid and that here and there in the interstices of the blue-green, upraised network there had appeared pale freckles, which darkened and broadened and multiplied; the skin was still silken and ivory, but it was redundant and lay too loosely on her fingers. That year, when she got to the sanitarium, she was in great distress, but she had confidence in her doctor.

Dr. Fleege-Althoff, however, though he was sincerely sorry, told her there was nothing he could do. Hands and legs, he said, could not be benefited by the waters of the fountain of youth. Sardonically, he recommended gloves, and, taking him literally, she was aghast. How could one wear gloves at a dinner table? What could be more parvenu, more telltale, than to lunch in gloves at a restaurant? Teasing her further, the vile little man proposed that she revive the style of wearing mitts, and tears of pain sprang to Angelica's eyes. Her voice was almost petulant when she protested against these grotesque prescriptions. The Doctor, nasty as he was, was wise, and in his unkind wisdom, accumulated through a lifetime of dealing with appearances, said, "Forgive my waggery. I'm tired today. Go get yourself loved, Mrs. London. I've dealt with women so many years that I can tell which of my patients have lovers or loving husbands and which have not—perhaps it will surprise you to know that very few of them have. Most have lost their men and come to me in the hope that the excision of crow's-feet will bring back the wanderers." He was sitting at his desk, facing her, his glasses hugely magnifying his intelligent, bitter eyes. "There is an aesthetic principle," he pursued, "that says beauty is the objectification of love. To be loved is to be beautiful, but to be beautiful is not necessarily to be loved. Imagine that, Mrs. London! Go and find a lover and obfuscate his senses; give him a pair of rose-colored glasses and he'll see your hands as superb—or, even better, he won't see your hands at all. Get loved by somebody—it doesn't matter who—and you'll get well."

"Get well?" said Angelica, amazed. "Am I ill?"

"If you are not ill, why have you come to me? I am a doctor," he said, and with a sigh he gestured toward the testimonials of his medical training that hung on the walls. The Doctor's fatigue gave him an air of melancholy that humanized him, despite his derisive voice, and momentarily Angelica pitied him in his ineluctable ugliness. Still, he was no more solitary in his hemisphere than she was in hers, and quickly she slipped away from her consideration of him to her own woe.

"But even if I weren't married, how could I find a lover at my age?" she cried.

He shook his head wearily and said, "Like most of

your countrywomen, you confound youth with value, with beauty, with courage—with everything. To you, youth and age are at the two poles, one positive, the other negative. *I* cannot tell you what to do. I am only an engineer—I am not the inventor of female beauty. I am a plastic surgeon—I am not God. All you can do now is cover your imperfections with *amour-propre*. You are a greedy woman, Mrs. London—a few spots appear on your hands and you throw them up and say 'This is the end.' What egotism!"

Angelica understood none of this, and her innocent and humble mind went round and round amongst his paradoxes, so savagely delivered. How could she achieve *amour-propre* when what she had most respected in herself was now irretrievably lost? And if she had not *amour-propre,* how could she possibly find anyone else to love her? Were not these the things she should have been told when she was a girl growing up? Why had no one, in this long life of hers, which had been peopled by such a multitude, warned her to lay up a store of good things against the famine of old age? Now, too late, she wrung her old-woman hands, and from the bottom of her simple heart she lamented, weeping and caring nothing that her famous eyes were smeared and their lids swollen.

At last the Doctor took pity on her. He came around to her side of the desk and put his hands kindly on her shaking shoulders. "Come, Mrs. London, life's not over," he said. "I've scheduled your planing for to-morrow morning at nine. Will you go through with it or do you want to cancel?"

She told him, through her tears, that she would go through with the operation, and he congratulated her.

"You'll rise from these depths," he said. "You'll learn, as we all learn, that there are substantial rewards in age."

That summer, Dr. Fleege-Althoff, who had grave problems of his own (he had a nagging wife; his only child, a son, was schizophrenic) and whose understanding was deep, did what he could to lighten Angelica's depression. He found that she felt obscurely disgraced and ashamed, as if she had committed a breach of faith, had broken a sacred trust, and could not expect anything but public dishonor. She had never been a happy woman, but until now she had been too diligent to be unhappy; the experience of unhappiness for the first time when one is growing old is one of the most malignant diseases of the heart. Poor soul! Her person was her personality. Often, when the Doctor had finished his rounds, he took Angelica driving in the pretty countryside; she was veiled against the ravages of the sun and, he observed, she wore gloves. As they drove, he talked to her and endeavored to persuade her that for each of the crucifixions of life there is a solace. Sometimes she seemed to believe him.

Sometimes, believing him, she took heart simply through the look of the trees and the feel of the air, but when they had returned to the sanitarium and the sun had gone down and she was alone with her crumpled hands—with her crumpled hands and her compassionate but helpless maid—she could not remember any of the reasons for being alive. She would think of what she had seen on their drive: children playing with boisterous dogs; girls and young men on horses or bicycles, riding along the back roads; peasant women in their gardens tending their cabbages and tending their sunning babies at the same time. The earth, in the ebullience of summertime, seemed more resplendent and refreshed than she could ever remember it. Finally, she could not bear to look at it or at all those exuberant young human beings living on it, and began to refuse the Doctor's invitations.

You might think that she would have taken to drink or to drugs, but she went on in her dogtrot way, taking care of her looks, remembering how drink hardens the skin and how drugs etiolate it.

That year, when Angelica arrived in Paris on her way back to New York, she was dealt an adventitious but crippling blow of mischance from which she never really recovered. She had arrived in midafternoon, and the lift in her hotel was crowded with people going up to their rooms after lunch. She had been one of the first to enter the car and she was standing at the back. At the front, separated from her by ten people or more, were two young men who had been standing in the lobby when she came into the hotel. They were Americans, effeminate and a little drunk, and one of them said to the other, "She must have been sixty—why, she could have been seventy!" His companion replied, "Twenty-eight. Thirty at the most." His friend said, "You didn't see her hands when she took off her gloves to register. They were old, I tell you. You can always tell by the hands."

Luckily for Angelica and luckily for them, the cruel, green boys got off first; as she rode up the remaining way to her floor, she felt dizzy and hot. Unused as she had been most of her life to emotion, she was embraced like a serpent by the desire to die (that affliction that most of us have learned to cope with through its reiteration), and she struggled for breath. She walked down the corridor to her room jerkily; all her resilience was gone. Immediately she telephoned the steamship line and booked the first passage home she could get. For two days, until the boat sailed, she lay motionless on her bed, with the curtains drawn, or she paced the floor, or sat and stared at her culprit hands. She saw no one and she spoke to no one except Dora, who told all the friends who called that her mistress was ill.

When these friends returned from Europe in the autumn, and others from the country, they learned, to their distress and puzzlement, that Angelica was not going out at all, nor was she receiving anyone. The fiction of her illness, begun in Paris, gained documentation and became fact, until at last no one was in doubt: she had cancer, far too advanced for cure or palliation; they assumed she was attended by nurses. Poor darling, they said, to have her love affair end this way! They showered her with roses, telephoning their florists before they went out to lunch; they wrote her tactful notes of sympathy, and it was through reading these that she guessed what they thought was the reason for her retirement.

The maisonette seemed huge to her, and full of echoes; for the first time since she had married, she began to think about her husband and, though he was a stranger, to long for his return. Perhaps he could become the savior Fleege-Althoff had told her to seek. But she was not strong enough to wait for him. The drawing room was still in its summer shrouds; the umbrageous dining room was closed. At first, she dined in the library, and then she began to have dinner on a tray in her bedroom, sitting before the fire. Soon after this, she started keeping to her bedroom and, at last, to her bed, never rising from it except for her twice-daily ritualistic baths. Her nightdresses and bed jackets were made by the dressmaker she had always used to supplement her Paris wardrobe; she wore her jewels for the eyes of her maid and her masseuse—that is, she wore earrings and necklaces, but she never adorned her hands. And, as if she were dying in the way they thought, she wrote brave letters to her friends, and sometimes, when her loneliness became unbearable, she telephoned them and inquired in the voice of an invalid about their parties and about the theatre, though she did not want to hear, but she refused all their kind invitations to come and visit, and she rang off saying, "Do keep in touch."

For a while, they did keep in touch, and then the flowers came less and less often and her mail dwindled away. Her panic gave way to inertia. If she had been able to rise from her bed, she would have run crying to them, saying, "I was faithful to your conception of me for all those years. Now take pity on me—reward me for my singleness of purpose." They would have been quick to console her and to laugh away her sense of failure. (She could all but hear them saying, "But my dear, how absurd! Look at your figure! Look at your face and your hair! What on earth do you mean by killing yourself simply because of your hands?") But she had not the strength to go to them and receive their mercy. They did not know and she could not tell them. They thought it was cancer. They would never have dreamed it was despair that she groped through sightlessly, in a vacuum everlasting and black. Their flowers and their letters and their telephone calls did not stop out of unkindness but out of forgetfulness; they were busy, they were living their lives.

Angelica began to sleep. She slept all night and all day, like a cat. Dreams became her companions and sleep became her food. She ate very little, but she did not waste away, although she was weakened—so weakened, indeed, that sometimes in her bath she had attacks of vertigo and was obliged to ring for Dora. She could not keep her mind on anything. The simplest words in the simplest book bewildered her, and she let her eyes wander drowsily from the page; before she could close the book and set it aside, she was asleep.

Just before Christmas, the drunken aunt, Angelica's only relative, came back to town after a lengthy visit to California. She had not heard from Angelica in months, but she had not been alarmed, for neither of them was a letter writer. The first evening she was back, she dined with friends and learned from them of her niece's illness; she was shocked into sobriety and bitterly excoriated herself for being so lazy that she had not bothered to write. She telephoned the doctor who had taken care of Angelica all her life and surprised him by repeating what she had heard—that the affliction had been diagnosed as cancer. At first, the doctor was offended that he had not been called in, and then, on second thought, he was suspicious, and he urged the aunt to go around as soon as she could and make a report to him.

The aunt did not warn Angelica that she was coming. She arrived late the next afternoon, with flowers and champagne and, by ill chance, a handsome pair of crocheted gloves she had picked up in a shop in San Francisco. She brought, as well, a bottle of Scotch, for her own amusement. The apartment was dark and silent, and in the wan light the servants looked spectral. The aunt, by nature a jovial woman—she drank for the fun of it—was oppressed by the gloom and went so quickly through the shadowy foyer and so quickly up the stairs that she was out of breath when she got to the door of Angelica's room. Dora, who had come more and more to have the deportment of a nurse, opened the door with nurselike gentleness and, seeing that her patient was, for a change, awake, said with nurselike cheer, "You have company, Madame! Just look at what Mrs. Armstrong has brought!" She took the flowers to put in water and the champagne to put on ice, and silently left the room.

The moment Angelica saw her aunt, she burst into tears and held out her arms, like a child, to be embraced,

and Mrs. Armstrong began also to cry, holding the unhappy younger woman in her arms. When the hurricane
was spent and the ladies had regained their voices, the
aunt said, "You must tell me the whole story, my pet,
but before you do, you must give me a drink and open
your present. I do pray you're going to like them—they
are so much *you*."

Angelica rang for glasses and ice, for the Scotch, and
then she undid the ribbon around the long box. When
she saw what was inside, all the blood left her face. "Get
out!" she said to her aunt, full of cold hatred. "Is that
why you came—to taunt me?"

Amazed, Mrs. Armstrong turned away from a book
she had been examining on a table in the window and
met her niece's angry gaze.

"*I* taunt you?" she cried. "Why, darling, are you out
of your mind? If you don't like the gloves, I'll give
them to someone else, but don't—"

"Yes, do that! Give them to some young beautiful
girl whose hands don't need to be hidden." And she
flung the box and the gloves to the floor in an infantile
fury. Twisting, she bent herself into her pillows and
wept again, heartbrokenly.

By the end of the afternoon, Mrs. Armstrong's heart
was also broken. She managed, with taste and tact, aided
by a good deal of whiskey, to ferret out the whole story,
and, as she said to her dinner companion later on, it
was unquestionably the saddest she had ever heard.
She blamed herself for her obtuseness and she blamed
Major Early for his, and, to a lesser extent, she blamed
Angelica's friends for never realizing that they, with
their constant and superlative praise of her looks, had
added to her burden, had forced her into so conventual

a life that she had been removed from most of experience. "The child has no memories!" exclaimed Mrs. Armstrong, appalled. "She wouldn't know danger if she met it head on, and she certainly wouldn't know joy. We virtually said to her, 'Don't tire your pretty eyes with looking at anything, don't let emotion harm a hair of your lovely head.' We simply worshipped and said, 'Let us look at you, but don't you look at us, for we are toads.' The ghastly thing is that there's nothing to be salvaged, and even if some miracle of surgery could restore her hands to her, it would do no good, for her disillusion is complete. I think if she could love anyone, if that talent were suddenly to come to her at this point in her life, she would love her ugly man in Normandy, and would love him *because* he was ugly."

When Angelica had apologized to her aunt for her tantrum over the gloves, she had then got out of bed and retrieved them and, in the course of her soliloquy, had put them on and had constantly smoothed them over each finger in turn as she talked.

She was still wearing the gloves when Dora came in to run her evening bath and found that her heart, past mending, had stopped.

A Reasonable Facsimile

Far from withering on the vine from apathy and loneliness after his retirement as chairman of the Philosophy Department at Nevilles College, Dr. Bohrmann had a second blooming, and it was observed amongst his colleagues and his idolatrous students that he would age with gusto and live to be a hundred. He looked on the end of his academic career—an impressive one that had earned him an international reputation in scholarly quarters—as simply the end of one phase of his life, and when he began the new one, he did so with fresh accoutrements, for, as he had been fond of saying to his students, "Change is the only stimulus." He took up the study of Japanese (he said with a smile that he would write hokku as tributes to his friends on stormy days); he took up engraving and lettering (designed a new bookplate, designed a gravestone for his dead wife); he began to grow Persian melons under glass; he took up mycology, and mycophagy as well, sending his fidgety housekeeper off into shrill protests as he flirted with death by eating mushrooms gathered in cow pastures and on golf links. He abandoned chess for bridge, and two evenings a week played a cutthroat game with Miss Blossom Duveen, the bursar's blond and bawdy secretary, as his partner and as his opponents Mr. Street, the logician, and Mr. Street's hopelessly scatterbrained wife.

But the radical thing about his new life was the house he had had built for himself in the spring semester of his last year at the college. It was a house of tomorrow— cantilevered, half glass—six miles out on the prairies that confronted the mountain range in whose foothills lay Adams, the town where the college was. The house, though small and narrow, was long, and it looked like a ship, for there was a deck that went all the way around it; from certain points Dr. Bohrmann could see Pikes Peak, a hundred and fifty miles away, and from every point he could watch the multiform weather: there dark rain, here blinding sunshine, yonder a sulphurous dust storm, haze on the summit of one peak, a pillow of cloud concealing a second, hyaline light on the glacier of a third. The house amazed that nondescript, stick-in-the-mud Western town, which, from the day it was founded, had been putting up the worst eyesores it could think of. Whoever on earth would have dreamed that the professor, absentminded and old, riding a bicycle, wearing oldfangled gaiters and an Old World cape, would make such an angular nest for himself and drastically paint it bright pink? The incongruity between the man and his habitat could not possibly have been greater. He belonged in and had, in fact, spent most of his life in fusty parlors where stout, permanent furniture (bookcases with glass fronts, mahogany secretaries with big claw feet, lounges upholstered in quilted black leather, ottomans, immovable bureaus, round tables as heavy as lead) bulked larger than life in the dim-orange light of hanging lamps with fringe. You could see him cleaving through those portières people used to have that were made of long strands of brown wooden beads; you could see him hanging his hat on a much ramified hatrack. Imagine, then, this character, with his silver beard, wearing a hazel coat-sweater from J. C. Penney, and a mussed green tweed suit, those gaiters, a stiff-collared shirt, a Tyrolian hat—dressed, in general, for an altogether different *mise en scène*—sitting in a black sling chair on the front deck of this gleaming, youthful house, drinking ginger beer out of an earthenware mug and looking through binoculars at eagles and the weather. Or look at him pottering in his pretty Oriental garden (it had a steeply arching bridge over a lily pond and a weeping willow, and a deformed pine tree that he had brought down from up near the timber line), shading himself with the kind of giant black bumbershoot one associates with hotel doormen in a pouring rain. See him in his sleek, slender blond dining room eating a mutton chop or blood pudding with red cabbage, drinking *dunkles Bier* from a stein. No matter where you placed him in that house, he simply would not match. It was the joke of Adams, but a good-natured one, for Dr. Bohrmann was the pet of the town.

Dr. Bohrmann and his wife, who died two years before his retirement, had arrived in Colorado from Freiburg by way of Montreal, where, just as he was beginning to make his presence felt at the university, he was halted in his stride by a sudden, astounding hemorrhage of the lungs. When, after seventeen wan, lengthy months, he was discharged from the sanitarium, not as cured but as arrested, his careful doctors counselled him to go West, to the Rocky Mountains, under whose blue, bright skies he could, in time, rout the last bacterium. On their further recommendation, he applied for an appointment at Nevilles College, since Adams was famous for the particular salubrity of its air. And providence was pleased to accommodate him, having a few months earlier created a vacancy on the staff through the death—from tuberculosis—of a young instructor. Adams was high above sea level and its prospect of soaring palisades and pinnacles of rock was magnificent, if, at first, dismaying to European eyes that had been accustomed to grandeur on a smaller scale. Moreover, the faculty of its college was remarkable— was, in part, illustrious—because so many of its members had come here for Dr. Bohrmann's reason; if their distemper had been of a different nature, they would have lectured in much grander but moister groves—in New Haven or Princeton, in Oxford or Bonn. For the most part, they accepted their predicament with grace— it is no myth that the tubercular is by and large a sanguine fellow—and lived urbanely in rented houses, year by year meaning it less and less when they stated their resolve that as soon as their health was completely restored they would go back to the East or to their foreign fatherlands. Although their New York *Times* came four days late, and although perhaps they were not in the thick of things, neither did their minds abide in Shangri-La. Visiting lecturers and vacationing friends were bound to admit that the insular community was remarkably *au courant* and that within it there was an exchange of ideas as brilliant and constant as the Colorado sun.

At first, when the Bohrmanns came, in 1912, they had no intention of lingering any longer than was absolutely necessary. But after little more than a year, neither of them could imagine living anywhere else; the immaculate air was deliciously inebriating and the sun, in those superlative heavens, fed them with the vibrancy of youth. They daily rejoiced in their physical existence, breathed deeply, and slept like children. They liked to walk on the mesas, gathering kinnikin- nick in the winter and pasqueflowers in the spring; sometimes they rented sweet-faced burros and rode up to a waterfall of great temperament and beauty. They admired the turbulent colors of the sunsets, the pro- found snows of winter, the plangent thunderstorms of summer. There was, they said, some sort of spell upon the place that bound them to it; roving the tablelands, whence one could gaze for miles on miles upon the works of God, they paused in silence, their hands upon their quickened, infatuated hearts. And besides the land, they loved the people of it, both the autochthonous Town and the dislocated Gown; students thronged their house at the *gemütlich* coffee hour, and their coevals and their elders came at night to drink hot wine or beer and, endlessly, in witty, learned periods, to talk.

Sometimes Dr. Bohrmann and Hedda spoke of summering in Europe—in spite of their contentment, they were often grievously homesick for Freiburg—and occasionally they went so far as to book passage, but something always prevented them from going. One year, Wolfgang was engaged in writing a monograph on Maimonides for the *Hibbert Journal,* another year Hedda was bedridden for a long while after a miscarriage that doomed them, to their everlasting sorrow, to childlessness. After the Second World War, they no longer even spoke of going back, for the thought of how Freiburg now must look sickened them.

All in all, they had an uncommonly happy life and they so much enjoyed each other that when Hedda died, with no warning at all, of heart disease, Wolfgang's friends were afraid that he, too, might die, of grief. And, indeed, he asked for a semester's leave and spent the whole of it indoors, seldom answering his doorbell and never answering his telephone. But, at the end of that time, he emerged as companionable and as exuberant as ever, as much at home with life.

It was then, upon his return to the mild and miniature hurly-burly of the campus, that he began to lay in his supplies against the lean times when his rank would be emeritus. He started Japanese with Professor Sy mington, the historian, who, until he had got tuberculosis, had been an Orientalist resident in Kyoto; he read Goren and Culbertson on bridge; he studied every magazine on architecture that was published, and throughout that winter he worked on designs for his new house. In the beginning, when he went to the builders, they dismissed his plans as the work of a visionary—all that expanse of window, they said, was impractical in a cold climate; they said he would rue the day he put a flat roof over his head. If it had been anyone but Dr. Bohrmann, they probably never would have come round, but Dr. Bohrmann had a way about him that could persuade a river to stand still or a builder to build a pavilion at the North Pole. So, in the end, they took on the job, and they admitted, grudgingly but still with fondness, that he had not faltered in his specifications by so much as a fraction of an inch. While the house was going up, he rode out on his bicycle each afternoon at tremendous speed, his romantic mantle billowing, the brim of his hat standing straight up in the wind, to watch the installation of his windows and the progress of his grass; he was like a mother watching, in pride and fascination, the extraordinary daily changes in her first-born.

In June, after his last Commencement, he moved out of the house in which he and Hedda had lived all those years, and he transferred to the new house his vast polylingual library, his busts of Plato and Lucretius and Aesculapius and Kant, his collection of maps and of antique firearms, and Hedda's pure-linen sheets. He sold or gave away the durable, lubberly furniture he and Hedda had accumulated and all those souvenirs of another time—antimacassars, needlepoint cushions, afghans, porcelain umbrella stands, Lalique bud vases. He transplanted his tuberous begonias to the terrace on the west side of the new house and, at the back, he put in mountain-ash trees, a row of eight Lombardy poplars, and an ambitious kitchen garden, bordered with herbs, pinks, primroses, and bachelor's-buttons.

On the morning he moved, after the vans had gone, Dr. Bohrmann got on his bicycle, with his fiddle strapped in its case behind him and his ginger cat in a basket in front of him, and he pedalled out to the plains, singing "Gaudeamus Igitur" in a rich, if untrue, baritone. Street, the logician, saw him wheeling past his house and later said on the telephone to Symington, the historian, "You should have seen *mein Herr Doktor Professor* this morning, with his cat and his fiddle, singing hi-diddle-diddle, ready to hop right over the moon." Symington, with a laugh, rejoined, "When we're pushing up daisies, he'll be learning jujitsu." Blossom Duveen saw him, too; she drove past him in her brash crimson convertible on her way to Denver and a flicker of interest started a flame in her heart; he was really a dear, she thought, and by no means all that old. She wouldn't mind in the least little bit going to live in that snappy, streamlined house.

The moving men, aided by Mrs. Pritchard, the housekeeper who had taken care of Dr. Bohrmann since Hedda's death, and by a crew of students who were staying on for the summer term, had everything in place by midday and had even cleared away the excelsior and the cartons and barrels, and, on the dot of noon, the jocund old professor fired a shot into the sky from a harquebus he himself had restored to working order, the boys gave a cheer, and Dr. Bohrmann opened up a keg of beer. To each of his helpers in turn he genially raised his glass and said *"Prosit."* Momentarily, as he saluted them, he wished he had bedrooms enough to lodge every one of these warmhearted lads who talked like cow hands but whose minds were critical and tough and appreciative of his own appreciations. He was sorry, so very sorry, that he had no sons. But he erased his useless regret by telling himself that the next best thing to a son was a student and the Lord knew he had a host of those.

When the beer was gone, and the last raffish jalopy had roared away, and Mrs. Pritchard was in the kitchen making his lunch, he went into his new library, handsomely appointed in blackwood and saffron upholstery, and, sitting before his windows that commanded a view from the plains to the tundra, he smiled on everything as if he were smiling on a gathering of intimate friends. Then his smile ebbed and his eyes grew grave, for he realized that in a year or two there would be no more of his students to come and match wits with him as they ate apples and pecans and fanned the fire on his hearth with bellows. Once they were out in the world, they seldom came back to Adams, and when they did, they were not the same, for they had outgrown their lucubrations; they were no longer so fervent as they had been, and often their eyes strayed to their wristwatches in the midst of a conversation. Dr. Bohrmann sighed at his sad loss of the young, and he sighed again, sorely missing Hedda; she had laughed so charmingly, he had liked her so extremely well. He thought of her sitting opposite him over a backgammon board, her fingers approaching and then withdrawing from the men, and his heart broke with longing for the sweet look of her perplexity. But then he chided himself for his unphilosophical egocentricity, and reminded himself of the marvels that were to emerge in his gardens and of the quotidian pleasure he was to know in this house with its kingly prospects, and, ashamed that he had brooded even for a minute, he resolutely turned to the morning mail, separating the journals and bulletins from the letters.

For many years, Dr. Bohrmann had kept up a prodigious correspondence with all manner of people all over the world—with a handful of relatives scattered by war and pogroms, with the friends he had known at Freiburg and in Montreal, with his fellow-invalids and the doctors in the tuberculosis sanitarium, with philosophers he had argued with at meetings of learned societies. And besides these, he wrote to a great many people he had never met. His was a nature so benign, so full of generous heart, that whenever he read a book he liked, or a short story or a poem in a magazine, whenever he heard on the radio a piece of music by a contemporary composer, he wrote the author a letter of congratulation—a careful, specific letter that showed he had read or listened with diligence and discrimination. More often than not this ingratiating overture led to a lasting friendship by mail, and, through the years, Dr. Bohrmann grew as conversant with these friends' families and pets and illnesses and sorrows and triumphs as if he had frequently dined at their houses. One time, Rosalind Throop, the greatly gifted young woman novelist in Johannesburg, flatteringly asked him to send a photograph of himself, saying, "Since the shape of your heart is now so clear to me, I am impelled to know the shape of your face as well." He sent a snapshot of himself and Hedda, up to their knees in columbines, a grand reach of snowy peaks behind them, and Mrs. Throop wrote by return mail, "What are these flowers you and the *Frau Professor* wade in? Only last night, before the photograph came, I dreamed I met you in a meadow in the Cotswolds abloom with Michaelmas daisies, and you said to me, 'We must gather our daisies quickly, for the snows are on their way.' And here in the picture you stand in flowers and at your back there is snow!" Thereafter, in their letters they made allusions to their pastoral encounter in England, where neither of them had ever been, until it no longer seemed fantasy.

To South Africa and to Japan, to Scotland and France, to Israel and Germany, he sent presents of books and subscriptions to magazines and CARE packages; to his friends' children he sent arrowheads and feathered Indian headbands. His correspondents sent him presents in return, and now and then someone dedicated a book to him. When he had been obliged to write of Hedda's death, they mourned sincerely and worried over his solitude, but they took heart once again when he started building his house, of which he sent them photographs.

There was another side to the coin, for often an admiring reader wrote him an appreciation of or an objection to an essay of his that had appeared in the

Journal of the History of Ideas or in *Revue de Méta-physique et de Morale;* he was a prolific writer and, by his own wry, rueful admission, a prolix one. (Once he had written to Mrs. Throop, "I have read your new novel with the monster's green eye. How you write! If I had but a tittle of talent! I have instead a galloping *cacoëthes scribendi* and you don't go to Heaven on the strength of that! May I be summoned by the Gabriel horn when I'm about a modest business—gathering toadstools, e.g., or making Jap squiggles.") But in spite of the turgid vocabulary and the Germanic, backward syntax of his monographs, Dr. Bohrmann had a wide following, and really nothing in the world pleased him more than a letter from someone who had read him through to the end.

At the time he withdrew from society, after Hedda's death, he acquired a new correspondent, a young man named Henry Medley, who taught English at a college in Florida, and who had come across Dr. Bohrmann's "A Reinquiry into Burke's Aesthetic." This princely lad (Dr. Bohrmann did not stint in his use of laudatory adjectives when he described his partisans) had been inspired to look further into the philosopher's work, and painstakingly he compiled a complete bibliography, which included early studies that Dr. Bohrmann had forgotten altogether and, in some cases, would have preferred to disown. Medley's dossier, gradually revealed in the course of a two-year exchange of letters, was this: he came from the upper regions of New York State and he was in his early twenties; he was the only child of a lawyer father, who had been dead for many years, and of a pedigreed but impecunious mother, who had been reduced to the status of paid companion to "a dragon nearly ninety who hurles her hideous taile about a Hudson-River-Bracketed den. It's here I spend my holidays, keeping a civil tongue in my head." He had worked his way through Harvard by tutoring the rich and retarded, and he had caught swift glimpses of Europe one summer when he had escorted a band of adolescents on a bicycle tour. He wrote Miltonic epics and Elizabethan songs which, someday, when the time and the poems were ripe, he hoped to show Dr. Bohrmann.

Medley had apparently read everything and forgotten nothing, and his immense letters, written on onionskin in a hand so fine that it could only be properly seen through a magnifying glass, were the most learned Dr. Bohrmann had ever got from anyone. When he mentioned that he was taking up Japanese, Medley sent him a list of "musts" to read; when he announced that he was going to build a modern house, Medley wrote at length on Frank Lloyd Wright vs. Miës van der Rohe; he knew about opera, medicine (he could quote from Sydenham, Pliny the Elder, René Théophile Hyacinthe Laënnec), painting, horticulture ("You speak of planting peonies and I presume to warn you, lest you don't know, that they are extremely crotchety. They detest any direct contact with manure and they detest being encroached upon by the roots of trees. And plant shallow!"). He knew movies and jazz and Marx and Freud and Catullus and the Koran, military strategy, iconography, geography, geology, anthropology, theology; he was amused by such cryptosciences as phrenology, alchemy, and astrology; he knew about wines and fish and cheese; he read German, French, Italian, Latin, Greek. He played tennis, swam among coral reefs, and during his Christmas vacations in the North he skied; he repaired the dragon's electrical appliances and designed his mother's clothes. Dr. Bohrmann wrote him once that his name was so apt it could have been taken from the dramatis personae of an allegorical play.

Once in a while, when Medley replied in five close-written pages to something that in Dr. Bohrmann's letter had been virtually no more than a parenthetical musing, Dr. Bohrmann was annoyed and brought him to book for his excess. One time he wrote, "I think you have made a Jungfrau out of the hill of a pygmy mole. My reflections don't *all* deserve such attention, dear boy, and I fear I must have expressed myself more abominably than usual to inspire you to this support of my wisecrack about Euripides. I can't possibly agree with you that he has 'the shabbiest mind in history.' My joke was no good to begin with and I am much ashamed." By return post came an apology so abject that Dr. Bohrmann was further ashamed; nevertheless, he continued to scold Medley whenever he committed that sin he so much deplored—of impassioned, uncritical agreement.

It had been a challenging interchange; the chap was brilliant, though undisciplined and incorrigibly high-falutin. "Don't be so hard on the dumb blondes in your classes," Dr. Bohrmann once wrote him. "What sort of world would it be if we didn't have the Philistines to judge ourselves by? God bless 'em." After that, Medley barely mentioned his trials when he confronted girls in his classrooms who had never heard of Aristotle. But while Medley's voracity was greater than his digestion, Dr. Bohrmann was sure that time would balance his chemistry. No one, these days, was mature at twenty-four. Often, after some especially felicitous letter—for when the boy was at his best and dropped his airs, he was a charmer—Dr. Bohrmann was moved to wish that Henry Medley had been his son. What a delight it would have been to nurture and prune a mind like that! To have a son in whose lineaments he could read dear Hedda's face and his own mind—ah, *that* would be a harvest for the autumn of an old philosopher's life!

Today, as if to salute him on his first day in his new house, there was a letter from Medley, as thick as ever, and sent, as always, by airmail. It was posted from the Hudson River town, since his teaching in Florida was over until fall, and he was back with his mother and the dragon, who had got, he wrote, "a barkless dog to match the dummy piano, on which for years she has been playing the Ballades of Chopin. That is, she *says* she is playing Chopin." The first five pages of the letter— there were seven altogether, written in that microscopic hand—gave an account of a few days he had spent in New York on his way up from Florida; he had gone to the museums, and reported his reactions to Matisse and Rembrandt, he had heard some contemporary chamber music, and he had found a set of the eleventh edition of the Encyclopaedia Britannica for twenty dollars. He enjoined Dr. Bohrmann to read the article on the alphabet without delay, and from that he went on to say that he had resumed his study of philology and that he found Holthausen's glossary to "Beowulf" far inferior to Klaeber's.

As he read on, Dr. Bohrmann shifted his position from time to time to ease the arthritic pain in his left hip, remembering that in the confusion of moving today, he had forgotten to take his pain-killing pills. He was, on the whole, in remarkably good health for a man of his age, but he was wearing out in the joints and the eyes—not grievously but in a bothersome way. The energy expended on Medley's New York stay made his legs and his heart ache. Page six of the letter began, "Now for the surprise, which I hope you will accept with as much pleasure as I take in the telling of it." We all like surprises and Dr. Bohrmann was no different from the rest of us; hoping for news of the arrival of a box of oranges from Florida perhaps, or something edible that was indigenous to upstate New York, he polished the magnifying glass and read on. He learned that Medley was getting a free automobile ride to the West with some former Harvard classmates who were going out to dig in Arizona, and that he would like to propose himself, "as our English cousins say, for a week or two weeks, or however long you enjoy me as your vis-à-vis. I will come with my own quarters (pup tent), and my own kitchen (portable grill), and hope you will give me houseroom in your back yard, though, should I detract from the aspect, I'll go up to your famous mesa. If my calculations are correct, and if we are not hindered by any act of God, and *if,* etc., I should be on your doorstep, with my camp, my typewriter, a change of shirt, and a sheaf of poems, on the 25th of June." He went on to say that he was anxious to do some mountain climbing and visit a cattle ranch and tour the ghost towns; that he had all sorts of ideas for Dr. Bohrmann's Oriental garden, which he would disclose on his arrival; that he had enough questions to ask, and theories to expound, and half theories to solidify, to last "til two each morning for a lifetime." He added, in a postscript, "Since I'm leaving tomorrow, I'm afraid there will be no way for you to put me off. But the cordiality of your letters, dear sir, gives me confidence in your welcome. I cherish the prospect of your midnight oil."

In all his life, Dr. Bohrmann had never had a house guest (it would, of course, be unthinkably infra dig to let the kid pitch a tent in the yard when there was an unused bedroom), not through any want of hospitality but because it was a matter that had never arisen, and he was so surprised by Medley's precipitous and inexorable assignment to him of the role of host that, while he never drank before five and seldom then drank spirits, he called to Mrs. Pritchard for the whiskey bottle and a glass.

Mrs. Pritchard, who was shaped like a pear and wore a blue mustache under a fleshy and ferocious bill, was punctual to the point of addiction (the professor said that she suffered from "chronic chronomania"), and, moreover, the slightest breach in routine sent her into a flushed and flustered minor nervous breakdown. "Whiskey? In the middle of the day?" she shouted from the kitchen, appalled. "But you've already had your beer, and I'm putting the soufflé in. This nice soufflé with chives in will be a fizzle." But she came bustling into the library anyhow with the whiskey and some ice, and, setting them down beside him, she said, "I declare!

Are we going to have meals any which way just because we've moved into a modernistic house?"

"I don't know," said Dr. Bohrmann thoughtfully. "I don't know what our life is going to be from now on, Mrs. Pritchard. We have a guest arriving—a Mr. Henry Medley."

"A guest for lunch? You *might* have told me!"

"No, no. Not a guest for lunch today. On Friday a young man is arriving to spend several days—perhaps weeks. Who knows? He offers to live in a wigwam under the trees. But we'll give him the spare room, Mrs. Pritchard."

Mrs. Pritchard gaped like a landed fish, but all she managed to say was, "He can't come Friday. Friday is your night for bridge, and the Streets and Miss Duveen are coming to dinner. You might have remembered that when you invited him."

"Well, the fact is, I didn't exactly invite him," said Dr. Bohrmann. "He is dropping out of the blue, so to speak. He is springing full grown out of the Hudson River."

"You mean you don't know him? Do you mean to tell me that I am to fetch and carry for a total stranger? A strange *young man?*" Mrs. Pritchard keenly disliked the young, and when students came to call, she was as rude to them as she could possibly be without actually boxing their ears.

Dr. Bohrmann, flinching under his housekeeper's snapping eyes, timorously said, "If we don't like him, we'll turn him out. But I think we're going to like him. I think we're going to find him a man of parts."

"Then why do you have to have whiskey just the selfsame minute I've put my soufflé in the oven?" Mrs.

Pritchard, as she often said of herself, was nobody's fool. With this retort, she went back to the kitchen, and the needless bangings and crashes that came from it indicated plainly that she did not mean to take Medley's intrusion lying down.

As the professor drank, he was in a tumult of emotions, a most uncommon condition for him, a placid man. He was a little uneasy at contemplating a change of pace in his life (the remark about the midnight oil alarmed him; he had gone to bed at ten o'clock ever since he could remember), and he was a little scared of Medley's erudition; part of the pleasure, shameful to be sure, of teaching at Nevilles had been that for the most part his students were as green as grass. But, on the other hand, he was touched to think of having a daily companion of such enthusiasm; they could walk together on the mesas and dispute matters pertaining to God and man and, in lighter moods, they could go to the movies. He began to consider how he might influence and temper his young friend's thought; in his imagination Henry Medley became so malleable that Dr. Bohrmann, with tenderness and tact, molded him into one of the most impressive figures on the intellectual scene of the twentieth century. How about adopting him? He could be a sort of monument to Dr. Bohrmann after Dr. Bohrmann's bones were laid to rest, beside Hedda's.

He caught himself up in the midst of his daydream and said to himself, "Come off it, Bohrmann," and turned aside to read a lighthearted scenic postcard from Mrs. Throop, sent from Durban, where she was having a holiday with her children. "I like gathering sea shells beside the Indian Ocean so very much better than writing novels," she wrote in a relaxed and generous hand, "and I do it so much better. These lovely shells! Jon is making a collection of them, to repay you for the arrowheads. You see, you're a daily part of our life."

Darling Mrs. Throop! He wished he could adopt *her*. He wished that all his distant friends were coming to bless his house.

When Henry Medley arrived, at about dusk, he greeted his host in a torrent of epigrammatic and perfect Hanoverian German, refused the offer of the spare bedroom, and then, cajoled, accepted it. And he began to unload his gear from the taxi that had brought him up from the interurban station. (He had parted with his companions in Denver.) Besides the tent and the portable grill and the sleeping bag, he had brought two bulging Gladstones, a typewriter, a tennis racket, a pair of skis, a rifle, a fishing rod and tackle box, a recorder, a green baize bag full of books, extensive photographic equipment, and two large boxes of cuttings of field flowers from the Hudson Valley. At the sight of the skis, Mrs. Pritchard's eyebrows disappeared into her hair; there would be no skiing near Adams for three months. Before Medley went up to his room, he produced two bottles of Bernkasteler Doktor from the depths of one of the Gladstones and asked Mrs. Pritchard, with ineffable sweetness, to make a *Bowle* (for which he gave her the recipe), so that he could toast "the most distinguished scholar in America." Such was his sweetness and such, also, his air of authority that Mrs. Pritchard, that virago and nobody's fool, was disarmed, and trotted obediently to the kitchen and began to cut up fruit.

Before Dr. Bohrmann had got any real impression of the youth at all—beyond the fact that he lived like a gale—he found himself sitting on the western deck, sipping the wine (how had Medley guessed that this was his favorite of all Mosels—the *Bowle* was delicious), and answering Medley's rapid and knowledgeable questions about the differences between ground and push moraines, about glacier flora, about the mining history of this region. The young man listened to the old man's answers as closely as a doctor listening to a heartbeat through a stethoscope, and Dr. Bohrmann had the feeling that he was indelibly recording every fact and every speculation, however irrelevant or tenuous. It is flattering to be so closely attended and so respected, and Dr. Bohrmann glowed as he talked, slaking this burning student's thirst.

Henry Medley wore glasses and a beard, and a beholder, looking at the two from afar, would have said they bore a close resemblance. Nearer at hand, it would have been observed that the frames of the young man's glasses were of thick tortoise shell and that the old man's were gold, that Medley's curly beard was black and Dr. Bohrmann's was straight and frosty. An eavesdropper would have said their German was the same, but an expert would have heard the academy in Medley's inflections and his stilted usages, and would, in Dr. Bohrmann's accent, have heard a southern softening.

At first, dismissing the beard as an amusing coincidence, Dr. Bohrmann's view of the boy was an agree-

able one. Henry Medley was small, constructed thriftily
and well, and he emanated indestructibility from the
soles of his neat little feet, shod in immaculate white
sneakers, to the top of his shapely and close-cropped
head. His hands were quick and nervous, and darkly
stained with nicotine, for he smoked cigarettes ceaselessly, down to nothing; his clever eyes glinted as they
swiftly detached themselves from one focus and fixed
upon the next. His voice was high and tended to be
phrenetic. Despite the voice, despite the crew cut, despite the lissome limbs, Medley gave the impression of
having existed on the earth for much more than twenty-
four years, and Dr. Bohrmann was sure that at seventy
he would not look much different from the way he did
now. He was, thought Dr. Bohrmann as the sun began
to set, darkening Henry Medley's face and whitening
his perfect teeth, like a spruce, goodlooking, ageless
imp. He was respectful, responsive, articulate, enthusi-
astic, astoundingly catholic in his information. Dr.
Bohrmann, however, was pleased to note that he wasn't
perfect: there was somewhere in him a lack—a lack of a
quality an imp did not need but a man could not live
without. For example, when Dr. Bohrmann inquired
about his journey, really wanting to know, Medley was
perfunctory. "The Lincoln Highway is as hot as
Tophet, and as ugly as sin—the trip was no Odyssey to
put into dactylic hexameters," and then asked Dr. Bohrmann how he would evaluate Croce as a historian.
Generally people of this age were so self-centered that
one was obliged to defend oneself against autobiography
with the greatest diplomacy. But Medley was so unself-
centered that Dr. Bohrmann began to wonder if he had
a self at all. He would discuss his plans, but not his

aspirations; he would talk about his ideas on a subject, but not his feelings on it; he would quote from "Voyage of the 'Beagle,' " but would not say that he longed to go on a voyage himself. It comes from having no father, and only a mother and a dragon and dumb little blondes, said Dr. Bohrmann to himself, and he resolved to rear this orphan imp into a human creature.

That evening, at dinner, Medley was a smashing success. As Mr. Street said afterward, he had never found anyone who had so fully grasped Whitehead and Russell; the ladies were delighted with his droll descriptions of Hudson River Bracketed and his account of a meeting with a manufacturer of embalming supplies. When Medley praised the *coq au vin,* Mrs. Pritchard fell head over heels in love; when he gave a short talk on the viticulture of the Rhine, the Hochheimer in their glasses turned to nectar. After dinner, when the bridge game began, he sat quietly in a distant corner of the library reading the "Diary of William Dunlap" until Blossom Duveen protested and archly told her host that he was rude. Thereafter, at the end of each rubber, someone sat out, and, in the end, as it happened, Medley was always at the table. He played, said the overwhelmed logician Street, like a rattlesnake.

At half past nine, as his elders were yawning, having had enough bridge and having finished the one weak highball they allowed themselves, Medley said, "I don't suppose you'd like me to teach you ombre? I learned it after a close reading of 'The Rape of the Lock.' "

And so, for two more hours, the company spent a stimulating, if puzzling, time with a pack of forty cards, learning—or, rather, failing to learn—such terms as *manille* and *basto,* and being reminded every so often by their teacher that "There is no *ponto* in black trumps, and this is most important to remember."

When the Streets and Miss Duveen departed, they were seen to the door not only by their host but by Medley as well, who warmly shook hands with them all and cordially said he hoped they would meet again soon. Back in the library, he tidied up, emptying ashtrays, putting away the cards, plumping up the cushions. Suddenly, in the midst of his housewifery, his eyes began to water, and then he sneezed explosively and repeatedly; in the lacunae between these detonations, he grimaced painfully and mopped his face and made a sort of moaning sound.

"Poor chap," said Dr. Bohrmann. "I expect it's some pollen or other from the prairie. We've been very dry this year."

"Not pollen," gasped Medley. "That!" And with a quivering forefinger he pointed at Grimalkin, the ginger cat, who had apparently come into the house through his own entrance, which Dr. Bohrmann had had cut into the kitchen door, and was sitting on the window sill, looking with interest at the shaking and sneezing and wheezing stranger.

What a way for the visit to begin and the evening to end! Breathing with difficulty, Medley told Dr. Bohrmann that from earliest childhood, cats had affected him thus. What was there to do? Plainly Grimalkin, an admirable cat and the lord of the manor, would not dream of changing his habits. And Dr. Bohrmann would not dream of Medley's going up to the mesa with his tent or—for Medley, in his discomfort that was mixed with fear, proposed this—of his returning at once to the dragon and her barkless dog.

"But look here," said Dr. Bohrmann. "My beast has never set foot in the spare room—I assure you it's innocent of his dangerous dander. Come along upstairs and let's see if you don't feel better."

Once in his bedroom, Medley gulped down antihistamines of divers colors and did presently feel better. He said he would stay out of the cat's way, and Dr. Bohrmann, very unhappy over the contretemps, said that he and Mrs. Pritchard would do what they could to keep Grimalkin out of the house; at this time of year he had a good deal of business outdoors, what with hunting shrews and smelling flowers. Dr. Bohrmann would board up the cat door first thing the next day.

In the morning, as Dr. Bohrmann was going through the upper hall, he found the corpse of a gopher on the floor in front of Medley's door. In spite of himself he smiled, and when he went into the dining room and found Grimalkin in his accustomed chair, opposite his own, he stroked the tom's big manly head and said, "Rotten cat! Wicked cat! How did you get in?" though he knew perfectly well Grimalkin had got in through his own private door. The cat, according to his lifetime habit, had his breakfast of corn flakes, well saturated with heavy cream. His purr, as he ate, was loud and smug.

Mrs. Pritchard had, since Dr. Bohrmann had known her, loved three creatures: Hedda, himself, and Grimalkin. For the cat she bought toys at the five-and-ten, grew catnip in a flowerpot in the kitchen, made special dishes (he was particularly fond of corn pudding); she brushed him, scratched him behind the ears, petted him, talked to him, suffered him to involve himself in her knitting. And when Dr. Bohrmann, strengthening himself with an unwonted third cup of coffee, announced to her that he was going to board up the cat door, and that Grimalkin must henceforth live outside because of Medley's disaffection, she was outraged.

"What next!" she cried. "I've been giving that boy some second thoughts. For all his kowtowing and his mealy mouth and his 'Sublime chicken, Mrs. Pritchard' and his 'After you, Dr. Bohrmann,' there's something about him that tells me he's sneaky. Put Grimalkin out of the house indeed! And what if milord takes a scunner to me? Will my door be boarded up, too?"

"Oh, come, Mrs. Pritchard," said Dr. Bohrmann. "It's summer and Grimalkin has plenty to do outdoors. He won't mind for a few days."

"A few days! Did you see those skis? Whoever heard of skiing here before October? To my way of thinking, Mr. Henry Medley brought his entire worldly goods with him and means to stay till kingdom come."

"Oh, lady, be good!" said Dr. Bohrmann, and he sighed. He was not used to domestic trouble and it embarrassed him. Moreover, he was not entirely sure that Mrs. Pritchard was wrong about Medley and he found himself hoping that the boy slept late; he did not feel like a deep conversation just now.

"Very well," said Mrs. Pritchard. "But we shall see what we shall see." And she closed her mouth firmly, scooped Grimalkin up in her loving arms, and marched to the kitchen.

Henry Medley stayed with Dr. Bohrmann for three weeks and was, during this lengthy time, the most sedulous of apes. He rented a bicycle and he bought a Tyrolian hat; he appropriated Dr. Bohrmann's politics and his taste in music and food; in company, he quoted his host continually but did not acknowledge his source. On the second day of his visit, Dr. Bohrmann began to tire of him; on the third day he began to avoid him; on the fourth, he begged a ride to Denver with Blossom Duveen, where he went to a double-feature Western while she was shopping. But Henry Medley was not aware that he bored his host; on the contrary, he often observed that their meeting of minds was enough almost to make him believe in a magnanimous God. He was very busy. Besides tirelessly picking Dr. Bohrmann's brains, he gardened ferociously, moved the porch furniture about, played his recorder and Dr. Bohrmann's fiddle, read his poems aloud (they were awful and long), took hundreds of photographs. At the end of the first week, Dr. Bohrmann, worn out with company and conversation, suggested that Medley join an organized tour that was going to the ghost towns, but Medley replied that unless

Dr. Bohrmann went with him, he would prefer to stay at home. He did not go fishing, because Dr. Bohrmann did not fish; he did not play tennis, because Dr. Bohrmann was too old for the courts. They were invited out as a pair, and when Dr. Bohrmann had guests, Medley did the honors. "We are giving you a Piesporter tonight," he would say, or, "We prevailed upon Mrs. Pritchard to make cold sorrel soup." It was *us* and *our* and *we* until Dr. Bohrmann began to feel that his identity was ebbing away from him. Or that he had attached to his side an unmovable homunculus, who, by the way, now spoke German with a Breisgau accent and who mimicked his every thought and every gesture. The gratification he had felt on that first afternoon when Medley had seemed to listen so wisely and so well never returned.

Mrs. Pritchard would not speak to Medley. Her hatred was murderous; it was evident that she would have liked to put arsenic in his food. And it was Mrs. Pritchard who in the end—guileful, beloved thing that she was—dislodged him. Mrs. Pritchard, ably assisted by Grimalkin. She accomplished this through the simple expedient of taking away the board that had immobilized the swinging cat door. But she was very sly. Later on, she confessed that each night she waited up until the young man had gone to bed and then she would creep down to the kitchen and take away the board; in the morning, long before either of the men got up, she nailed it on again.

One night, Dr. Bohrmann was in a restive sleep,
troubled by his arthritis and wakened often by the
brightness of the moon. He was distressed, moreover,
about Medley, for this was the first time in his long life
that he had ever really disliked anyone; he had come to
detest that bearded and permanent fixture almost as
keenly as Mrs. Pritchard did. And what was the matter
with him, a man full of years and of experience, that he
could not gracefully remove himself from this dilemma?
He dozed, and woke, and dozed again. He dreamed
sadly of Hedda. They were cycling, he and Hedda,
through the Schwarzwald, toiling up a hill but talking
continually, though they had little breath. "Aunt Ger-
trude will be cross because we're late for tea and I promised to bring the butter," said Hedda. Her worry at last
made her weep, then sob tragically, and Wolfgang comforted her in shouts; he tried to lower his voice but he
could not, and he woke himself by yelling, "We're not
too late, my darling! We have until the sun goes down."
Startled by the sound of his own voice, he switched on
the light. Medley was standing in the doorway.

"Is the cat in here?" he said.

"Look here, Medley," said Dr. Bohrmann in an amazing burst of courage. "I don't like having people walk
into my bedroom in the middle of the night."

"I'm sorry, sir, I wouldn't have, only—" and he was
seized with a violent paroxysm of sneezes. His red eyes
streamed and his breathing, after the sneezes, was sterto-
rous. Obviously he was in for an asthma attack.

Dr. Bohrmann sat up in bed and he grasped at a
straw. "Poor chap," he said kindly. "I'm afraid my old
ginger tomcat has outwitted us. That's the way they are,
you know—foxy."

Medley, in a choked voice, said, "I have concealed this from you, sir, but every morning for a week now, that cat has brought some unspeakable piece of carrion to my bedroom door. Tonight, though, it went the limit. It got into my room through some diabolical system of its own, and now the room will be dangerous for me for days."

Dr. Bohrmann smiled behind his concealing hand. "I'm sorry for that," he said, and clucked his tongue.

"I don't suppose you would . . . No, I don't suppose you would."

"Would what, Medley?"

"Would—oh, no, sir, I won't propose it."

"Get rid of Grimalkin? Is that what you're trying to say?"

"Well, in a manner of speaking."

"No, I would not. I've had my handsome ginger tom-cat for fifteen years, and I'll have him till he dies."

"Then, if he's to have the run of the house," said Medley, "I'd better move out to the yard."

"Well, I'll tell you, Medley," said Dr. Bohrmann, ashamed of his cunning and pleased as punch with it, "if Grimalkin has got your number, and it's plain that he has, moving outdoors won't do a particle of good. He'll get into your tent and plague you there. No, Medley, my boy, I'm afraid Grimalkin has us over a barrel."

A frenzy of sneezes—the intellectual face turned red and blue. When the storm was over, Medley leaned weakly against the door and groaned. When he spoke again, there was a decided testiness in his voice. "If I had known you had a cat," he said, "I wouldn't have made this trip. Isn't there *anything* we can do?"

"I'm afraid not," said Dr. Bohrmann. "I'm just afraid there isn't a thing we can do."

"I could go up to the mesa, I suppose?"

"I wouldn't recommend that," said Dr. Bohrmann. "It's rattlesnake time."

"Then what shall I do?" He was plaintive and pathetic, and for a split second Dr. Bohrmann almost weakened, but he remembered in time the sapping tedium of Medley's monologues and interrogations, and the feeling he had that Medley had robbed him of his own personality, and he said, "It looks like Hudson River Bracketed and the barkless dog for you."

In the morning, when they met at breakfast, Henry Medley was pale and shaky; obviously he had had a very bad night. Dr. Bohrmann, who had slept excellently after his visitor left his room, tried to start a conversation about Spanish cave drawings. But the wind was out of Medley's sails; he smiled wanly and asked to be excused.

The taxi came an hour later, and Medley piled his mountain of belongings into the back seat. Mrs. Pritchard, beaming, brought him a box lunch. Grimalkin, sitting in a lake of sun under the weeping-willow tree, was cleaning a shoulder blade.

"Now you write to me," said Dr. Bohrmann heartily. "Now *auf Wiederschen,* Medley."

"Goodbye," said Medley sorrowfully. "To think that a cat . . . I might almost think there was a plan behind it."

"Have a good trip, son," said Dr. Bohrmann, and shuddered at the appellation.

At last, sulkily, Medley got into the taxi, and then he rallied and his old self reappeared. He said, in German with a South German accent, "If Grimalkin ever goes to join his ancestors, perhaps you will invite me again? We haven't scratched the surface of our common interests."

But happily the driver started the motor and went off before Dr. Bohrmann was obliged to reply. Mrs. Pritch-ard had gone into the house and now came out again with a dish of sardines, which, without a word, she handed to Dr. Bohrmann; he received it without a word and took it to the heroic tom, who accepted it with an open diapason of purrs. The old man, squatting on his heels beside the cat, surveyed his pretty garden with delight and looked at his house with amazement. How beautiful and bountiful was life! How charming it was of accident to cause contrast: it was good to be cold, so that one could get warm; it was good to wear out so that one could renew oneself; it was really a lovely thing that Medley had come and had gone. With these heartwarming and reasonable thoughts, Dr. Bohrmann watched his cat finish the last fishtail, and then, fetching his big black umbrella, he began to work in his garden. He uprooted the field flowers Medley had brought from the Hudson Valley, not in anger but because they had never really belonged with the rest of the planting, and just as he threw them into the lily pond, Blossom Duveen drove up.

"Came by to remind you it's bridge night," she called out in her vulgar, brassy voice. "No goulashes tonight, I hope, I hope."

As he strolled over to talk to her, Dr. Bohrmann listed

to himself some of the other pleasures of life: this dumb dear, for example, after Medley with his hellbent enlightenment; bridge after ombre; a contented Mrs. Pritchard.

"What gives?" said Miss Duveen. "You look like the cat that swallowed the canary."

"I am," said Dr. Bohrmann, grinning conspiratorially at Grimalkin who was washing the top of his brainy head.

In the Zoo

Keening harshly in his senility, the blind polar bear slowly and ceaselessly shakes his head in the stark heat of the July and mountain noon. His open eyes are blue. No one stops to look at him; an old farmer, in passing, sums up the old bear's situation by observing, with a ruthless chuckle, that he is a "back number." Patient and despairing, he sits on his yellowed haunches on the central rock of his pool, his huge toy paws wearing short boots of mud.

The grizzlies to the right of him, a conventional family of father and mother and two spring cubs, alternately play the clown and sleep. There is a blustery, scoundrelly, half-likable bravado in the manner of the black bear on the polar's left; his name, according to the legend on his cage, is Clancy, and he is a rough-and-tumble, brawling blowhard, thundering continually as he paces back and forth, or pauses to face his audience of children and mothers and release from his great, gray-tongued mouth a perfectly Vesuvian roar. If he were to be reincarnated in human form, he would be a man of action, possibly a football coach, probably a politician. One expects to see his black hat hanging from a branch of one of his trees, at any moment he will light a cigar.

The polar bear's next-door neighbors are not the only ones who offer so sharp and sad a contrast to him. Across a reach of scrappy grass and litter is the convocation of conceited monkeys, burrowing into each other's necks and chests for fleas, picking their noses with their long, black, finicky fingers, swinging by their gifted tails on the flying trapeze, screaming bloody murder. Even when they mourn—one would think the male orangutan was on the very brink of suicide—they are comedians; they only fake depression, for they are firmly secure in their rambunctious tribalism and in their appalling insight and contempt. Their flibbertigibbet gambolling is a sham, and, stealthily and shiftily, they are really watching the pitiful polar bear ("Back number," they quote the farmer. "That's *his* number all right," they snigger), and the windy black bear ("Life of the party. Gasbag. Low I.Q.," they note scornfully on his dossier), and the stupid, bourgeois grizzlies ("It's feed the face and hit the sack for them," the monkeys say). And they are watching my sister and me, two middle-aged women, as we sit on a bench between the exhibits, eating popcorn, growing thirsty. We are thoughtful.

A chance remark of Daisy's a few minutes before has turned us to memory and meditation. "I don't know why," she said, "but that poor blind bear reminds me of Mr. Murphy." The name "Mr. Murphy" at once returned us both to childhood, and we were floated far and fast, our later lives diminished. So now we eat our popcorn in silence with the ritualistic appetite of childhood, which has little to do with hunger; it is not so much food as a sacrament, and in tribute to our sisterliness and our friendliness I break the silence to say that this is the best popcorn I have ever eaten in my life. The extravagance of my statement instantly makes me feel self-indulgent, and for some time I uneasily avoid looking at the blind bear. My sister does not agree or disagree; she simply says that popcorn is the only food she has ever really liked. For a long time, then, we eat without a word, but I know, because I know her well and know her similarity to me, that Daisy is thinking what I am thinking; both of us are mournfully remembering Mr. Murphy, who, at one time in our lives, was our only friend.

This zoo is in Denver, a city that means nothing to my sister and me except as a place to take or meet trains. Daisy lives two hundred miles farther west, and it is her custom, when my every-other-year visit with her is over, to come across the mountains to see me off on my eastbound train. We know almost no one here, and because our stays are short, we have never bothered to learn the town in more than the most desultory way. We know the Burlington uptown office and the respectable hotels, a restaurant or two, the Union Station, and, beginning today, the zoo in the city park.

But since the moment that Daisy named Mr. Murphy by name our situation in Denver has been only corporeal; our minds and our hearts are in Adams, fifty miles north, and we are seeing, under the white sun at its pitiless meridian, the streets of that ugly town, its parks and trees and bridges, the bandstand in its dreary park, the roads that lead away from it, west to the mountains and east to the plains, its mongrel and multitudinous churches, its high school shaped like a loaf of bread, the campus of its college, an oasis of which we had no experience except to walk through it now and then, eying the woodbine on the impressive buildings. These things are engraved forever on our minds with a legibility so insistent that you have only to say the name of the town aloud to us to rip the rinds from our nerves and leave us exposed in terror and humiliation.

We have supposed in later years that Adams was not so bad as all that, and we know that we magnified its ugliness because we looked upon it as the extension of the possessive, unloving, scornful, complacent foster mother, Mrs. Placer, to whom, at the death of our parents within a month of each other, we were sent like Dickensian grotesqueries—cowardly, weak-stomached, given to tears, backward in school. Daisy was ten and I was eight when, unaccompanied, we made the long trip from Marblehead to our benefactress, whom we had never seen and, indeed, never heard of until the pastor of our church came to tell us of the arrangement our father had made on his deathbed, seconded by our mother on hers. This man, whose name and face I have forgotten and whose parting speeches to us I have not forgiven, tried to dry our tears with talk of Indians and of buffaloes; he spoke, however, at much greater length, and in preaching cadences, of the Christian goodness of Mrs. Placer. She was, he said, childless and fond of children, and for many years she had been a widow, after the lingering demise of her tubercular husband, for whose sake she had moved to the Rocky Mountains. For his support and costly medical care, she had run a boarding house, and after his death, since he had left her nothing, she was obliged to continue running it. She had been a girlhood friend of our paternal grandmother, and our father, in the absence of responsible relatives, had made her the beneficiary of his life insurance on the condition that she lodge and rear us. The pastor, with a frankness remarkable considering that he was talking to children, explained to us that our father had left little more than a drop in the bucket for our care, and he enjoined us to give Mrs. Placer, in return for her hospitality and sacrifice, courteous help and eternal thanks. "Sacrifice" was a word we were never allowed to forget.

And thus it was, in grief for our parents, that we came cringing to the dry Western town and to the house where Mrs. Placer lived, a house in which the square, uncushioned furniture was cruel and the pictures on the walls were either dour or dire and the lodgers, who lived in the upper floors among shadowy wardrobes and chiffoniers, had come through the years to resemble their landlady in appearance as well as in deportment.

After their ugly-colored evening meal, Gran—as she bade us call her—and her paying guests would sit, rangy and aquiline, rocking on the front porch on spring and summer and autumn nights, tasting their delicious grievances: those slights delivered by ungrateful sons and daughters, those impudences committed by trolley-car conductors and uppity salegirls in the ready-to-wear, all those slurs and calculated elbow-jostlings that were their daily crucifixion and their staff of life. We little girls, washing the dishes in the cavernous kitchen, listened to their even, martyred voices, fixed like leeches to their solitary subject and their solitary creed—that life was essentially a matter of being done in, let down, and swindled.

At regular intervals, Mrs. Placer, chairwoman of the victims, would say, "Of course, I don't care; I just have to laugh," and then would tell a shocking tale of an intricate piece of skulduggery perpetrated against her by someone she did not even know. Sometimes, with her avid, partial jury sitting there on the porch behind the bitter hopvines in the heady mountain air, the cases she tried involved Daisy and me, and, listening, we travailed, hugging each other, whispering, "I wish she wouldn't! Oh, how did she find out?" How *did* she? Certainly we never told her when we were snubbed or chosen last on teams, never admitted to a teacher's scolding or to the hoots of laughter that greeted us when we bit on silly, unfair jokes. But she knew. She knew about the slumber parties we were not invited to, the beefsteak fries at which we were pointedly left out; she knew that the singing teacher had said in so many words that I could not carry a tune in a basket and that the sewing superintendent had said that Daisy's fingers were all thumbs. With our teeth chattering in the cold of our isolation, we would hear her protestant, litigious voice defending our right to be orphans, paupers, wholly dependent on her—except for the really ridiculous pittance from our father's life insurance—when it was all she could do to make ends meet. She did not care, but she had to laugh that people in general were so small-minded that they looked down on fatherless, motherless waifs like us and, by association, looked down on her. It seemed funny to her that people gave her no credit for taking on these sickly youngsters who were not even kin but only the grandchildren of a friend.

If a child with braces on her teeth came to play with us, she was, according to Gran, slyly lording it over us because our teeth were crooked, but there was no money to have them straightened. And what could be the meaning of our being asked to come for supper at the doctor's house? Were the doctor and his la-di-da New York wife and those pert girls with their solid-gold barrettes and their Shetland pony going to shame her poor darlings? Or shame their poor Gran by making them sorry to come home to the plain but honest life that was all she could provide for them?

There was no stratum of society not reeking with the effluvium of fraud and pettifoggery. And the school system was almost the worst of all: if we could not understand fractions, was that not our teacher's fault? And therefore what right had she to give us F? It was as plain as a pikestaff to Gran that the teacher was only covering up her own inability to teach. It was unlikely, too— highly unlikely—that it was by accident that time and time again the free medical clinic was closed for the day just as our names were about to be called out, so that nothing was done about our bad tonsils, which meant that we were repeatedly sick in the winter, with Gran fetching and carrying for us, climbing those stairs a jillion times a day with her game leg and her heart that was none too strong.

Steeped in these mists of accusation and hidden plots and double meanings, Daisy and I grew up like worms. I think no one could have withstood the atmosphere in that house where everyone trod on eggs that a little bird had told them were bad. They spied on one another, whispered behind doors, conjectured, drew parallels beginning "With all due respect . . ." or "It is a matter of indifference to *me* but . . ." The vigilantes patrolled our town by day, and by night returned to lay their goodies at their priestess's feet and wait for her oracular interpretation of the innards of the butcher, the baker, the candlestick maker, the soda jerk's girl, and the barber's unnatural deaf white cat.

Consequently, Daisy and I also became suspicious. But it was suspicion of ourselves that made us mope and weep and grimace with self-judgment. Why were we not happy when Gran had sacrificed herself to the bone for us? Why did we not cut dead the paper boy who had called her a filthy name? Why did we persist in our willful friendliness with the grocer who had tried, unsuccessfully, to overcharge her on a case of pork and beans?

Our friendships were nervous and surreptitious; we sneaked and lied, and as our hungers sharpened, our debasement deepened; we were pitied; we were shifty-eyed, always on the lookout for Mrs. Placer or one of her tattletale lodgers; we were hypocrites.

Nevertheless, one thin filament of instinct survived, and Daisy and I in time found asylum in a small menagerie down by the railroad tracks. It belonged to a gentle alcoholic ne'er-do-well, who did nothing all day long but drink bathtub gin in rickeys and play solitaire and smile to himself and talk to his animals. He had a little, stunted red vixen and a deodorized skunk, a parrot from Tahiti that spoke Parisian French, a woebegone coyote, and two capuchin monkeys, so serious and humanized, so small and sad and sweet, and so religious-looking with their tonsured heads that it was impossible not to think their gibberish was really an ordered language with a grammar that someday some philologist would under-stand.

Gran knew about our visits to Mr. Murphy and she did not object, for it gave her keen pleasure to excoriate him when we came home. His vice was not a matter of guesswork; it was an established fact that he was half-seas over from dawn till midnight. "With the black Irish," said Gran, "The taste for drink is taken in with the mother's milk and is never mastered. Oh, I know all about those promises to join the temperance movement and not to touch another drop. The way to Hell is paved with good intentions."

We were still little girls when we discovered Mr. Murphy, before the shattering disease of adolescence was to make our bones and brains ache even more pain-fully than before, and we loved him and we hoped to marry him when we grew up. We loved him, and we loved his monkeys to exactly the same degree and in ex-actly the same way; they were husbands and fathers and brothers, these three little, ugly, dark, secret men who minded their own business and let us mind ours. If we stuck our fingers through the bars of the cage, the monkeys would sometimes take them in their tight, tiny hands and look into our faces with a tentative, somehow

absent-minded sorrow, as if they terribly regretted that
they could not place us but were glad to see us all the
same. Mr. Murphy, playing a solitaire game of cards
called "once in a blue moon" on a kitchen table in his
back yard beside the pens, would occasionally look up
and blink his beautiful blue eyes and say, "You're
peaches to make over my wee friends. I love you for it."
There was nothing demanding in his voice, and nothing
sticky; on his lips the word "love" was jocose and forth-
right, it had no strings attached. We would sit on either
side of him and watch him regiment his ranks of cards
and stop to drink as deeply as if he were dying of thirst
and wave to his animals and say to them, "Yes, lads,
you're dandies."

Because Mr. Murphy was as reserved with us as the
capuchins were, as courteously noncommittal, we were
surprised one spring day when he told us that he had a
present for us, which he hoped Mrs. Placer would let us
keep; it was a puppy, for whom the owner had asked
him to find a home—half collie and half Labrador re-
triever, blue-blooded on both sides.

"You might tell Mrs. Placer—" he said, smiling at the
name, for Gran was famous in the town. "You might tell
Mrs. Placer," said Mr. Murphy, "that this lad will make
a fine watchdog. She'll never have to fear for her spoons
again. Or her honor." The last he said to himself, not
laughing but tucking his chin into his collar; lines
sprang to the corners of his eyes. He would not let us see
the dog, whom we could hear yipping and squealing inside his shanty, for he said that our disappointment
would weigh on his conscience if we lost our hearts to
the fellow and then could not have him for our own.

That evening at supper, we told Gran about Mr.

Murphy's present. A dog? In the first place, why a dog? Was it possible that the news had reached Mr. Murphy's ears that Gran had just this very day finished planting her spring garden, the very thing that a rampageous dog would have in his mind to destroy? What sex was it? A male! Females, she had heard, were more trustworthy; males roved and came home smelling of skunk; such a consideration as this, of course, would not have crossed Mr. Murphy's fuddled mind. Was this young male dog housebroken? We had not asked? That was the limit!

Gran appealed to her followers, too raptly fascinated by Mr. Murphy's machinations to eat their Harvard beets. "Am I being farfetched or does it strike you as decidedly queer that Mr. Murphy is trying to fob off on my little girls a young cur that has not been trained?" she asked them. "If it were housebroken, he would have said so, so I feel it is safe to assume that it is not. Perhaps cannot *be* housebroken. I've heard of such cases."

The fantasy spun on, richly and rapidly, with all the skilled helping hands at work at once. The dog was tangibly in the room with us, shedding his hair, biting his fleas, shaking rain off himself to splatter the walls, dragging some dreadful carcass across the floor, chewing up slippers, knocking over chairs with his tail, gobbling the chops from the platter, barking, biting, fathering, fighting, smelling to high heaven of carrion, staining the rug with his muddy feet, scratching the floor with his claws. He developed rabies; he bit a child, two children! Three! Everyone in town! And Gran and her poor darlings went to jail for harboring this murderous, odoriferous, drunk, Roman Catholic dog.

And yet, astoundingly enough, she came around to agreeing to let us have the dog. It was, as Mr. Murphy had predicted, the word "watchdog" that deflected the course of the trial. The moment Daisy uttered it, Gran halted, marshalling her reverse march; while she rallied and tacked and reconnoitred, she sent us to the kitchen for the dessert. And by the time this course was under way, the uses of a dog, the enormous potentialities for investigation and law enforcement in a dog trained by Mrs. Placer, were being minutely and passionately scrutinized by the eight upright bloodhounds sitting at the table wolfing their brown Betty as if it were fresh-killed rabbit. The dog now sat at attention beside his mistress, fiercely alert, ears cocked, nose aquiver, the protector of widows, of orphans, of lonely people who had no homes. He made short shrift of burglars, homicidal maniacs, Peeping Toms, gypsies, bogus missionaries, Fuller Brush men with a risqué spiel. He went to the store and brought back groceries, retrieved the evening paper from the awkward place the boy had meanly thrown it, rescued cripples from burning houses, saved children from drowning, heeled at command, begged, lay down, stood up, sat, jumped through a hoop, ratted.

Both times—when he was a ruffian of the blackest delinquency and then a pillar of society—he was full-grown in his prefiguration, and when Laddy appeared on the following day, small, unsteady, and whimpering lonesomely, Gran and her lodgers were taken aback; his infant, clumsy paws embarrassed them, his melting eyes were unapropos. But it could never be said of Mrs. Placer, as Mrs. Placer her own self said, that she was a woman who went back on her word, and her darlings were going to have their dog, softheaded and feckless as he might be. All the first night, in his carton in the kitchen, he wailed for his mother, and in the morning, it was true, he had made a shambles of the room—fouled the floor, and pulled off the tablecloth together with a ketchup bottle, so that thick gore lay everywhere. At breakfast, the lodgers confessed they had had a most amusing night, for it had actually been funny the way the dog had been determined not to let anyone get a wink of sleep. After that first night, Laddy slept in our room, receiving from us, all through our delighted, sleepless nights, pats and embraces and kisses and whispers. He was our baby, our best friend, the smartest, prettiest, nicest dog in the entire wide world. Our soft and rapid blandishments excited him to yelp at us in pleased bewilderment, and then we would playfully grasp his muzzle, so that he would snarl, deep in his throat like an adult dog, and shake his head violently, and, when we freed him, nip us smartly with great good will.

He was an intelligent and genial dog and we trained him quickly. He steered clear of Gran's radishes and lettuce after she had several times given him a brisk come-uppance with a strap across the rump, and he soon left off chewing shoes and the laundry on the line, and he outgrew his babyish whining. He grew like a weed; he lost his spherical softness, and his coat, which had been sooty fluff, came in stiff and rusty black; his nose grew aristocratically long, and his clever, pointed ears stood at attention. He was all bronzy, lustrous black except for an Elizabethan ruff of white and a tip of white at the end of his perky tail. No one could deny that he was exceptionally handsome and that he had as well, great personal charm and style. He escorted Daisy and me to school in the morning, laughing interiorly out of the enormous pleasure of his life as he gracefully cantered ahead of us, distracted occasionally by his private interest in smells or unfamiliar beings in the grass but, on the whole, engrossed in his role of chaperon. He made friends easily with other dogs, and sometimes he went for a long hunting weekend into the mountains with a huge and bossy old red hound named Mess, who had been on the county most of his life and had made a good thing of it, particularly at the fire station.

It was after one of these three-day excursions into the high country that Gran took Laddy in hand. He had come back spent and filthy, his coat a mass of cockleburs and ticks, his eyes bloodshot, loud *râles* in his chest; for half a day he lay motionless before the front door like someone in a hangover, his groaning eyes explicitly saying "Oh, for God's sake, leave me be" when we offered him food or bowls of water. Gran was disapproving, then affronted, and finally furious. Not, of course, with Laddy, since all inmates of her house enjoyed immunity, but with Mess, whose caddish character, together with that of his nominal masters, the firemen, she examined closely under a strong light, with an air of detachment, with her not caring but her having, all the same, to laugh. A lodger who occupied the back west room had something to say about the fire chief and his nocturnal visits to a certain house occupied by a certain group of young women, too near the same age to be sisters and too old to be the daughters of the woman who claimed to be their mother. What a story! The exophthalmic librarian—she lived in one of the front rooms— had some interesting insinuations to make about the deputy marshal, who had borrowed, significantly, she thought, a book on hypnotism. She also knew—she was, of course, in a most useful position in the town, and from her authoritative pen in the middle of the library her mammiform and azure eyes and her eager ears missed nothing—that the fire chief's wife was not as scrupulous as she might be when she was keeping score on bridge night at the Sorosis.

There was little at the moment that Mrs. Placer and her disciples could do to save the souls of the Fire Department and their families, and therefore save the town from holocaust (a very timid boarder—a Mr. Beaver, a newcomer who was not to linger long—had sniffed throughout this recitative as if he were smelling burning flesh), but at least the unwholesome bond between Mess and Laddy could and would be severed once and for all. Gran looked across the porch at Laddy, who lay stretched at full length in the darkest corner, shuddering and baying abortively in his throat as he chased jack rabbits in his dreams, and she said, "A dog can have morals like a human." With this declaration Laddy's randy, manly holidays were finished. It may have been telepathy that woke him; he lifted his heavy head from his paws, laboriously got up, hesitated for a moment, and then padded languidly across the porch to Gran. He stood docilely beside her chair, head down, tail drooping as if to say, "O.K., Mrs. Placer, show me how and I'll walk the straight and narrow."

The very next day, Gran changed Laddy's name to Caesar, as being more dignified, and a joke was made at the supper table that he had come, seen, and conquered Mrs. Placer's heart—for within her circle, where the magnanimity she lavished upon her orphans was daily demonstrated, Mrs. Placer's heart was highly thought of. On that day also, although we did not know it yet, Laddy ceased to be our dog. Before many weeks passed,

indeed, he ceased to be anyone we had ever known. A
week or so after he became Caesar, he took up residence
in her room, sleeping alongside her bed. She broke him
of the habit of taking us to school (temptation to low
living was rife along those streets; there was a chow—
well, never mind) by the simple expedient of chaining
him to a tree as soon as she got up in the morning. This
discipline, together with the stamina-building cuffs she
gave his sensitive ears from time to time, gradually but
certainly remade his character. From a sanguine, affectionate, easygoing Gael (with the fits of melancholy that
alternated with the larkiness), he turned into an over-
bearing, military, efficient, loud-voiced Teuton. His
bark, once wide of range, narrowed to one dark, glottal
tone.

Soon the paper boy flatly refused to serve our house
after Caesar efficiently removed the bicycle clip from his
pants leg; the skin was not broken, or even bruised, but
it was a matter of principle with the boy. The milkman
approached the back door in a seizure of shakes like St.
Vitus's dance. The metermen, the coal men, and the
garbage collector crossed themselves if they were Catholics and, if they were not, tried whistling in the dark.
"Good boy, good Caesar," they carolled, and, unctu-
ously lying, they said they knew his bark was worse than
his bite, knowing full well that it was not, considering
the very nasty nip, requiring stitches, he had given a
representative of the Olson Rug Company, who had
had the folly to pat him on the head. Caesar did not
molest the lodgers, but he disdained them and he did
not brook being personally addressed by anyone except
Gran. One night, he wandered into the dining room,
appearing to be in search of something he had mislaid,

and, for some reason that no one was ever able to divine, suddenly stood stock-still and gave the easily upset Mr. Beaver a long and penetrating look. Mr. Beaver, trembling from head to toe, stammered, "Why—er, hello there, Caesar, old boy, old boy," and Caesar charged. For a moment, it was touch and go, but Gran saved Mr. Beaver, only to lose him an hour later when he departed, bag and baggage, for the Y.M.C.A. This rout and the consequent loss of revenue would more than likely have meant Caesar's downfall and his deportation to the pound if it had not been that a newly widowed druggist, very irascible and very much Gran's style, had applied for a room in her house a week or so before, and now he moved in delightedly, as if he were coming home.

Finally, the police demanded that Caesar be muzzled and they warned that if he committed any major crime again—they cited the case of the Olson man—he would be shot on sight. Mrs. Placer, although she had no respect for the law, knowing as much as she did about its agents, obeyed. She obeyed, that is, in part; she put the muzzle on Caesar for a few hours a day, usually early in the morning when the traffic was light and before the deliveries had started, but the rest of the time his powerful jaws and dazzling white sabre teeth were free and snapping. There was between these two such preternatural rapport, such an impressive conjugation of suspicion, that he, sensing the approach of a policeman, could convey instantly to her the immediate necessity of clapping his nose cage on. And the policeman, sent out on the complaint of a terrorized neighbor, would be greeted by this law-abiding pair at the door.

Daisy and I wished we were dead. We were divided be-

tween hating Caesar and loving Laddy, and we could
not give up the hope that something, someday, would
change him back into the loving animal he had been
before he was appointed vice-president of the Placerites.
Now at the meetings after supper on the porch he took
an active part, standing rigidly at Gran's side except
when she sent him on an errand. He carried out these
assignments not with the air of a servant but with that
of an accomplice. "Get me the paper, Caesar," she
would say to him, and he, dismayingly intelligent and a
shade smart-alecky, would open the screen door by himself and in a minute come back with the *Bulletin,* from
which Mrs. Placer would then read an item, like the
Gospel of the day, and then read between the lines of it,
scandalized.

In the deepening of our woe and our bereavement
and humiliation, we mutely appealed to Mr. Murphy.
We did not speak outright to him, for Mr. Murphy
lived in a state of indirection, and often when he used
the pronoun "I," he seemed to be speaking of someone
standing a little to the left of him, but we went to see
him and his animals each day during the sad summer,
taking what comfort we could from the cozy, quiet indo-
lence of his back yard, where small black eyes encountered ours politely and everyone was half asleep. When
Mr. Murphy inquired about Laddy in his bland, inat-
tentive way, looking for a stratagem whereby to shift the
queen of hearts into position by the king, we would say,
"Oh, he's fine," or "Laddy is a nifty dog." And Mr.
Murphy, reverently slaking the thirst that was his talent
and his concubine, would murmur, "I'm glad."

We wanted to tell him, we wanted his help, or at least
his sympathy, but how could we cloud his sunny world?

It was awful to see Mr. Murphy ruffled. Up in the calm clouds as he generally was, he could occasionally be brought to earth with a thud, as we had seen and heard one day. Not far from his house, there lived a bad troublemaking boy of twelve, who was forever hanging over the fence trying to teach the parrot obscene words. He got nowhere, for she spoke no English and she would flabbergast him with her cold eye and sneer, *"Tant pis."* One day, this boorish fellow went too far; he suddenly shot his head over the fence like a jack-in-the-box and aimed a water pistol at the skunk's face. Mr. Murphy leaped to his feet in a scarlet rage; he picked up a stone and threw it accurately, hitting the boy square in the back, so hard that he fell right down in a mud puddle and lay there kicking and squalling and, as it turned out, quite badly hurt. "If you ever come back here again, I'll kill you!" roared Mr. Murphy. I think he meant it, for I have seldom seen an anger so resolute, so brilliant, and so voluble. "How dared he!" he cried, scrambling into Mallow's cage to hug and pet and soothe her. "He must be absolutely mad! He must be the Devil!" He did not go back to his game after that but paced the yard, swearing a blue streak and only pausing to croon to his animals, now as frightened by him as they had been by the intruder, and to drink straight from the bottle, not bothering with fixings. We were fascinated by this unfamiliar side of Mr. Murphy, but we did not want to see it ever again, for his face had grown so dangerously purple and the veins of his forehead seemed ready to burst and his eyes looked scorched. He was the closest thing to a maniac we had ever seen. So we did not tell him about Laddy; what he did not know would not hurt him, although it was hurting us, throbbing in us like a great, bleating wound.

But eventually Mr. Murphy heard about our dog's conversion, one night at the pool hall, which he visited from time to time when he was seized with a rare but compelling garrulity, and the next afternoon when he asked us how Laddy was and we replied that he was fine, he tranquilly told us, as he deliberated whether to move the jack of clubs now or to bide his time, that we were sweet girls but we were lying in our teeth. He did not seem at all angry but only interested, and all the while he questioned us, he went on about his business with the gin and the hearts and spades and diamonds and clubs. It rarely happened that he won the particular game he was playing, but that day he did, and when he saw all the cards laid out in their ideal pattern, he leaned back, looking disappointed, and he said, "I'm damned." He then scooped up the cards, in a gesture unusually quick and tidy for him, stacked them together, and bound them with a rubber band. Then he began to tell us what he thought of Gran. He grew as loud and apoplectic as he had been that other time, and though he kept repeating that he knew *we* were innocent and he put not a shred of the blame on us, we were afraid he might suddenly change his mind, and, speechless, we cowered against the monkeys' cage. In dread, the monkeys clutched the fingers we offered to them and made soft, protesting noises, as if to say, "Oh, stop it, Murphy! Our nerves!"

As quickly as it had started, the tantrum ended. Mr. Murphy paled to his normal complexion and said calmly that the only practical thing was to go and have it out with Mrs. Placer. "At once," he added, although he said he bitterly feared that it was too late and there would be no exorcising the fiend from Laddy's misused spirit. And because he had given the dog to us and not to her, he required that we go along with him, stick up for our rights, stand on our mettle, get up our Irish, and give the old bitch something to put in her pipe and smoke.

Oh, it was hot that day! We walked in a kind of delirium through the simmer, where only the grasshoppers had the energy to move, and I remember wondering if ether smelled like the gin on Mr. Murphy's breath. Daisy and I, in one way or another, were going to have our gizzards cut out along with our hearts and our souls and our pride, and I wished I were as drunk as Mr. Murphy, who swam effortlessly through the heat, his lips parted comfortably, his eyes half closed. When we turned in to the path at Gran's house, my blood began to scald my veins. It was so futile and so dangerous and so absurd. Here we were on a high moral mission, two draggletailed, gumptionless little girls and a toper whom no one could take seriously, partly because he was little more than a gurgling bottle of booze and partly because of the clothes he wore. He was a sight, as he always was when he was out of his own yard. There, somehow, in the carefree disorder, his clothes did not look especially strange, but on the streets of the town, in the barbershop or the post office or on Gran's path, they were fantastic. He wore a pair of hound's tooth pants, old but maintaining a vehement pattern, and with them he wore a collarless blue flannelette shirt. His hat was the silliest of all, because it was a derby three sizes too big. And as if Shannon, too, was a part of his funny-paper costume, the elder capuchin rode on his shoulder, tightly embracing his thin red neck.

Gran and Caesar were standing side by side behind the screen door, looking as if they had been expecting us all along. For a moment, Gran and Mr. Murphy faced each other across the length of weedy brick between the gate and the front porch, and no one spoke. Gran took no notice at all of Daisy and me. She adjusted her eye-glasses, using both hands, and then looked down at Caesar and matter-of-factly asked, "Do you want out?"

Caesar flung himself full-length upon the screen and it sprang open like a jaw. I ran to meet and head him off, and Daisy threw a library book at his head, but he was on Mr. Murphy in one split second and had his monkey on his shoulder and had broken Shannon's neck in two shakes. He would have gone on nuzzling and mauling and growling over the corpse for hours if Gran had not marched out of the house and down the path and slapped him lightly on the flank and said, in a voice that could not have deceived an idiot, "Why, Caesar, you scamp! You've hurt Mr. Murphy's monkey! Aren't you ashamed!"

Hurt the monkey! In one final, apologetic shudder, the life was extinguished from the little fellow. Bloody and covered with slather, Shannon lay with his arms suppliantly stretched over his head, his leather fingers curled into loose, helpless fists. His hind legs and his tail lay limp and helter-skelter on the path. And Mr. Murphy, all of a sudden reeling drunk, burst into the kind of tears that Daisy and I knew well—the kind that time alone could stop. We stood aghast in the dark-red sunset, killed by our horror and our grief for Shannon and our unforgivable disgrace. We stood upright in a dead faint, and an eon passed before Mr. Murphy picked up Shannon's body and wove away, sobbing, "I don't believe it! I don't *believe it!*"

The very next day, again at morbid, heavy sunset, Caesar died in violent convulsions, knocking down two tall hollyhocks in his throes. Long after his heart had stopped, his right hind leg continued to jerk in aimless reflex. Madly methodical, Mr. Murphy had poisoned some meat for him, had thoroughly envenomed a whole pound of hamburger, and early in the morning, before sunup, when he must have been near collapse with his hangover, he had stolen up to Mrs. Placer's house and put it by the kitchen door. He was so stealthy that Caesar never stirred in his fool's paradise there on the floor by Gran. We knew these to be the facts, for Mr. Murphy made no bones about them. Afterward, he had gone home and said a solemn Requiem for Shannon in so loud a voice that someone sent for the police, and they took him away in the Black Maria to sober him up on strong green tea. By the time he was in the lockup and had confessed what he had done, it was far too late, for Caesar had already gulped down the meat. He suffered an undreamed-of agony in Gran's flower garden, and Daisy and I, unable to bear the sight of it, hiked up to the red rocks and shook there, wretchedly ripping to shreds the sand lilies that grew in the cracks. Flight was the only thing we could think of, but where could we go? We stared west at the mountains and quailed at the look of the stern white glacier; we wildly scanned the prairies for escape. "If only we were something besides kids! Besides girls!" mourned Daisy. I could not speak at all; I huddled in a niche of the rocks and cried.

No one in town, except, of course, her lodgers, had the slightest sympathy for Gran. The townsfolk allowed that Mr. Murphy was a drunk and was fighting Irish, but he had a heart and this was something that could never be said of Mrs. Placer. The neighbor who had called the police when he was chanting the *Dies Irae* before breakfast in that deafening monotone had said, "The poor guy is having some kind of a spell, so don't be rough on him, hear?" Mr. Murphy became, in fact, a kind of hero; some people, stretching a point, said he was a saint for the way that every day and twice on Sunday he sang a memorial Mass over Shannon's grave, now marked with a chipped, cheap plaster figure of Saint Francis. He withdrew from the world more and more, seldom venturing into the streets at all, except when he went to the bootlegger to get a new bottle to snuggle into. All summer, all fall, we saw him as we passed by his yard, sitting at his dilapidated table, enfeebled with gin, graying, withering, turning his head ever and ever more slowly as he maneuvered the protocol of the kings and the queens and the knaves. Daisy and I could never stop to visit him again.

It went on like this, year after year. Daisy and I lived in a mesh of lies and evasions, baffled and mean, like rats in a maze. When we were old enough for beaux, we connived like sluts to see them, but we would never admit to their existence until Gran caught us out by some trick. Like this one, for example: Once, at the end of a long interrogation, she said to me, "I'm more relieved than I can tell you that you *don't* have anything to do with Jimmy Gilmore, because I happen to know that he is after only one thing in a girl," and then, off guard in the loving memory of sitting in the movies the night before with Jimmy, not even holding hands, I defended him and defeated myself, and Gran, smiling with success, said, "I *thought* you knew him. It's a pretty safe rule of thumb that where there's smoke there's fire." That finished Jimmy and me, for afterward I was nervous with him and I confounded and alarmed and finally bored him by trying to convince him, although the subject had not come up, that I did not doubt his good intentions.

Daisy and I would come home from school, or, later, from our jobs, with a small triumph or an interesting piece of news, and if we forgot ourselves and, in our exuberance, told Gran, we were hustled into court at once for cross-examination. Once, I remember, while I was still in high school, I told her about getting a part in a play. How very nice for me, she said, if that kind of make-believe seemed to me worth while. But what was my role? An old woman! A widow woman believed to be a witch? She did not care a red cent, but she did have to laugh in view of the fact that Miss Eccles, in charge of dramatics, had almost run her down in her car. And I would forgive her, would I not, if she did not come to see the play, and would not think her eccentric for not wanting to see herself ridiculed in public?

My pleasure strangled, I crawled, joy-killed, to our third-floor room. The room was small and its monstrous furniture was too big and the rag rugs were repulsive, but it was bright. We would not hang a blind at the window, and on this day I stood there staring into the mountains that burned with the sun. I feared the mountains, but at times like this their massiveness consoled me; they, at least, could not be gossiped about.

Why did we stay until we were grown? Daisy and I ask ourselves this question as we sit here on the bench in the municipal zoo, reminded of Mr. Murphy by the polar bear, reminded by the monkeys not of Shannon but of Mrs. Placer's insatiable gossips at their post-prandial feast.

"But how could we have left?" says Daisy, wringing her buttery hands. "It was the depression. We had no money. We had nowhere to go."

"All the same, we could have gone," I say, resentful still of the waste of all those years. "We could have come here and got jobs as waitresses. Or prostitutes, for that matter."

"I wouldn't have wanted to be a prostitute," says Daisy.

We agree that under the circumstances it would have been impossible for us to run away. The physical act would have been simple, for the city was not far and we could have stolen the bus fare or hitched a ride. Later, when we began to work as salesgirls in Kress's, it would have been no trick at all to vanish one Saturday afternoon with our week's pay, without so much as going home to say goodbye. But it had been infinitely harder than that, for Gran, as we now see, held us trapped by our sense of guilt. We were vitiated, and we had no choice but to wait, flaccidly, for her to die.

You may be sure we did not unlearn those years as soon as we put her out of sight in the cemetery and sold her house for a song to the first boob who would buy it. Nor did we forget when we left the town for another one, where we had jobs at a dude camp—the town where Daisy now lives with a happy husband and two happy sons. The succubus did not relent for years, and I can still remember, in the beginning of our days at the Lazy S 3, overhearing an edgy millionaire say to his wife, naming my name, "That girl gives me the cold shivers. One would think she had just seen a murder." Well, I had. For years, whenever I woke in the night in fear or pain or loneliness, I would increase my suffering by the memory of Shannon, and my tears were as bitter as poor Mr. Murphy's.

We have never been back to Adams. But we see that house plainly, with the hopvines straggling over the porch. The windows are hung with the cheapest grade of marquisette, dipped into coffee to impart to it an unwilling color, neither white nor tan but individual and spitefully unattractive. We see the wicker rockers and the swing, and through the screen door we dimly make out the slightly veering corridor, along one wall of which stands a glass-doored bookcase; when we were children, it had contained not books but stale old cardboard boxes filled with such things as W.C.T.U. tracts and anti-cigarette literature and newspaper clippings relating to sexual sin in the Christianized islands of the Pacific.

Even if we were able to close our minds' eyes to the past, Mr. Murphy would still be before us in the apotheosis of the polar bear. My pain becomes intolerable, and I am relieved when Daisy rescues us. "We've got to go," she says in a sudden panic. "I've got asthma coming on." We rush to the nearest exit of the city park and hail a cab, and, once inside it, Daisy gives herself an injection of adrenalin and then leans back. We are heartbroken and infuriated, and we cannot speak.

Two hours later, beside my train, we clutch each other as if we were drowning. We ought to go out to the nearest policeman and say, "We are not responsible women. You will have to take care of us because we cannot take care of ourselves." But gradually the storm begins to lull.

"You're sure you've got your ticket?" says Daisy. "You'll surely be able to get a roomette once you're on."

"I don't know about that," I say. "If there are any V.I.P.s on board, I won't have a chance. 'Spinsters and Orphans Last' is the motto of this line."

Daisy smiles. "I didn't care," she says, "but I had to laugh when I saw that woman nab the redcap you had signalled to. I had a good notion to give her a piece of my mind."

"It will be a miracle if I ever see my bags again," I say, mounting the steps of the train. "Do you suppose that blackguardly porter knows about the twenty-dollar gold piece in my little suitcase?"

"Anything's possible!" cries Daisy, and begins to laugh. She is so pretty, standing there in her bright-red linen suit and her black velvet hat. A solitary ray of sunshine comes through a broken pane in the domed vault of the train shed and lies on her shoulder like a silver arrow.

"So long, Daisy!" I call as the train begins to move.

She walks quickly along beside the train. "Watch out for pickpockets!" she calls.

"You, too!" My voice is thin and lost in the increasing noise of the speeding train wheels. "Goodbye, old dear!"

I go at once to the club car and I appropriate the writing table, to the vexation of a harried priest, who snatches up the telegraph pad and gives me a sharp look. I write Daisy approximately the same letter I always write her under this particular set of circumstances, the burden of which is that nothing for either of us can ever be as bad as the past before Gran mercifully died. In a postscript I add: "There is a Roman Catholic priest (that is to say, he is *dressed* like one) sitting behind me although all the chairs on the opposite side of the car are empty. I can only conclude that he is looking over my shoulder, and while I do not want to cause you any alarm, I think you would be advised to be on the lookout for any appearance of miraculous medals, scapulars, papist booklets, etc., in the shops of your town. It really makes me laugh to see the way he is pretending that all he wants is for me to finish this letter so that he can have the table."

I sign my name and address the envelope, and I give up my place to the priest, who smiles nicely at me, and then I move across the car to watch the fields as they slip by. They are alfalfa fields, but you can bet your bottom dollar that they are chockablock with marijuana.

I begin to laugh. The fit is silent but it is devastating; it surges and rattles in my rib cage, and I turn my face to the window to avoid the narrow gaze of the Filipino bar boy. I must think of something sad to stop this unholy giggle, and I think of the polar bear. But even his bleak tragedy does not sober me. Wildly I fling open the newspaper I have brought and I pretend to be reading something screamingly funny. The words I see are in a Hollywood gossip column: "How a well-known starlet can get get a divorce in Nevada without her crooner husband's consent, nobody knows. It won't be worth a plugged nickel here."

Cops and Robbers

The child, Hannah, sitting hidden on the attic steps, listened as her mother talked on the telephone to Aunt Louise.

"Oh, there's no whitewashing the incident. The child's hair is a sight, and it will be many moons, I can tell you, before I'll forgive Hugh Talmadge. But listen to me. The worst of it is that this baby of five has gone into a decline like a grown woman—like you or me, dear, at our most hysterical. Sudden fits of tears for no apparent reason and then simply hours of brooding. She won't eat, she probably doesn't sleep. I can't stand it if she's turning mental."

The door to the bedroom, across the hall, was half open, and through the crack of the door at the foot of the attic steps Hannah saw that in the course of the night her parents had disarrayed the pale-green blanket cover and now, half off the bed, drooping and askew, it looked like a great crumpled new leaf, pulled back here and there to show the rosy blankets underneath. In the bedroom it is spring, thought Hannah, and outdoors it is snowing on the Christmas trees; that is a riddle.

Her mother lay in the center of the big bed, which was as soft and fat as the gelded white Persian cat who dozed at her side, his scornful head erect, as if he were arrested not so much by sleep as by a coma of boredom and disgust. A little earlier, before he struck this pose, he had sniffed and disdained the bowl of cream on his mistress's breakfast tray, and when she had tried to cajole him into drinking it, he had coolly thrashed his tail at her. In the darkness of her enclosure, Hannah yearned, imagining herself in the privileged cat's place beside her mother, watching the mellowing, pillowing, billowing snow as it whorled down to meet the high tips of the pine trees that bordered the frozen formal garden. If she were Nephew, the cat, she would burrow into the silky depths of the bed up to her eyes and rejoice that she was not outside like a winter bird coming to peck at suet and snowy crumbs at the feeding station.

It was ugly and ungenerous here where she was, on the narrow, splintery stairs, and up in the attic a mouse or a rat scampered on lightly clicking claws between the trunks; some hibernating bees buzzed peevishly in their insomnia. Stingy and lonesome like old people, the shut-ins worried their grievances stealthily. And Hannah, spying and eavesdropping (a sin and she knew it), felt the ends of her cropped hair and ran a forefinger over her freshly combed boy's cut—the subject of her mother's conversation. Something like sleep touched her eyeballs, though this was early morning and she had not been awake longer than an hour. But it was tears, not drowsiness, that came. They fell without any help from her; her cheeks did not rise up as they usually did when she cried, to squeeze themselves into puckers like old apples, her mouth did not open in a rent of woe, no part of her body was affected at all except the eyes themselves, from which streamed down these mothering runnels.

"Why did he do it?" Her mother's question into the telephone was an impatient scream. "Why do men do half the things they do? Why does Arthur treat you in public as if you were an enlisted man? I swear I'll someday kill your rear admiral for you. Why does Eliot brag to Frances that he's unfaithful? Because they're sadists, every last one of them. I am very anti-man today."

"What is antiman?" whispered Hannah.

The stools on either side of the fireplace in the den were ottomans, and sometimes Hannah and her mother sat on them in the late afternoon, with a low table between them on which were set a Chinese pot of verbena tisane, two cups, and a plate of candied orange rind. At the thought of her mother's golden hair in the firelight, and the smell of her perfume in the intimate warmth, and the sound of her voice saying, "Isn't this gay, Miss Baby?" the tears came faster, for in her heavy heart Hannah felt certain that now her hair was cut off, her mother would never want to sit so close to her again.

Unable to see through the narrow opening of the door any longer, she leaned her face against the wall and felt her full tears moistening the beaverboard as she listened to her mother's recital of Saturday's catastrophe.

"On the face of it, the facts are innocent enough. He took her to town on Saturday to buy her a pair of shoes, having decided for his own reasons that I have no respect for my children's feet—the shoes he got are too odious, but that's another story. Then when he brought her back, here she was, cropped, looking like a rag doll. He said she'd begged to have it done. Of course she'd done nothing of the kind. To put the most charitable construction on the whole affair, I *could* say that when he went into the barbershop to have his own hair cut, he'd had a seizure of amnesia and thought he had Andy with him, or Johnny, or Hughie, and decided to kill two birds with one stone. And then afterward he was afraid of what I'd say and so cooked up this canard—and more than likely bribed her to bear him out. The way men will weasel out of their missteps! It isn't moral. It shocks me."

He did *not* think I was Andy or Johnny or Hughie, Hannah said to herself. In the barbershop at her father's club there had been no one but grown men and a fat stuffed skunk that stood in front of the mirror between two bottles of bay rum, its leathery nose pointed upward as if it were trying to see the underside of its chin in the looking glass. Through a steaming towel, her father had muttered, "Just do as I say, Homer, cut it off," and the barber, a lean man with a worried look on his red face, flinched, then shrugged his shoulders and began to snip off Hannah's heavy curls, frowning with disapproval and remarking once under his breath that women, even though they were five years old, were strictly forbidden on these premises. On the drive home, her peeled head had felt cold and wet, and she had not liked the smell that gauzily hovered around her, growing more cloying as the heater in the car warmed up. At a red light, her father had turned to her and, patting her on the knee, had said, "You look as cute as a button, young fellow." He had not seemed to hear her when she said, "I do not. I'm not a young fellow," nor had he noticed when she moved over against the door, as far away from him as she could get, hating him bitterly and hating her nakedness. Presently, he'd turned on the radio to a news broadcast and disputed out loud with the commentator. Hannah, left all alone, had stared out the window at the wolfish winter. In one snow-flattened field she saw tall flames arising from a huge wire trash basket, making the rest of the world look even colder and whiter and more unkind. Her father scowled, giving the radio what for, swearing at the slippery roads—carrying on an absentminded tantrum all by himself. Once, halted by a woman driver whose engine was stalled, he'd said, "Serves her right. She ought to be home at this time of day tending to business." As they turned in their own drive, he said a lie: "That was a fine idea of yours to have your hair cut off." She had never said any such thing; all she had said, when they were having lunch in a brown, cloudy restaurant, was that she would rather go to the barbership with him than wait at Grandma's. But she had not contradicted him, for he did not countenance contradiction from his children. "I'm an old-fashioned man," he announced every morning to his three sons and his two daughters. "I am the autocrat of this breakfast table." And though he said it with a wink and a chuckle, it was clear that he meant business. Johnny, who was intellectual, had told the other children that an autocrat was a person like Hitler, and he had added sarcastically, "That sure is something to brag about, I must say."

The voice speaking into the phone took on a new tone, and Hannah, noticing this, looked out through the crack again. "What? Oh, please don't change the subject, pet, I really want your help. It isn't a trifle, it's terribly important, I really think it is the *final* effrontery. . . . All right, then, if you promise that we can come back to it." With her free hand, Hannah's mother lightly stroked the cat, who did not heed, and she lay back among her many pillows, listening to her sister but letting her eyes rove the room as if she were planning changes in its decoration. "Yes, I did hear it but I can't remember where," she said inattentively. Then, smiling in the pleasure of gossip, forgetting herself for a moment, she went on, "Perhaps I heard it from Peggy the night she came to dinner with that frightful new man of hers. That's it—it was from *him* I heard it, and automatically discounted it for no other reason than that I took an instantaneous dislike to him. If he is typical of his department, the C.I.A. must be nothing more nor less than the Gestapo."

Hannah's head began to ache and she rolled it slowly, looking up the steep, ladderlike steps into the shadowy attic. She was bored now that the talk was not of her, and she only half heard her mother's agile voice rising, descending, laughing quickly, pleading, "Oh, no! It's not *poss*ible!" and she sucked her fingers, one by one. Her tears had stopped and she missed them as she might have missed something she had lost. Like her hair, like all her golden princess curls that the barber had gazed at sadly as they lay dead and ruined on the tiled floor.

Now that Hannah's hair was short, her days were long: it was a million hours between breakfast and lunch, and before, it had been no time at all, because her mother, still lying in her oceanic bed, had every morning made Hannah's curls, taking her time, telling anyone who telephoned that she would call back, that just now she was busy "playing with this angel's hair."

Today was Wednesday, and Hannah had lived four lifetimes since Saturday afternoon. Sunday had been endless, even though her brothers and her sister had been as exciting as ever, with their jokes and contests and their acrobatics and their game of cops-and-robbers that had set the servants wild. But even in their mad preoccupation it had been evident that the sight of Hannah embarrassed them. "The baby looks like a skinned cat," said Andy, and Hughie said, "It was a dopey thing to do. The poor little old baby looks like a mushroom." The parents did nothing to stop this talk, for all day long they were fighting behind the closed door of the den, not even coming out for meals, their voices growing slower and more sibilant as they drank more. "I hate them," Johnny had said in the middle of the long, musty afternoon, when the cops were spent and the robbers were sick of water-pistol fights. "When they get stinking, I hate them," said Johnny. "I bet a thousand dollars he had had a couple when he had them cut the baby's hair." Janie shouted, "Oh, that baby, baby, baby, baby! Is that goofy baby the only pebble on the beach? Why do they have to mess up Sunday fighting over her? I'm going crazy!" And she ran around in a circle like a dog, pulling at her hair with both hands.

On Monday morning, when Hannah's father took the older children off to Marion Country Day School on his way to the city, she had nearly cried herself sick, feeling that this Monday the pain of their desertion was more than she could bear. She would not let go of Janie's hand, and she cried, "You'll be sorry if you come back and find I'm dead!" Janie, who was ten and hot-blooded—she took after Daddy, who had Huguenot blood—had slapped Hannah's hand and said, "The nerve of some people's children!" Hannah had stood under the porte-cochere, shivering in her wrapper and slippers, until the car went out the driveway between the tulip trees; she had waved and called, "Goodbye, dearest Janie and Johnny and Andy and Hughie!" Only Johnny had looked back; he rolled down the window and leaned out and called, "Ta-ta, half pint." They were all too old and busy to pay much attention to her, though often they brought her presents from school—a jawbreaker or a necklace made of paper clips. The four older children were a year apart, starting with John, who was thirteen, and ending with Janie, and when family photographs were taken, they were sometimes lined up according to height; these were called "stair-step portraits," and while Hannah, of course, was included, she was so much smaller than Janie that she spoiled the design, and one time Uncle Harry, looking at a picture taken on Palm Sunday when all five children were sternly holding their palms like spears, had said, pointing to Hannah, "Is that the runt of the litter or is it a toy breed?" Andy, who was Uncle Harry's pet, said, "We just keep it around the house for its hair. It's made of spun gold, you know, and very invaluable." This evidently was something the barber had not known, for he had swept the curls into a dustpan and thrown them into a chute marked "Waste." She wondered how long they would keep her now that her sole reason for existence was gone.

In the other days, after Daddy and the children left and the maids began their panicky, silent cleaning, flinging open all the windows to chill the house to its heart, Hannah would run upstairs to the big bedroom to sit on the foot of the bosomy bed and wait while her mother drank her third cup of coffee and did the crossword puzzle in the *Tribune*. When she was stuck for a definition, she would put down her pencil and thoughtfully twist the diamond ring on her finger; if it caught the sun, Hannah would close her eyes and try to retain the flashing swords of green and purple, just as she unconsciously tried to seal forever in her memory the smell of the strong Italian coffee coming in a thin black stream out of the silver pot. Hannah remembered one day when her mother said to the cat, "What is that wretched four-letter word that means 'allowance for waste,' Nephew? We had it just the other day." Finally, when the puzzle was done and Edna had taken away the tray, she stretched out her arms to Hannah, who scrambled into her embrace, and she said, "I suppose you want your tawny tresses curled," and held her at arm's length and gazed at her hair with disbelieving eyes. "Bring us the brush, baby." All the while she brushed, then combed, then made long, old-fashioned sausage curls, turning and molding them on her index finger, she talked lightly and secretly about the dreams she had had and Christmas plans and what went on inside Nephew's head and why it was that she respected but could not bear Andy's violin teacher. She included Hannah, as if she were thirty years old, asking for her opinion or her corroboration of something. "Do you agree with me that Nephew is the very soul of Egypt? Or do you think there are Chinese overtones in his style?" After telling a dream (her dreams were full of voyages; one time she sailed into Oslo in Noah's ark and another time she went on the Queen Mary to Southampton in her night clothes without either luggage or a passport), she said, "What on earth do you suppose that means, Hannah? My id doesn't seem to know where it is at." Bewitching, indecipherable, she always dulcified this hour with her smoky, loving voice and her loving fingers that sometimes could not resist meandering over Hannah's head, ruining a curl by cleaving through it as she exclaimed, "Dear Lord, I never saw such stuff as this!" Actually, her own hair was the same vivacious color and the same gentle texture as Hannah's, and sometimes her hands would leave the child's head and go to her own, to stroke it lovingly.

Lately now, for this last month, when the afternoons were snug and short and the lamps were turned on early and the hearth fires smelled of nuts, there had been another hour as well when Hannah and her hair had been the center of attention. Every day at half past two, she and her mother drove in the toylike English car over to Mr. Robinson Fowler's house, three miles away, on the top of a bald and beautiful hill from which it was possible, on a clear day, to see the beaches of Long Island. In a big, dirty studio, jammed with plaster casts and tin cans full of turpentine and stacked-up canvases and nameless metal odds and ends, Mr. Fowler, a large, quiet man who mumbled when he talked, was painting a life-size portrait of Hannah and her mother. Her mother, wearing a full skirt of scarlet felt and a starched white Gibson-girl shirt and a black ribbon in her hair, sat on a purple Victorian sofa, and Hannah, in a blue velvet jacket trimmed with black frogs and a paler-blue accordion-pleated skirt, stood leaning against her knee. In the picture, these colors were all different, all smudgy and gray, and the point of this, said Mr. Fowler, was to accent the lambencies of the hair. Before they took their pose, all the morning's careful curls were combed out, for Mr. Fowler wanted to paint Hannah's hair, he murmured in his closed mouth, "in a state of nature." Occasionally, he emerged from behind his easel and came across to them with his shambling, easygoing, friendly gait, to push back a lock of hair that had fallen over Hannah's forehead, and the touch of his fingers, huge as they were, was as light as her mother's.

Hannah liked the heat of the studio, and the smell of the tea perpetually brewing on an electric grill, and the sight of the enormous world of hills and trees and farms and rivers through the enormous windows, and she liked the quiet, which was broken only once or twice in the course of the hour's sitting by an exchange of a casual question and answer between Mr. Fowler and her mother, half the time about her hair. "It must never be cut," said the painter one day. "Not a single strand of it." After the sitting was over and Hannah and her mother had changed back into their regular clothes, Mr. Fowler drew the burlap curtains at the windows and turned on the soft lamps. Then he and her mother sat back in two scuffed leather armchairs drinking whiskey and talking in a leisurely way, as if all the rest of the time in the world were theirs to enjoy in this relaxed geniality. Hannah did not listen to them. With her cup of mild, lemony tea, she sat on a high stool before a blackboard at the opposite end of the room and drew spider webs with a nubbin of pink chalk. Mr. Fowler and her mother never raised their voices or threw things at each other or stormed out of the room, banging doors, and Hannah was sorry when it was time to go home where that kind of thing went on all the time, horrifying the housemaids, who never stayed longer than two months at the most, although the cook, who had a vicious tongue herself, had been with them ever since Johnny could remember.

The picture, when it was finished, was going to hang in the drawing room over an heirloom lowboy, where now there hung a pair of crossed épées, used by Hannah's father and his adversary in a jaunty, bloody *Studentenmensur* at Freiburg the year he went abroad to learn German. The lilac scar from the duel was a half moon on his round right cheek.

Now the picture would never be finished, since Hannah's corn-tassel hair was gone, and the sunny hour at the start of the day and the teatime one at the end were gone with it.

Hannah, sitting on the attic stairs, began to cry again as she thought of the closed circle of her days. Even her sister's and her brothers' return from school was not the fun it had been before; her haircut had become a household issue over which all of them squabbled, taking sides belligerently. Janie and Andy maintained it did not matter; all right, they said, what if the baby did look silly? After all, she didn't go to school and nobody saw her. Johnny and Hughie and the cook and the maids said that it did matter, and Johnny, the spokesman for that camp, railed at his father behind his back and called him a dastard. But all the same, no one paid any attention to Hannah; when they spoke of "the baby," they might have been speaking of the car or a piece of furniture; one would never have known that she was in the room, for even when they looked directly at her, their eyes seemed to take in something other than Hannah. She felt that she was already shrinking and fading, that all her rights of being seen and listened to and caressed were ebbing away. Chilled and exposed as she was, she was becoming, nonetheless, invisible.

The tears came less fast now, and she heard her mother say, "How can I *help* looking at it closely? I shall eventually have to go to an analyst, as you perfectly well know, if I am to continue this marriage until the children are reasonably grown. But in the meantime, until I get my doctor, who can I talk to but you? I wouldn't talk to you if you weren't my sister, because I don't think you're discreet at all." Sad, in her covert,

Hannah saw that her mother was now sitting up straight against the headboard and was smoking a cigarette in long, meditative puffs; the smoke befogged her frowning forehead.

"Forget it, darling," she continued. "I know you are a tomb of silence. Look, do let me spill the beans and get it over with. It will put me into a swivet, I daresay, and I'll have to have a drink in my bath, but the way I feel, after these nights I've had, that's in the cards anyhow. . . . Oh, Christ, Louise, don't preach to me!"

Briefly, she put down the telephone and dragged Nephew to her side. Then she resumed, "Excuse me. I was adjusting my cat. Now, dear, right now, you can forget my 'charitable construction' because, of course, that's rot. At this juncture, neither one of us does anything by accident. I cannot believe that criminals are any more ingenious than wives and husbands when their marriages are turning sour. Do you remember how fiendish the Irelands were?

"Well, the night before the haircutting, we had a row that lasted until four, starting with Rob and going on from him to all the other men I know—he thinks it's bad form (and that's exactly how he puts it) that I still speak fondly of old beaux. He suspects me of the direst things with that poor pansy the decorators sent out to do the carpets on the stairs, and he's got it firmly rooted in his mind that Rob and I are in the middle of a red-hot affair. He doesn't know the meaning of friendship. He's got a sand dune for a soul. He suggested loathsomely that Rob and I were using Hannah as a blind—oh, his implications were too cynical to repeat.

"All this went on and on until I said that I would leave him. You know *that* old blind alley where any feint is useless because when five children are involved, one's hands are tied. Unless one can be proved mad. If only I could be! I would give my eyes to be sent away for a while to some insane asylum like that one Elizabeth loved so.

"It was hideous—the whole battle. We were so squalid with drink. We drink prodigiously these days. The ice ran out and we didn't even take time to go get more, so we drank whiskey and tap water as if we were in a cheap hotel, and I kept thinking, How demeaning this is. But I couldn't stop. This was the worst quarrel we've ever had—by far the most fundamental. The things we said! We could have killed each other. In the morning, not even our hangovers could bring us together. And let me tell you, they were shattering. If I hadn't known it was a hangover, I would have sent for an ambulance without thinking twice. Hugh sidled around like a wounded land crab and swore he had fractured his skull. Fortunately, the children, all except the baby, had been asked to the Fosters' to skate, so at least we didn't have to put up appearances—we do that less and less as it is. But finally we began to pull ourselves together about noon with Bloody Marys, and when he proposed that he take Hannah into town and buy her lunch and some shoes, I almost forgave him everything, I was so delighted to have the house to myself. I would not rise to that bait about my neglecting the welfare of my children's feet. All I could think of was just being alone.

"I should have known. I think I might have sensed what was up if I hadn't been so sick, because as they were about to leave, the baby asked why I hadn't curled her hair and Hugh said, 'You leave that to me today.' Now, looking back on it, I can see that he rolled his eyes in that baleful, planning way of his and licked one corner of his mouth. But even if I had noticed, I still would never have dreamed he would be so vile.

"It goes without saying that we have been at swords' points ever since, and it doesn't help matters to see the child so woebegone, wearing this look of 'What did I do to deserve this?' How can one explain it away as an accident to a child when one perfectly knows that accident is not involved? Her misery makes me feel guilty. I am as shy of her as if I had been an accessory. I can't console her without spilling all the beans about Hugh. Besides, you can't say to a child, 'Darling, you are only a symbol. It was really *my* beautiful hair that was cut off, not yours.' . . .

"Rob *crushed?* Oh, for God's sake, no, not crushed— that's not Rob's style. He's outraged. His reaction, as a matter of fact, annoys me terribly, for he takes the whole thing as a personal affront and says that if Hugh had wanted to make an issue of my afternoons in his studio, he should have challenged him to a duel with the Freiburg swords. His theory, you see, is that Hugh has been smoldering at the thought of these testimonials of his manliness being replaced by the portrait. Rob claims that Hugh hates art—as of course he does—and that it is the artist in him, Rob, not the potential rival, that he is attacking. Needless to say, this gives him a heaven-sent opportunity to berate me for living in the camp of the enemy. He was horrid on Monday. He called me an opportunist and a brood mare. It depresses me that Rob, who is so intuitive about most things, can't see that *I* am the victim, that *my* values have been impugned. Today I hate all men.

"What am I going to do? What *can* I do? I'm taking

her this afternoon to Angelo to see what he can salvage out of the scraps that are left. I'll get her a new doll—one with short hair. That's all I can do now. The picture will never be finished, so the duelling swords will stay where they are. And I will stay where I am—Oh, there's no end! Why on earth does one have children?"

For a minute or two her mother was silent, leaning back with her eyes closed, listening to Aunt Louise. Hannah no longer envied the cat curled into her mother's arm; she hated his smug white face and she hated her mother's sorrowful smile. Hot and desolate and half suffocated, she wished she were one of the angry bees. If she were a bee, she would fly through the crack of the attic door and sting Nephew and her mother and her father and Janie and Andy and Mr. Fowler. "Zzzzzzz," buzzed the child to herself.

After the telephone conversation was over and her mother had got up and gone to run her bath, Hannah let herself silently out the door into the hall and went downstairs to the kitchen. The cook was dicing onions, weeping. "There's my baby," she said as Hannah came to stand beside her, "my very own baby." She put down her knife and wiped her hands and her eyes on her apron and scooped Hannah up in a bear hug.

"I love you, Mattie," said Hannah.

The cook's teary face looked surprised and she put the

child down and said, "Run along now, kiddikins—Mattie's got work to do."

Hannah went into the den and kneeled on the window seat to watch the snow settling deeply on the branches of the trees. "I love you, snow," she said. It fell like sleep.

The Liberation

On the day Polly Bay decided to tell her Uncle Francis and his sister, her Aunt Jane, that in a week's time she was leaving their house and was going East to be married and to live in Boston, she walked very slowly home from Nevilles College, where she taught, dreading the startled look in their eyes and the woe and the indignation with which they would take her news. Hating any derangement of the status quo, her uncle, once a judge, was bound to cross-examine her intensively, and Aunt Jane, his perfect complement, would bolster him and

baffle her. It was going to be an emotional and argu-
mentative scene; her hands, which now were damp,
would presently be dripping. She shivered with appre-
hension, fearing her aunt's asthma and her uncle's po-
lemic, and she shook with rebellion, knowing how they
would succeed in making her feel a traitor to her family,
to the town, and to Colorado, and, obscurely, to her
country.

Uncle Francis and Aunt Jane, like their dead kins-
men, Polly's father and her grandfather and her great-
grandmother, had a vehement family and regional
pride, and they counted it virtue in themselves that they
had never been east of the Mississippi. They had looked
on the departures of Polly's sisters and her cousins as
acts of betrayal and even of disobedience. They had
been distressed particularly by removals to the East,
which were, they felt, iconoclastic and, worse, rude;
how, they marvelled, could this new generation be so
ungrateful to those intrepid early Bays who in the forties, had toiled in such peril and with such fortitude
across the plains in a covered wagon and who with such
perseverance had put down the roots for their traditions
in this town that they had virtually made? Uncle Francis
and Aunt Jane had done all in their power—through
threats and sudden illnesses and cries of "Shame!"—to
prevent these desertions, but, nevertheless, one by one,
the members of the scapegrace generation had managed
to fly, cut off without a penny, scolded to death, and
spoken of thereafter as if they were unredeemed, trea-
sonous, and debauched. Polly was the last, and her position, therefore, was the most uncomfortable of all; she
and her aunt and uncle were the only Bays left in
Adams, and she knew that because she was nearly thirty,

they had long ago stopped fearing that she, too, might go. As they frequently told her, in their candid way, they felt she had reached "a sensible age"—it was a struggle for them not to use the word "spinster" when they paid her this devious and crushing compliment. She knew perfectly well, because this, too, they spoke of, that they imagined she would still be teaching *Immensee* in German I years after they were dead, and would return each evening to the big, drafty house where they were born, and from which they expected to be carried in coffins ordered for them by Polly from Leonard Harper, the undertaker, whose mealy mouth and shifty eye they often talked about with detestation as they rocked and rocked through their long afternoons.

Polly had been engaged to Robert Fair for five months now and had kept his pretty ring in the desk in her office at college; she had not breathed a word to a soul. If she had spoken out when she came back from the Christmas holidays in her sister's Boston house, her uncle and aunt, with a margin of so much time for their forensic pleas before the college year was over, might have driven her to desperate measures; she might have had to flee, without baggage, in the middle of the night on a bus. Not wanting to begin her new life so haphazardly, she had guarded her secret, and had felt a hypocrite.

But she could not keep silent any longer; she had to tell them and start to pack her bags. She did not know how to present her announcement—whether to disarm them with joy or to stun them with a voice of adamant intention. Resenting the predicament, which so occupied her that her love was brusquely pushed aside, and feeling years younger than she was—an irritable adolescent, nerve-racked by growing pains—she now snatched leaves from the springtime bushes and tore them into shreds. It was late May and the purple lilacs were densely in blossom, offering their virtuous fragrance on the wind; the sun was tender on the yellow willow trees; the mountain range was blue and fair and free of haze. But Polly's senses were not at liberty today to take in these demure delights; she could not respond today at all to the flattering fortune that was to make her a June bride; she could not remember of her fiancé anything beyond his name, and, a little ruefully and a little cynically, she wondered if it was love of him or boredom with freshmen and with her aunt and uncle that had caused her to get engaged to him.

Although she loitered like a school child, she had at last to confront the house behind whose drawn blinds her aunt and uncle awaited her return, innocent of the scare they were presently to get and anticipating the modest academic news she brought each day to serve them with their tea. She was so unwilling that when she came in sight of the house, she sat down on a bench at a trolley stop, under the dragging branches of a spruce tree, and opened the book her uncle had asked her to bring from the library. It was *The Heart of Midlothian.* She read with distaste; her uncle's pleasures were different from her own.

Neither the book, though, nor the green needles could hide from her interior eye that house where she had lived for seven years, since her father had died; her mother had been dead for many years and her sisters had long been gone—Fanny to Washington and Mary to Boston—but she had stayed on, quiet and unquestioning. Polly was an undemanding girl and she liked to

teach and she had not been inspired to escape; she had
had, until now, no reason to go elsewhere although, to
be sure, these years had not been exclusively agreeable.
For a short time, she had lived happily in an apartment
by herself, waking each morning to the charming nov-
elty of being her own mistress. But Uncle Francis and
Aunt Jane, both widowed and both bereft of their
heartless children, had cajoled her and played tricks
upon her will until she had consented to go and live
with them. It was not so much because she was weak as
it was because they were so extremely strong that she
had at last capitulated out of fatigue and had brought
her things in a van to unpack them, sighing, in two
wallpapered rooms at the top of the stout brown house.
This odious house, her grandfather's, was covered with
broad, unkempt shingles; it had a turret, and two bow
windows within which begonia and heliotrope fed on
the powerful mountain sun. Its rooms were huge, but
since they were gorged with furniture and with garnish-
ments and clumps and hoards of artifacts of Bays, you
had no sense of space in them and, on the contrary, felt
cornered and nudged and threatened by hanging lamps
with dangerous dependencies and by the dark, bucolic
pictures of Polly's forebears that leaned forward from
the walls in their insculptured brassy frames.

The house stood at the corner of Oxford Street and
Pine, and at the opposite end of the block, at the corner
of Pine and Plato (the college had sponsored the brainy
place-names), there was another one exactly like it. It
had been built as a wedding present for Uncle Francis by
Polly's grandfather, and here Uncle Francis and his
wife, Aunt Lacy, had reared an unnatural daughter and

two unnatural sons, who had flown the coop, as he crossly said, the moment they legally could; there was in his tone the implication that if they had gone before they had come of age, he would have haled them back, calling on the police if they offered to resist. Uncle Francis had been born litigious; he had been predestined to arraign and complain, to sue and sentence.

Aunt Jane and Uncle Richard had lived in Grandpa's house, and their two cowed, effeminate sons had likewise vanished when they reached the age of franchise. When both Uncle Richard and Aunt Lacy had been sealed into the Bay plot, Uncle Francis had moved down the street to be with his sister for the sake of economy and company, taking with him his legal library, which, to this day, was still in boxes in the back hall, in spite of the protests of Mildred, their truculent housekeeper. Uncle Francis had then, at little cost, converted his own house into four inconvenient apartments, from which he derived a shockingly high income. A sign over the front door read, "The Bay Arms."

Polly's parents' red brick house, across the street from Uncle Francis's—not built but bought for them, also as a wedding present—had been torn down. And behind the trolley bench on which she sat there was the biggest and oldest family house of all, the original Bay residence, a vast grotesquerie of native stone, and in it, in the beginning of Polly's life, Great-Grandmother had imperiously lived, with huge, sharp diamonds on her fichus and her velvet, talking without pause of red Indians and storms on the plains, because she could remember nothing else. The house was now a historical museum; it was called, not surprisingly, the Bay. Polly never looked at it without immediately remembering the intricate smell of the

parlor, which had in it moss, must, belladonna, dry
leaves, wet dust, oil of peppermint, and something that
bound them all together—a smell of tribal history, perhaps, or the smell of a house where lived a half-cracked
and haughty old woman who had come to the end of the
line.

In those early days, there had been no other houses in
this block, and the Bay children had had no playmates
except each other. Four generations sat down to Sunday
midday dinner every week at Great-Grandmother's
enormous table; the Presbyterian grace was half as long
as a sermon; the fried rabbit was dry. On Christmas Eve,
beneath a towering tree in Grandpa's house, sheepish
Uncle Richard, as Santa Claus, handed round the presents while Grandpa sat in a central chair like a king on a
throne and stroked his proud goatee. They ate turkey
on Thanksgiving with Uncle Francis and Aunt Lacy,
shot rockets and pinwheels off on the Fourth of July in
Polly's family's back yard. Even now, though one of the
houses was gone and another was given over to the dis-
play of minerals and wagon wheels, and though pressed-
brick bungalows had sprung up all along the block,
Polly never entered the street without the feeling that
she came into a zone restricted for the use of her blood
kin, for there lingered in it some energy, some air, some
admonition that this was the territory of Bays and that
Bays and ghosts of Bays were, and forever would be, in
residence. It was easy for her to vest the wind in the
spruce tree with her great-grandmother's voice and to
hear it say, "Not a one of you knows the sensation of
having a red Indian arrow whiz by your sunbonnet with
wind enough to make the ribbons wave." On reflection,
she understood the claustrophobia that had sent her sis-

ters and cousins all but screaming out of town; horrified, she felt that her own life had been like a dream of smothering.

She was only pretending to read Walter Scott and the sun was setting and she was growing cold. She could not postpone any longer the discharge of the thunderbolt, and at last she weakly rose and crossed the street, feeling a convulsion of panic grind in her throat like a hard sob. Besides the panic, there was a heavy depression, an ebbing away of self-respect, a regret for the waste of so many years. Generations should not be mingled for daily fare, she thought; they are really contemptuous of one another, and the strong individuals, whether they belong to the older or the younger, impose on the meek their creeds and opinions, and, if they are strong enough, brook no dissent. Nothing can more totally subdue the passions than familial piety. Now Polly saw, appalled and miserably ashamed of herself, that she had never once insisted on her own identity in this house. She had dishonestly, supinely (thinking, however, that she was only being polite), allowed her aunt and uncle to believe that she was contented in their house, in sympathy with them, and keenly interested in the minutiae that preoccupied them: their ossifying arteries and their weakening eyes, their dizzy spells and migrant pains, their thrice-daily eucharist of pills and drops, the twinges in their old, uncovered bones. She had never disagreed with them, so how could they know that she did not, as they did, hate the weather? They assumed that she was as scandalized as they by Uncle Francis's tenants' dogs and children. They had no way of knowing that she was bored nearly to frenzy by their vicious quarrels with Mildred over the way she cooked their food.

In the tenebrous hall lined with closed doors, she took off her gloves and coat, and, squinting through the shadows, saw in the mirror that her wretchedness was plain in her drooping lips and her frowning forehead; certainly there was no sign at all upon her face that she was in love. She fixed her mouth into a bogus smile of courage, she straightened out her brow; with the faintest heart in the world she entered the dark front parlor, where the windows were always closed and the shades drawn nearly to the sill. A coal fire on this mild May day burned hot and blue in the grate.

They sat opposite each other at a round, splayfooted table under a dim lamp with a beaded fringe. On the table, amid the tea things, there was a little mahogany casket containing the props with which, each day, they documented their reminiscences of murders, fires, marriages, bankruptcies, and of the triumphs and the rewards of the departed Bays. It was open, showing cracked photographs, letters sallow-inked with age, flaccid and furry newspaper clippings, souvenir spoons flecked with venomous green, little white boxes holding petrified morsels of wedding cake. As Polly came into the room, Aunt Jane reached out her hand and, as if she were pulling a chance from a hat, she picked a newspaper clipping out of the box and said, "I don't think you have ever told Polly the story of the time you were in that train accident in the Royal Gorge. It's such a yarn."

Her uncle heard Polly then and chivalrously half rose from his chair; tall and white-haired, he was distinguished, in a dour way, and dapper in his stiff collar and his waistcoat piped with white. He said, "At last our strayed lamb is back in the fold." The figure made Polly shiver.

"How late you are!" cried Aunt Jane, thrilled at this small deviation from routine. "A department meeting?" If there had been a department meeting, the wreck in the Royal Gorge might be saved for another day.

But they did not wait for her answer. They were impelled, egocentrically and at length, to tell their own news, to explain why it was that they had not waited for her but had begun their tea. Uncle Francis had been hungry, not having felt quite himself earlier in the day and having, therefore, eaten next to nothing at lunch, although the soufflé that Mildred had made was far more edible than customary. He had several new symptoms and was going to the doctor tomorrow; he spoke with infinite peace of mind. Painstakingly then, between themselves, they discussed the advisability of Aunt Jane's making an appointment at the beauty parlor for the same hour Uncle Francis was seeing Dr. Wilder; they could in this way share a taxi. And what was the name of that fellow who drove for the Town Taxi whom they both found so cautious and well-mannered? Bradley, was it? They might have him drive them up a little way into the mountains for the view; but, no, Francis might have got a bad report and Jane might be tired after her baking under the dryer. It would be better if they came straight home. Sometimes they went on in this way for hours.

Polly poured herself a cup of tea, and Aunt Jane said, as she had said probably three thousand times in the past seven years, "You may say what you like, there is simply nothing to take the place of a cup of tea at the end of the day."

Uncle Francis reached across the table and took the newspaper clipping from under his sister's hand. He adjusted his glasses and glanced at the headlines, smiling. "There was a great deal of comedy in that tragedy," he said.

"Tell Polly about it," said Aunt Jane. Polly knew the details of this story by heart—the number of the locomotive and the name of the engineer and the passenger's injuries, particularly her uncle's, which, though minor, had been multitudinous.

Amazing herself, Polly said, "Don't!" And, amazed by her, they stared.

"Why Polly, what an odd thing to say!" exclaimed Aunt Jane. "My dear, is something wrong?"

She decided to take them aback without preamble—it was the only way—and so she said, "Nothing's wrong. Everything's right at last. I am going to be married ten days from today to a teacher at Harvard and I am going to Boston to live."

They behaved like people on a stage; Aunt Jane put her teacup down, rattling her spooon, and began to wring her hands; Uncle Francis, holding his butter knife as if it were a gavel, glared.

"What are you talking about, darling?" he cried. "Married? What do you mean?"

Aunt Jane wheezed, signalling her useful asthma, which, however, did not oblige her. "Boston!" she gasped. "What ever for?"

Polly returned her uncle's magisterial look, but she did so obliquely, and she spoke to her cuffs when she said, "I mean 'married,' the way you were married to Aunt Lacy and the way Aunt Jane was married to Uncle

Richard. I am in love with a man named Robert Fair and *he* is with *me* and we're going to be married."

"How lovely," said Aunt Jane, who, sight unseen, hated Robert Fair.

"Lovely perhaps," said Uncle Francis the magistrate, "and perhaps not. You might, if you please, do us the honor of enlightening us as to the qualifications of Mr. Fair to marry and export you. To the best of my knowledge, I have never heard of him."

"I'm quite sure we don't know him," said Aunt Jane; she coughed experimentally, but her asthma was still in hiding.

"No, you don't know him," Polly said. "He has never been in the West." She wished she could serenely drink her tea while she talked, but she did not trust her hand. Fixing her eyes on a maidenhair fern in a brass jardiniere on the floor, she told them how she had first met Robert Fair at her sister Mary's cottage in Edgartown the summer before.

"You never told us," said Uncle Francis reprovingly. "I thought you said the summer had been a mistake. Too expensive. Too hot. I thought you agreed with Jane and me that summer in the East was hard on the constitution." (She had; out of habit she had let them deprecate the East, which she had loved at first sight, had allowed them to tell her that she had had a poor time when, in truth, she had never been so happy.)

Shocked by her duplicity, Aunt Jane said, "We ought to have suspected something when you went back to Boston for Christmas with Mary instead of resting here beside your own hearth fire."

Ignoring this sanctimonious accusation, Polly continued, and told them as much of Robert Fair as she thought they deserved to know, eliding some of his history—for there was a divorce in it—but as she spoke, she could not conjure his voice or his face, and he remained as hypothetical to her as to them, a circumstance that alarmed her and one that her astute uncle sensed.

"You don't seem head over heels about this Boston fellow," he said.

"I'm nearly thirty," replied his niece. "I'm not sixteen. Wouldn't it be unbecoming at my age if I *were* lovesick?" She was by no means convinced of her argument, for her uncle had that effect on her; he could make her doubt anything—the testimony of her own eyes, the judgments of her own intellect. Again, and in vain, she called on Robert Fair to materialize in this room that was so hostile to him and, through his affection, bring a persuasive color to her cheeks. She did not question the power of love nor did she question, specifically, the steadfastness of her own love, but she did observe, with some dismay, that, far from conquering all, love lazily sidestepped practical problems; it was no help in this interview; it seemed not to cease but to be temporarily at a standstill.

Her uncle said, "Sixteen, thirty, sixty, it makes no difference. It's true I wouldn't like it if you were wearing your heart on your sleeve, but, my Lord, dear, I don't see the semblance of a light in your eye. You look quite sad. Doesn't Polly strike you as looking downright blue, Jane? If Mr. Fair makes you so doleful, it seems to me you're better off with us."

"It's not a laughing matter," snapped Aunt Jane, for Uncle Francis, maddeningly, had chuckled. It was a way he had in disputation; it was intended to enrage and thereby rattle his adversary. He kept his smile, but for a moment he held his tongue while his sister tried a different tack. "What I don't see is why you have to go to Boston, Polly," she said. "Couldn't he teach Italian at Nevilles just as well as at Harvard?"

Their chauvinism was really staggering. When Roddy, Uncle Francis's son, went off to take a glittering job in Brazil, Aunt Jane and his father had nearly reduced this stalwart boy to kicks and tears by reiterating that if there had been anything of worth or virtue in South America, the grandparent Bays would have settled there instead of in the Rocky Mountains.

"I don't think Robert would like it here," said Polly.

"What wouldn't he like about it?" Aunt Jane bridled. "I thought our college had a distinguished reputation. Your great-grandfather, one of the leading founders of it, was a man of culture, and unless I am sadly misinformed, his humanistic spirit is still felt on the campus. Did you know that his critical study of Isocrates is *highly* esteemed amongst classical scholars?"

"I mean I don't think he would like the West," said Polly, rash in her frustration.

She could have bitten her tongue out for the indiscretion, because her jingoistic uncle reddened instantly and menacingly, and he banged on the table and shouted, "How does he know he doesn't like the West? You've just told us he's never been farther west than Ohio. How does he dare to presume to damn what he doesn't know?"

"I didn't say he damned the West. I didn't even say he didn't like it. I said *I* thought he wouldn't."

"Then *you* are presuming," he scolded. "I am impatient with Easterners who look down their noses at the West and call us crude and barbaric. But Westerners who renounce and denounce and derogate their native ground are worse."

"Far worse," agreed Aunt Jane. "What can have come over you to turn the man you intend to marry against the land of your forebears?"

Polly had heard it all before. She wanted to clutch her head in her hands and groan with helplessness; even more, she wished that this were the middle of next week.

"We three are the last left of the Bays in Adams," pursued Aunt Jane, insinuating a quaver into her firm, stern voice. "And Francis and I will not last long. You'll only be burdened and bored with us a little while longer."

"We have meant to reward you liberally for your loyalty," said her uncle. "The houses will be yours when we join our ancestors."

In the dark parlor, they leaned toward her over their cups of cold tea, so tireless in their fusillade that she had no chance to deny them or to defend herself. Was there to be, they mourned, at last not one Bay left to lend his name and presence to municipal celebrations, to the laying of cornerstones and the opening of fairs? Polly thought they were probably already fretting over who would see that the grass between the family graves was mown.

Panicked, she tried to recall how other members of her family had extricated themselves from these webs of casuistry. Now she wished that she had more fully explained her circumstances to Robert Fair and had told him to come and fetch her away, for he, uninvolved, could afford to pay the ransom more easily than she. But she had wanted to spare him such a scene as this; they would not have been any more reticent with him; they would have, with this same arrogance—and this underhandedness—used their advanced age and family honor to twist the argument away from its premise.

Darkness had shrunk the room to the small circle where they sat in the thin light of the lamp; it seemed to her that their reproaches and their jeremiads took hours before they recommenced the bargaining Aunt Jane had started.

Reasonably, in a judicious voice, Uncle Francis said, "There is no reason at all, if Mr. Fair's attainments are as you describe, that he can't be got an appointment to our Romance Language Department. What is the good of my being a trustee if I can't render such a service once in a way?"

As if this were a perfectly wonderful and perfectly surprising solution, Aunt Jane enthusiastically cried, "But of course you can! That would settle everything. Polly can eat her cake and have it, too. Wouldn't you give them your house, Francis?"

"I'd propose an even better arrangement. Alone here, Jane, you and I would rattle. Perhaps we would move into one of my apartments and the Robert Fairs could have this house. Would that suit you?"

"It would, indeed it would," said Aunt Jane. "I have been noticing the drafts here more and more."

"I don't ask you to agree today, Polly," said Uncle Francis. "But think it over. Write your boy a letter tonight and tell him what your aunt and I are willing to do for him. The gift of a house, as big a house as this, is not to be scoffed at by young people just starting out."

Her "boy," Robert, had a tall son who in the autumn

would enter Harvard. "Robert has a house," said Polly, and she thought of its dark-green front door with the brilliant brass trimmings; on Brimmer Street, at the foot of Beacon Hill, its garden faced the Charles. Nothing made her feel more safe and more mature than the image of that old and handsome house.

"He could sell it," said her indomitable aunt.

"He could rent it," said her practical uncle. "That would give you additional revenue."

The air was close; it was like the dead of night in a sealed room and Polly wanted to cry for help. She had not hated the West till now, she had not hated her relatives till now; indeed, till now she had had no experience of hate at all. Surprising as the emotion was—for it came swiftly and authoritatively—it nevertheless cleared her mind and, outraged, she got up and flicked the master switch to light up the chandelier. Her aunt and uncle blinked. She did not sit down again but stood in the doorway to deliver her valediction. "I don't want Robert to come here because I don't want to live here any longer. I want to live my own life."

"Being married is hardly living one's own life," said Aunt Jane.

At the end of her tether now, Polly all but screamed at them, "We *won't* live here and that's that! You talk of my presuming, but how can *you* presume to boss not only me but a man you've never even seen? I don't want your houses! I hate these houses! It's true—I hate, I despise, I abominate the West!"

So new to the articulation of anger, she did it badly and, ashamed to death, began to cry. Though they were hurt, they were forgiving, and both of them rose and came across the room, and Aunt Jane, taking her in a spidery embrace, said, "There. You go upstairs and have a bath and rest and we'll discuss it later. Couldn't we have some sherry, Francis? It seems to me that all our nerves are unstrung."

Polly's breath toiled against her sobs, but all the same she took her life in her hands and she said, "There's nothing further to discuss. I am leaving. I am not coming back."

Now, for the first time, the old brother and sister exchanged a look of real anxiety; they seemed, at last, to take her seriously; each waited for the other to speak. It was Aunt Jane who hit upon the new gambit. "I mean, dear, that we will discuss the wedding. You have given us very short notice but I daresay we can manage."

"There is to be no wedding," said Polly. "We are just going to be married at Mary's house. Fanny is coming up to Boston."

"Fanny has known all along?" Aunt Jane was insulted. "And all this time you've lived under our roof and sat at our table and have never told *us* but told your sisters, who abandoned you?"

"Abandoned me? For God's sake, Aunt Jane, they had their lives to lead!"

"Don't use that sort of language in this house, young lady," said Uncle Francis.

"I apologize. I'm sorry. I am just so sick and tired of—"

"Of course you're sick and tired," said the adroit old woman. "You've had a heavy schedule this semester. No wonder you're all nerves and tears."

"Oh, it isn't that! Oh, leave me alone!"

And, unable to withstand a fresh onslaught of tears, she rushed to the door. When she had closed it upon them, she heard her aunt say, "I simply can't believe it. There must be some way out. Why, Francis, we would be left altogether *alone*," and there was real terror in her voice.

Polly locked the door to her bedroom and dried her eyes and bathed their lids with witch hazel, the odor of which made her think of her Aunt Lacy, who, poor simple creature, had had to die to escape this family. Polly remembered that every autumn Aunt Lacy had petitioned Uncle Francis to let her take her children home for a visit to her native Vermont, but she had never been allowed to go. Grandpa, roaring, thumping his stick, Uncle Francis bombarding her with rhetoric and using the word "duty" repeatedly, Polly's father scathing her with sarcasm, Aunt Jane slyly confusing her with red herrings had kept her an exhausted prisoner. Her children, as a result, had scorned their passive mother and had wounded her, and once they finally escaped, they had not come back—not for so much as a visit. Aunt Lacy had died not having seen any of her grandchildren; in the last years of her life she did nothing but cry. Polly's heart ached for the plight of that gentle, frightened woman. How lucky *she* was that the means of escape had come to her before it was too late! In her sister's Boston drawing room, in a snowy twilight, Robert Fair's proposal of marriage had seemed to release in her an inexhaustible wellspring of life; until that moment she had not known that she was dying, that she was being killed—by inches, but surely killed—by her aunt and uncle and by the green yearlings in her German classes and by the dogmatic monotony of the town's provincialism. She shuddered to think of her narrow escape from wasting away in these arid foothills, never knowing the cause or the name of her disease.

Quiet, herself again, Polly sat beside the window and looked out at the early stars and the crescent moon. Now that she had finally taken her stand, she was invulnerable, even though she knew that the brown sherry was being put ceremoniously on a tray, together with ancestral Waterford glasses, and though she knew that her aunt and uncle had not given up—that they had, on the contrary, just begun. And though she knew that for the last seven days of her life in this house she would be bludgeoned with the most splenetic and most defacing of emotions, she knew that the worst was over; she knew that she would survive, as her sisters and her cousins had survived. In the end, her aunt and uncle only *seemed* to survive; dead on their feet for most of their lives, they had no personal history; their genesis had not been individual—it had only been a part of a dull and factual plan. And they had been too busy honoring their family to love it, too busy defending the West even to look at it. For all their pride in their surroundings, they had never contemplated them at all but had sat with the shades drawn, huddled under the steel engravings. They and her father had lived their whole lives on the laurels of their grandparents; their goal had already been reached long before their birth.

The mountains had never looked so superb to her. She imagined a time, after Uncle Francis and Aunt Jane were dead, when the young Bays and their wives and husbands might come back, free at last to admire the landscape, free to go swiftly through the town in the foothills without so much as a glance at the family memorials and to gain the high passes and the peaks and the glaciers. They would breathe in the thin, lovely air of summits, and in their mouths there would not be a trace of the dust of the prairies where, as on a treadmill, Great-Grandfather Bay's oxen plodded on and on into eternity.

The next days were for Polly at once harrowing and delightful. She suffered at the twilight hour (the brown sherry had become a daily custom, and she wondered if her aunt and uncle naïvely considered getting her drunk and, in this condition, persuading her to sign an unconditional indenture) and all through dinner as, by turns self-pitying and contentious, they sought to make her change her mind. Or, as they put it, "come to her senses." At no time did they accept the fact that she was going. They wrangled over summer plans in which she was included; they plotted anniversary speeches in the Bay museum; one afternoon Aunt Jane even started making a list of miners' families among whom Polly was to distribute Christmas baskets.

But when they were out of her sight and their nagging voices were out of her hearing, they were out of her mind, and in it, instead, was Robert Fair, in his rightful place. She graded examination papers tolerantly, through a haze; she packed her new clothes into her new suitcases and emptied her writing desk completely. On these starry, handsome nights, her dreams were charming, although, to be sure, she sometimes woke from them to hear the shuffle of carpet slippers on the floor below her as her insomniac aunt or uncle paced. But before sadness or rue could overtake her, she burrowed into the memory of her late dream.

The strain of her euphoria and her aunt's and uncle's

antipodean gloom began at last to make her edgy, and she commenced to mark the days off on her calendar and even to reckon the hours. On the day she met her classes for the last time and told her colleagues goodbye and quit the campus forever, she did not stop on the first floor of the house but went directly to her room, only pausing at the parlor door to tell Aunt Jane and Uncle Francis that she had a letter to get off. Fraudulently humble, sighing, they begged her to join them later on for sherry. "The days are growing longer," said Aunt Jane plaintively, "but they are growing fewer."

Polly had no letter to write. She had a letter from Robert Fair to read, and although she knew it by heart already, she read it again several times. He shared her impatience; his students bored him, too; he said he had tried to envision her uncle's house, so that he could imagine her in a specific place, but he had not been able to succeed, even with the help of her sister. He wrote, "The house your malicious sister Mary describes could not exist. Does Aunt Jane *really* read Ouida?"

She laughed aloud. She felt light and purged, as if she had finished a fever. She went to her dressing table and began to brush her hair and to gaze, comforted, upon her young and loving face. She was so lost in her relief that she was pretty, and that she was going to be married and was going away, that she heard neither the telephone nor Mildred's feet upon the stairs, and the housekeeper was in the room before Polly had turned from her pool.

"It's your sister calling you from Boston," said Mildred with ice-cold contempt; she mirrored her employers. "I heard those operators back East giving themselves *some* airs with their la-di-da way of talking."

Clumsy with surprise and confusion (Mary's calls to her were rare and never frivolous), and sorry that exigency and not calm plan took her downstairs again, she reeled into that smothering front hall where hat trees and cane stands stood like people. The door to the parlor was closed, but she knew that behind it Aunt Jane and Uncle Francis were listening.

When Mary's far-off, mourning voice broke to Polly the awful, the impossible, the unbelievable news that Robert Fair had died that morning of the heart disease from which he had intermittently suffered for some years, Polly, wordless and dry-eyed, contracted into a nonsensical, contorted position and gripped the telephone as if this alone could keep her from drowning in the savage flood that had come from nowhere.

"Are you there, Polly? Can you hear me, darling?" Mary's anxious voice came louder and faster. "Do you want me to come out to you? Or can you come on here now?"

"I can't come now," said Polly. "There's nothing you can do for me." There had always been rapport between these sisters, and it had been deeper in the months since Robert Fair had appeared upon the scene to rescue and reward the younger woman. But it was shattered; the bearer of ill tidings is seldom thanked. "How can you help me?" Polly demanded, shocked and furious. "You can't bring him back to life."

"I can help bring you back to life," her sister said. "You must get out of *there,* Polly. It's more important now than ever."

"Do you think that was why I was going to marry him? Just to escape this house and this town?"

"No, no! Control yourself! We'd better not try to talk any more now—you call me when you can."

The parlor door opened, revealing Uncle Francis with a glass of sherry in his hand.

"Wait, Mary! Don't hang up!" Polly cried. There was a facetious air about her uncle; there was something smug. "I'll get the sleeper from Denver tonight," she said.

When she hung up, her uncle opened the door wider to welcome her to bad brown sherry; they had not turned on the lights, and Aunt Jane, in the twilight, sat in her accustomed place.

"Poor angel," said Uncle Francis.

"I am so sorry, so very sorry," said Aunt Jane.

When Polly said nothing but simply stared at their impassive faces, Uncle Francis said, "I think I'd better call up Wilder. You ought to have a sedative and go straight to bed."

"I'm going straight to Boston," said Polly.

"But why?" said Aunt Jane.

"Because he's there. I love him and he's there."

They tried to detain her; they tried to force the sherry down her throat; they told her she must be calm and they asked her to remember that at times like this one needed the love and the support of one's blood kin.

"I am going straight to Boston," she repeated, and turned and went quickly up the stairs. They stood at the bottom calling to her: "You haven't settled your affairs. What about the bank?" "Polly, get hold of yourself! It's terrible, I'm heartbroken for you, but it's not the end of the world."

She packed nothing; she wanted nothing here—not even the new clothes she had bought in which to be a bride. She put on a coat and a hat and gloves and a scarf and put all the money she had in her purse and went downstairs again. Stricken but diehard, they were beside the front door.

"Don't go!" implored Aunt Jane.

"You need us now more than ever!" her uncle cried.

"And we need you. Does that make no impression on you, Polly? Is your heart that cold?"

She paid no attention to them at all and pushed them aside and left the house. She ran to the station to get the last train to Denver, and once she had boarded it, she allowed her grief to overwhelm her. She felt chewed and mauled by the niggling hypochondriacs she had left behind, who had fussily tried to appropriate even her own tragedy. She felt sullied by their disrespect and greed.

How lonely I have been, she thought. And then, not fully knowing what she meant by it but believing in it faithfully, she said half aloud, "I am not lonely now."

The Captain's Gift

Though it is wartime, it is spring, so there are boys down in the street playing catch. Babies and dogs are sunning in the square and here and there among them, on green iron benches under the trees, rabbis sit reading newspapers. Some stout women and some thin little girls have brought crusts of bread in paper bags and are casting crumbs to the pigeons. There is a fire in one of the wire trash baskets and bits of black ash fly upward, but there is no wind at all to carry them off and they slowly descend again. Out of the windows of the maternity hospital, new mothers, convalescent, wearing flowered wrappers, lean to call to their friends who stand in little clumps on the sidewalk, waving their arms and shouting up pleasantries and private jokes in Yiddish. They are loath to end the visit, but finally they must, for unseen nurses speak to the women at the windows and they retire, crying good-humoured farewells and naming each friend by name: Goodbye, Uncle Nathan! Goodbye, Mama! Goodbye, Isabel! Goodbye, Mrs. Leibowitz! Goodbye! In the pushcarts at the curb-stone are lilacs and mountain laurel, pots of grape hyacinth and petunias for window-boxes; between sales the venders rearrange their buckets and talk with the superintendents of the apartment buildings who idle, smoking, in the cellar entries where they lean against the tall ash cans. Six blocks away, the clock at St. Marks-in-the-Bouwerie strikes four.

Mrs. Chester Ramsey, the widow of the general, has one of the very few private houses in the neighborhood. At the window of her drawing room on the second floor, she is writing letters at a little desk that looks like a spinet. Now and then, pausing for a word, she glances through the marquisette curtains that blur the scene below and impart to it a quality she cannot name but which bewitches her at this time of day, especially in the spring. It separates her while it does not take her quite away; she becomes of and not of the spectacle. And then, too, it makes her nostalgic for the days, long ago, when young matrons, her friends, strolled through the square under their parasols, when trim French nursemaids wheeled babies, whose names she knew, in English prams; and little girls in sailor hats walked briskly with their governesses to confirmation class; when she herself was well-known there and was greeted and detained innumerable times in her passage through the flower-lined walks.

But there is no bitterness at all in her reflection; indeed, she enjoys the lazy turmoil of the anonymous crowd below. Often, on a nice day like this if no one is coming in to tea, she goes out to sit on one of the benches, and it is always thrillingly strange to her that no one notices her, even though she wears the sort of clothes her mother might have done when she was an old lady: a black taffeta dress with a long skirt and a tightly buttoned, high-necked jacket with a garnet brooch at the throat, a small velvet hat, black silk gloves. She is not in the least unconscious of her appearance, but she does not hope to be greeted with a flurry of surprise; rather, its absence is what she looks forward to, and she is like a child, who, dressed in her mother's clothes, is accepted as a grown-up. She is no more eccentric than the bearded rabbis or the brown gypsy women who occasionally waddle along the paths with their greasy striped skirts and their waist-long strings of beads. Sometimes, sitting there, she feels that she is invisible. Surely, she thinks, the people would remark on her if they could see her; they would certainly realize that in her reside memories of this square and this neighborhood older than some of the plane trees. She is surprised and not resentful that none of them knows that she alone belongs here.

The lady's friends and relatives, who live uptown, year after year try to dislodge her from her old and inconvenient house. It is, they feel nervously, much too close to Third Avenue with its swarming, staggering riff-raff, and living alone as she does with only two faithful maids (one of whom is deaf) and a choreman, she would be quite defenceless if burglars came. Moreover, the fire department has condemned her house as well as many others in the block, and they shudder to think of Mrs. Ramsey's being trapped in her bedroom at the back of the second floor, far from help. There is no question about it: she would be burned in her bed. But she baffles them with what they say is a paradox. She says, "I have never liked change, and now I am too old for it." They protest, unable sometimes to keep the note of exasperation out of their voices, that change is exactly what they want to preserve her from. They predict, with statistics to back them up, that the neighborhood will go still further downhill and soon will be another Delancey Street. She returns that while she is touched by their solicitude, she has no wish to move. She is, she thanks them, quite at home. Finally they have to give up and when they have accepted defeat with a sigh, they begin to admire her stubbornness all over again, and to say it is really heroic the way she has refused to acknowledge the death of the past. The ivory tower in which she lives is impregnable to the ill-smelling, rude-sounding, squalid-looking world which through the years has moved in closer and closer and now surrounds her on all sides. Incredibly, she has not been swallowed up. She has not gone out of her way to keep the streets in their place, but the streets have simply not dared to encroach upon her dignity. Take the matter of the smells, for example. Her visitors, stepping out of their taxis before her door, are almost overpowered by the rank, unidentifiable emanations from cellars and open windows: food smells (these people think of nothing but food) that are so strong and so foreign and so sickening that they call to

mind the worst quarters of the worst Near Eastern cities.
And yet, the moment the door of Mrs. Ramsey's house
closes upon them, shutting out the laden atmosphere,
they have forgotten the stink which a moment before
they had thought unforgettable, and are aware only of
aged pot-pourri, of lemon oil, and of desiccated lavender
in linen closets.

Despite her refusal to leave her inaccessible slums,
Mrs. Ramsey passes hardly a day without at least one
caller for she remains altogether charming, preserving
the grace of manner and the wit that marked her at her
first Assembly almost sixty years ago. She has not, that
is, kept even a suggestion of her beauty. The flesh has
worn away from her crooked bones and her white hair is
yellowish and rather thin; she has a filmy cataract over
one eye and in her skinny little face, her large nose has
an Hebraic look. Indeed, though she was famous for her
looks, no one on first meeting her ever says, "She must
have been a beauty in her day." It is quite impossible to
reconstruct her as she might have been since there is
nothing to go on; the skeleton seems quite a badly
botched job, and the face has no reminder in it of a
single good feature. One supposes, in the end, that she
was one of those girls whose details are not independ-
ently beautiful, but who are, nevertheless, a lovely com-
position. General Ramsey, on the other hand, five years
dead, was a handsome man at the very end of his life,
and the portrait painted just before his final illness,
shows him to be keen-eyed, imposing, with a long aristo-
cratic head on a pair of military shoulders, heavily
adorned.

A stranger, having heard of Mrs. Ramsey's charm,
thinks when he first sees her that it must lie in a tart wit

since she looks too droll, too much like a piquant chipmunk, to have a more expansive feminine elegance. But while the wit is there, bright and Edwardian, this is not the chief of her gifts. Rather, it is her tenderness and pity, her delicate and imaginative love, her purity that makes her always say the right thing. She is so wise a husbandman, so economical, that her smallest dispensations and her briefest words are treasure. She has neither enemies nor critics, so that like an angel she is unendangered by brutality or by "difficult situations." Even her sorrow at her husband's death and her loneliness afterwards seemed only to make sweeter her sweet life. She is an innocent child of seventy-five.

Among her friends, Mrs. Ramsey numbers many well-bred young men who, before the war, came to her house for tea or for lunch on Sunday. Now they are all in uniform and many of them are overseas, but they write to her frequently and she replies, in a wavy old-fashioned hand, on V-mail blanks. In spite of this substitution of the blanks for her own monogrammed letter paper, in spite of the military titles and the serial numbers which she copies down in the little box at the top of the page, in spite of the uniforms which she cannot help seeing in the square, and the newspapers and the War Bond drives, the blackout curtains at her windows and the buckets of sand in her fourth floor corridor and the ration books, Mrs. Ramsey is the one person, her friends say, to whom the cliché may accurately be applied: "She does not know there is a war on." Her daughter, who is a Red Cross supervisor and who comes in uniform once a week to dine with her mother, says she is "too good to be true," that she is a perfect asylum, that in her house one can quite delude oneself into believing that this tranquillity extends far beyond her doorstep, beyond the city, throughout the world itself, and that the catastrophes of our times are only hypothetical horrors. Her granddaughters, who are Waves, her grandson Ramsey who is an instructor in a pre-flight school, her son who manufactures precision instruments and has bought fifty thousand dollars' worth of bonds, her son-in-law, the military attaché, her daughter-in-law who works at the blood bank, all say the same thing of her. They say they frightfully pity people who cannot have a holiday from the war in her house. She continues to speak of Paris as if the only reason she does not go there is that she is too old and her health is too unsteady; she hopes that one of her favorite young men, wounded at Anzio, will enjoy Easter in Italy and she assumes that he will go to Rome to hear the Pope. She speaks of Germany and Japan as if they were still nothing more than two foreign countries of which she has affectionate memories. It is true that at times her blandness becomes trying. For example, if someone speaks of the mistakes of Versailles, she quite genuinely believes he refers to the way the flower beds are laid out in the palace gardens and she agrees warmly that they could have been ever so much nicer. But one has no business to be annoyed with her. Since there are so few years left to her (and since there is now no danger of our being bombed) it would be an unkind and playful sacrilege to destroy her illusion that the world is still good and beautiful and harmonious in all its parts. She need never know how barbarically civilization has been betrayed.

How refreshing must be her letters to the soldiers! She neither complains of their hardships nor gushes over their bravery. It must be marvelous, indeed, to

know that there is someone across whose lips the phrase
"the four freedoms" has never passed, someone whose
vocabulary is innocent of "fascism," someone who writes
calm reminiscences in her letters (even so! on the
printed V-mail form!) of summer band concerts in Sara-
toga Springs, of winter dinner parties at the Murray
Hill which, in reality as fusty as an old trunk, she thinks
is still the smartest hotel in town. Mothers of the soldiers are overjoyed: she is their link with the courtly
past, she is Mrs. Wharton at first hand.

Mrs. Ramsey has written five letters to soldiers and
sailors and a sixth is begun. But her eyes have started to
burn and since it is anyhow nearly time for tea, she rises
from her desk and prepares to go to her bedroom to
freshen up for her guests who today will be one of her
granddaughters and the fiancée of one of her young ad-
mirers. She looks down once more into the little park
and thinks that it is the loveliest in the city. It reminds
her of Bloomsbury Square. There she used to sit waiting
for her husband while he copied out notes and lists of
things in the British Museum whenever they visited
London. One of his avocations, perhaps the mildest of
them all, had been a study of English ballads and he
kept notebooks full of their variants. Great as was her
delight in his society, she was always glad when he
stayed away a long time, for she loved sitting there
alone, heedless of anything but the simple fact of her
being there. Perhaps it is the memory of those days that
now motivates her occasional afternoon in the square,
for the atmosphere is just as foreign and her presence
seems just as unusual as it used to be in London. The
difference is that in London she had been a visitor from

a distant country while here she is a visitor from a distant time. As she looks down she sees a little boy in a beret like a French sailor's. He is carrying a string shopping bag with a long loaf of bread sticking out of it. He walks beside his enormous mother who wears a red snood over a bun of hair as big as the loaf of bread in the bag. Mrs. Ramsey, for no reason, thinks how dearly she loves Europe and how sorry she is that there is no time left for her to go abroad again. If she were just a few years younger, she would be envious of the boys to whom she has been writing her letters.

She has just turned toward the door when she hears, far off, the bell at the street entrance and she makes a convulsive little gesture with her hand, afraid that the girls have come already and she is not prepared. She opens the door and waits beside it, listening, and then, hearing Elizabeth coming up the stairs alone, she steps out into the hall and calls down, "I am just going to dress, Elizabeth. Who was at the door?"

The plump middle-aged maid is deaf and she has not heard. She comes into sight on the stairs; she is carrying a parcel and seeing her mistress, she says, "The special delivery man brought it, Mrs. Ramsey, and I thought you would like to have it at once since it comes from overseas." She hands over the package, adding, "From Captain Cousins."

Mrs. Ramsey returns to the drawing room, saying to the maid, "Oh, I shan't wait to open *this!* If I am late and don't have time to dress, I am sure the young ladies won't mind." The maid beams, delighted with the look of pleasure in Mrs. Ramsey's face, and retires quietly as though she were leaving a girl to read her sweetheart's letter.

The little old lady sits down on a yellow and pink striped love-seat, holding the box in her hands, but she does not immediately open it. She sits remembering her grandson, Arthur Cousins, of all the young men, her favorite. He looks much as the General did as a youth and it is this resemblance, probably, that so endears him to her. She recalls him in exquisite detail and his image takes her breath away. He is as tall, as fair, as red-cheeked as a Swede. Before he went away, when he used to come to see her, he always seemed sudden and exotic, making her drawing room look dusky. Whenever she saw him and now whenever she thinks of him, she remembers, rapturously, the hot beaches of Naples, the blinding winter sun at Saint Moritz, the waves of heat rising from the gravel slope before the Pitti Palace. The sunlight he calls up is not parching but wonderfully rich and heady. His mind is as luminous as his skin and his hair; and he is so happy! She thinks of him leaning forward in his chair at a recital to watch a woman playing a lute, bending her head down to look at it with love, as if she were looking into a child's face; his lips are parted and his eyes shine. She sees him sitting beside her in church and she remembers the days when he was an altar boy. The very package that she holds seems to give off a warmth of summertime and she touches it lightly here and there with her fingertips.

Arthur, first in England, then in France and then in Italy has sent not only countless letters to his grandmother, but presents as well. Under the General's portrait, in a Chinese chest to which she wears the key on a gold chain round her neck, the letters lie in ribbon-bound packets and so do the gifts, still in their tissue-paper wrappings. From London, he sent Irish linen handkerchiefs and heliotrope sachets and a small pink marble shepherdess; from Paris, gloves and a silver box for oddments; from Italy, a leather writing case and two paste-studded shell combs. His affectionate letters which she reads and re-reads through a magnifying glass on a mother-of-pearl handle, tell of his homesickness, of his unwillingness to be so far away from her. He writes that on his return, they must go again, as they did on the last day of his last furlough, round Central Park in a carriage. "Only with you, my darling Grandma, is this not just a stunt," he writes. They must, he goes on, dine at the Lafayette where the *moules marinières* have been celebrated from her day until his; she must allow him to come every day to tea and must tell him stories of her girlhood. He knows that he will find her exactly the same as she was when he told her goodbye.

On the last little square photograph headed "Somewhere in Germany" he had written, "I am sending you the best present that I have found for you yet. It is something that Helena Rubenstein (as if you knew who she is!) would give a fortune for, but I'm not going to tell you what it is. I like thinking of you trying to guess as you sit there among all your lares and penates and your fresh flowers."

Mrs. Ramsey, repeating to herself the phrase "fresh flowers," regrets that she has not sent out for some lilacs, for the only things in bloom are two white African violets on the sideboard. She feels a little guilty as though she has betrayed Arthur's picture of her and she thinks of what her daughter, Arthur's mother, said at dinner last night, "With you, Arthur will not change because you are unchangeable. But in his letters to me, he is becoming more and more unrecognizable."

She had forbidden her daughter to pursue this subject: there was a hint of disloyalty in her voice, or was it a hint of fear? The whole last sentence of Arthur's letter now reechoes in her mind and a slight cloud comes over her face. She feels a touch of cold and decides that she must tell Elizabeth to lay a fire after all. When one is very old and fleshless, one is like a thermometer, registering the least change in temperature.

But the fire must wait until she has opened her present. She smiles. She knows who Helena Rubenstein is, but it pleases her that Arthur thinks she does not. Perhaps it is a bottle of some rare scent that would so much gratify both of them. The clock at St. Mark's strikes the quarter hour and she goes to her desk and brings back a pair of scissors. She is so happy that she does not any longer try to imagine what is inside; she rather hopes she has not guessed rightly, that it is not scent, that it will take her completely by surprise.

Under the outer wrappings there is a shoe-box, and in the box, a parcel in tissue paper, tied with a piece of string. It is something shapeless and even when she has taken it out and has held it a moment in her old wrinkled hands, she cannot tell what it is. It is not a bottle and not a box nor a case; it is rather heavy but its heaviness is of a curious kind: it seems to be a mass of something. She delays no longer and snips the string. There in her lap lies a braid of golden hair. At the top it is ruffled a little as though a girl, just fallen asleep, had tossed once or twice on her pillow; the rest of it is smooth, down to the end, which is tied with a little pink bow. It has been cut off cleanly at the nape of the neck, and it is so long that it must have hung below her waist. It is thick and it seems still so vital in the light that streams through the windows that Mrs. Ramsey feels its owner is concealed from her only by a vapour, that her head is here beside her on the love-seat: she is hidden from Mrs. Ramsey just as Mrs. Ramsey is hidden from the people in the square.

She pushes the tissue paper with the handle of the scissors and the braid slips to the grey carpet and lies there shining like a living snake. Now the old lady clasps her hands together to end their trembling, and looking at the African violets she admits to some distant compartment of her mind the fact that they are dying and must be removed tomorrow. She speaks aloud in the empty room. "How unfriendly, Arthur!" she says. "How unkind!" And as if there were a voice in the hair at her feet, she distinctly hears him saying, "There's a war on, hadn't you heard?"

A Reading Problem

One of the great hardships of my childhood—and there were many, as many, I suppose, as have ever plagued a living creature—was that I could never find a decent place to read. If I tried to read at home in the living room, I was constantly pestered by someone saying, "For goodness' sake, Emily, move where it's light. You're going to ruin your eyes and no two ways about it," or "You ought to be outdoors with the other youngsters getting some roses in your cheeks." Of course, I knew how to reply to these kill-joy injunctions; to the first I said, "They're *my* eyes," and to the second, "Getting some brains in my head is more important than getting any so-called roses in my cheeks." But even when I had settled the hash of that Paul Pry—Mother, usually, but sometimes a visiting aunt, or even a bossy neighbor—I was cross and could no longer concentrate. The bedroom I shared with my sister Stella was even worse, because Stella was always in it, making an inventory of her free samples out loud, singing Camp Fire Girl songs, practicing ballet steps and giggling whenever she made a mistake; she was one of the most vacant people I have ever known.

At one certain time of year, I could read up in the mountains, in any number of clearings and dingles and amphitheatres, and that was in the fall. But in the winter it was too cold, and in the spring there were wood ticks, and in the summer there were snakes. I had tried a pinewoods I was very fond of for several weeks one summer, but it was no good, because at the end of every paragraph I had to get up and stamp my feet and shout and describe an agitated circle on the ground with a stick to warn the rattlers to stay away from me.

The public library was better, but not much. The librarian, Mrs. Looby, a fussbudgety old thing in a yellow wig and a hat planted with nasturtiums, was so strict about the silent rule that she evicted children who popped their gum or cracked their knuckles, and I was a child who did both as a matter of course and constantly. Besides, she was forever coming into the children's section like a principal making rounds, and leaning over you to see what you were reading; half the time she disapproved and recommended something else, something either so dry you'd go to sleep reading it or so mushy you'd throw up. Moreover, our dog, Reddie, loved to follow me to the library, and quite often, instead of waiting outside under the lilac bush, as he was supposed to do, he would manage to get in when someone opened the door. He didn't come to see me; he came to tease Mrs. Looby, who abominated anything that walked on four legs. He would sit on his haunches in front of her desk, wagging his tail and laughing, with his long pink tongue hanging out. "Shoo!" Mrs. Looby would scream, waving her hands at him. "Emily Vanderpool, you get this pesky dog of yours out of here this minute! The very idea! Quick, Emily, or I'll call the dogcatcher! I'll call the dogcatcher. I will positively call the dogcatcher if a dog ever comes into my library again." I had to give up the library altogether after one unlucky occasion when Reddie stood on his hind legs and put his paws on top of her high desk. She had had her back to him, and, thinking she heard a customer, she turned, saying in her library whisper, "Good afternoon, and what may I do for you this afternoon?" and faced the grinning countenance of my dog. That time, in her wrath and dismay, she clutched her head in her hands and dislodged her hat and then her wig, so that a wide expanse of baldness showed, and everyone in the children's section dived into the stacks and went all to pieces.

For a while after that, I tried the lobby of the downtown hotel, the Goldmoor, where the permanent residents, who were all old men, sat in long-waisted rocking chairs, rocking and spitting tobacco juice into embossed cuspidors and talking in high, offended, lonesome voices about their stomach aches and their insomnia and how the times had changed. All in the world the old duffers had left was time, which, hour after hour, they had to kill. People like that, who are bored almost to extinction, think that everyone else is, too, and if they see someone reading a book, they say to themselves, "I declare, here's somebody worse off than I am. The poor soul's really hard up to have to depend on a book, and it's my bounden Christian duty to help him pass the time," and they start talking to you. If you want company on the streetcar or the bus or the interurban, open a book and you're all set. At first, the old men didn't spot me, because I always sat in one of the two bow windows in a chair that was half hidden by a potted sweet-potato plant, which, according to local legend, dated from the nineteenth century—and well it might have, since it was the size of a small-size tree. My chair was crowded in between this and a table on which was a clutter of seedy Western souvenirs—a rusted, beat-up placer pan with samples of ore in it, some fossils and some arrowheads, a tomahawk, a powder horn, and the shellacked tail of a beaver that was supposed to have been trapped by a desperado named Mountain Jim Nugent, who had lived in Estes Park in the seventies. It was this tabletop historical museum that made me have to give up the hotel, for one day, when I was spang in the middle of *Hans Brinker,* two of the old men came over to it to have a whining, cantankerous argument about one of the rocks in the placer pan, which one maintained was pyrites and the other maintained was not. (That was about as interesting as their conversations ever got.) They were so angry that if they hadn't been so feeble, I think they would have thrown the rocks at each other. And then one of them caught sight of me and commenced to cackle. "Lookit what we got here," he said.

"A little old kid in a middy reading windies all by her lonesome."

I had been taught to be courteous to my elders, so I looked up and gave the speaker a sickly smile and returned to my book, which now, of course, I could not follow. His disputant became his ally, and they carried on, laughing and teasing me as if I were a monkey that had suddenly entered their precincts for the sole purpose of amusing them. They asked me why I wasn't at the movies with my sweetheart, they asked me how I'd like to be paddled with that stiff old beaver tail of Mountain Jim's, and they asked me to sing them a song. All the other old men, delighted at this small interruption in their routine of spitting and complaining, started rubbernecking in my direction, grinning and chuckling, and a couple of them came shuffling over to watch the fun. I felt as if I had a fever of a hundred and five, because of the blush that spread over my entire person, including my insides. I was not only embarrassed, I was as mad as anything to be hemmed in by this phalanx of giggling old geezers who looked like a flock of turkey gobblers. "Maybe she ran away from home," said one of them. "Hasn't been any transients in this hotel since that last Watkins fella. Fella by the name of Fletcher. Is your name Fletcher, Missy?" Another said, "I think it's mighty nice of her to come and pay us a call instead of going to the show with her best beau," and when a third said, "I bet I know where there's a Hershey bar not a thousand miles from here," I got up and, in a panic, ducked through the lines and fled; taking candy from a strange old man was the quickest way to die like a dog from poison.

So the hotel after that was out. Then I tried the

depot, but it was too dirty and noisy; a couple of times I went and sat in the back of the Catholic church, but it was dark there, and besides I didn't feel right about it, because I was a United Presbyterian in good standing. Once, I went into the women's smoking room in the library at the college, but it was full of worried-looking old-maid summer-school students who came back year after year to work on their Master's degrees in Education, and they asked me a lot of solemn questions, raising their voices as if I were deaf. Besides, it was embarrassing to watch them smoke; they were furtive and affected, and they coughed a good deal. I could smoke better than that and I was only ten; I mean the one time I had smoked I did it better—a friend and I each smoked a cubeb she had pinched from her tubercular father.

But at last I found a peachy place—the visitors' waiting room outside the jail in the basement of the courthouse. There were seldom any visitors, because there were seldom any prisoners, and when, on rare occasions, there were, the visitors were too edgy or too morose to pay any heed to me. The big, cool room had nothing in it but two long benches and a wicker table, on which was spread out free Christian Science literature. The sheriff, Mr. Starbird, was very sympathetic with me, for he liked to read himself and that's what he did most of the time (his job was a snap; Adams was, on the whole, a law-abiding town) in his office that adjoined the waiting room; he read and read, not lifting his eyes from Sax Rohmer even when he was rolling a cigarette. Once, he said he wished his own daughters, Laverne, thirteen, and Ida, sixteen, would follow my example, instead of, as he put it, "rimfirin' around the county with paint on their faces and spikes on their heels and not caring two hoots for anything on God's green earth except what's got on pants." Mr. Starbird and I became good friends, although we did not talk much, since we were busy reading. One time, when were both feeling restless, he locked me up in a cell so I could see how it felt; I kind of liked it. And another time he put handcuffs on me, but they were too big.

At the time I discovered the jail, in the first hot days in June, I was trying to memorize the books of the Bible. If I got them by heart and could name them off in proper order and without hesitating or mispronouncing, I would be eligible to receive an award of a New Testament at Sunday school, and if there was one thing I liked, it was prizes. So every day for several weeks I spent the whole afternoon more or less in jail, reading whatever fun thing I had brought along (*Rebecca of Sunnybrook Farm, Misunderstood Betsy, Trudy Goes to Boarding School*) and then working away at I Samuel, II Samuel, I Kings, II Kings, whispering so as not to disturb Mr. Starbird. Sometimes, on a really hot day, he would send out for two bottles of Dr. Pepper.

One blistering Saturday, when I was as limp as a rag after walking through the sun down the hill and into the hot valley where the courthouse was, I got to the stairs leading to the waiting room and was met by the most deafening din of men yelling and bars rattling and Mr. Starbird hollering "Quiet there, you bastards!" at the top of his voice. I was shocked and scared but very curious, and I went on down the steps, hearing the vilest imaginable language spewing out from the direction of the cells. I had just sat down on the edge of one of the benches and was opening *Tom Sawyer Abroad* when Mr. Starbird, bright red in the face, came in, brushing his hands. Two sweating deputies followed him. "Not today, Emily," said Mr. Starbird when he saw me. "We got some tough customers today, worse luck. And me with a new Fu."

The prisoners were moonshiners, he told me as he led me by the arm to the stairs, whose still up in the mountains had been discovered, because they had drunk too much of their own rotgut and had got loose-tongued and had gone around bragging at the amusement park up at the head of the canyon. There were five of them, and they had had to be disarmed of sawed-off shotguns, although, as Mr. Starbird modestly pointed out, this wasn't much of a job, since they had been three sheets in the wind. "Whew!" said the sheriff. "They got a breath on 'em like the whole shootin' match of St. Louis before the Volstead Act." I told him I didn't mind (it would give me considerable prestige with my brother and my friends to be on hand if one of them should try to make a break, and I would undoubtedly get my name in the paper: "Emily Vanderpool, daughter of Mr. and Mrs. Peter Vanderpool, witnessed the attempted escape of the desperate criminals. Emily is to receive an award at the United Presbyterian Church on July 29th"), but Mr. Starbird told me, a little sharply, to go on now, and I had no choice but to go.

Go where? I had exhausted every possibility in town. I thought of going to the Safeway, where my father was the manager, and asking him if I could read in his office, but I knew how that would go over on a busy Saturday when the farmers and the mountain people were in town buying potatoes and side meat; my father didn't have Mr. Starbird's temperament. Then, vaguely, I considered the front porch of a haunted house at the top of Carlyle Hill but rejected it when I remembered a recent rumor that there was a nest of bats under the eaves; I didn't want them in my hair, using my pigtails to swing on. I wasn't too sure I could read anyhow, because I was so excited over the prisoners, but it was far too hot to roller-skate, too hot to explore the dump—to hot, indeed, for anything but sitting quietly beside the lockup.

I started in the direction of home in a desultory way, stopping at every drinking fountain, window-shopping, going methodically through the ten-cent stores, looking for money in the gutters. I walked down the length of the main street, going toward the mountains, over whose summits hung a pale heat haze; the pavement was soft, and when it and the shimmering sidewalk ended, I had to walk in the red dirt road, which was so dusty that after a few steps my legs, above the tops of my socks, looked burned—not sunburned, *burned*.

At the outskirts of town, beside the creek, there was a tourist camp where funny-looking people pitched tents and filled up the wire trash baskets with tin cans; sometimes, on a still night, you could hear them singing state songs, and now and again there was the sound of an accordion or a harmonica playing a jig. Today there was only one tent up in the grounds, a sagging, ragged white one, and it looked forlorn, like something left behind. Nearby was parked a Model T, dark red with rust where its sky-blue paint had worn off, and to it was attached a trailer; I knew how hot the leather seat of that car would be and I could all but hear the sun beating on the top of it like hailstones. There wasn't a soul in sight, and there wasn't a sound nearby except for a couple of magpies ranting at each other in the trees and the occasional digestive croak of a bullfrog. Along the creek, there was a line of shady cottonwoods, and I decided to rest there for a while and cool off my feet in the water.

After I had washed as well as I could, I leaned back against the tree trunk, my feet still in the water, and opened the Bible to the table of contents, and then I closed my eyes so that I wouldn't cheat; I started reciting, sofly and clearly and proud of myself. I had just got to Ezra, having gone so far very fast and without a hitch, when a noise caused me to fling back my eyelids and to discover that a man's big foot in a high buttoned shoe had materialized on the ground beside me. Startled, I looked up into the bearded face of a tall man in black clothes (black suit, black string tie, black-rimmed eyeglasses, black hat—the hat was dented in such a way that it looked like a gravy boat) and into the small brown eyes of a girl about Stella's age, who wore a tennis visor and a long, dirty white thing that looked like her nightgown.

"Greetings, Christian soldier," said the man, in a deep, rich Southern accent, and he offered me a large, warty hand. "Evangelist Gerlash is the name, and this is my girl, Opal."

Opal put her hand on my head and said, "Peace."

"Same to you," I said awkwardly, and took my feet out of the water. "You can have this tree if you want. I was just leaving."

I started to get up, but Evangelist Gerlash motioned me to stay where I was, and he said, "It uplifts my heavy heart and it uplifts Opal's to find a believer in our wanderings through this godless world. All too seldom do we find a person applying themself to the Book. Oh, sister, keep to this path your youthful feet have started on and shun the Sodoms *and* the Gomorrahs *and* the Baby lons!"

My youthful feet were so wet I was having a struggle to put on my socks, and I thought, Peace! That's all he knows about it. There's not an inch of peace or privacy in this whole town.

"Seek truth and *not* the fleshpots!" said the man. "Know light, *not* license! 'A little child shall lead them,' says the Book you hold in your small hands, as yet unused to woman's work. Perhaps *you* are that very child."

"Amen," said Opal, and with this they both sat down, tailor-fashion, on the bank of the stream. For some time, nothing more was said. The Gerlashes complacently scrutinized me, as if I were the very thing they had been looking for, and then they looked at each other in a congratulatory way, while I, breaking out in an itching rash of embarrassment, tried to think of an urgent bit of business that would excuse me from their company without being impolite. I could think only of the dentist or of a dancing class, but I was dressed for neither; some weeks before, my Uncle Will M'Kerrow, who

lived in Ridley, Missouri, had gone to a sale at the Army
and Navy store in St. Joe and had bought presents for
me and my brother and my two sisters, and today I was
wearing mine—khaki knickers and a khaki shirt and a
cavalry hat. I had perked up the hat by twining a multi-
colored shoelace around the band; the other shoelace I
had cut in two to tie the ends of my pigtails; over my
heart was sewn a red "C," a school letter that I had got
in the spring for collateral reading. The dentist, Dr.
Skeen, a humorist, would have died laughing if he had
seen me in these A.E.F. regimentals, and Miss Jorene
Roy, the dancing teacher, would have had kittens. Although the Gerlashes had no way of knowing the personality of either of them, I was so unskillful at useful
lies, and believed so firmly that my mind could be read,
that I did not dare pretend I was going to have a cavity
filled or to assume the five ballet positions. I said nothing and waited for an inspiration to set me free. People
who talked Bible talk like this made me ashamed for
them.

Evangelist Gerlash was immensely tall, and his bones
had only the barest wrapper of flesh; he made me think
of a tree with the leaves off, he was so angular and
gnarled, and even his skin was something like bark,
rough and pitted and scarred. His wild beard was the
color of a sorrel horse, but his long hair was black, and
so were the whiskers on the backs of his hands that im-
perfectly concealed, on the right one, a tattoo of a pea-
cock. His intense and watchful brown eyes were flecked
with green, and so were Opal's. Opal's hair was the color
of her father's beard and it fell ropily to her shoulders;
it needed a good brushing, and probably a fine comb
wouldn't have done it any harm.

Presently, the evangelist took his beard between his hands and squeezed as if he were strangling it, and he said, "We have had a weary journey, sister."

"You said a mouthful," said Opal, and hugely yawned,

"We come all the way from Arkansas this trip," said her father. "We been comin' since May."

"I liked it better last summer," said Opal, "up in Missouri and Iowa. I don't like this dry. Mountains give me the fantods." She looked over her shoulder up at the heat-hidden range and shuddered violently.

"We been roving like gypsies of the Lord, warning the wicked and helping the sick," her father went on, "We are pleased to meet up with a person who goes to the source of goodness and spiritual health. In other words, we are glad to make the acquaintance of a *friend*." And, still wringing his beard, he gave me an alarming smile that showed a set of sharp, efficient teeth. "Yes, sir, it gladdens me right down to the marrowbone to see a little girl on a summer day reading the word of God instead of messing with the vanities of this world *or* robbing the honest farmer of his watermelon *or* sassing her Christian mother."

"We stopped in nineteen towns and preached up a storm," said Opal. "You got any gum on you?"

Fascinated by the Gerlashes, although the piety the evangelist assigned to me discomfited me, since I was no more reading the Bible than your cat, I took a package of Beech-Nut out of the pocket of my knickers, and along with it came my hand-me-down Ingersoll that hadn't run for two years. Opal took a stick of gum, and her father, with his eye on my watch, said, "Don't mind if I do," and also took a stick. "That's a dandy timepiece you got there. Remember that nice old gold turnip I used to have, Opie?"

"Yeah," said Opal scornfully. "I remember you hocked that nice old gold turnip."

"Possessions are a woe and a heavy load of sin," said her father, and reached out for my watch. But after he had held it to his ear and fiddled with the stem for a while, he gave it back, saying, "Was a dandy timepiece. Ain't nothing now but a piece of tin and isinglass." Then he returned to his thesis. "I reckon this is the one and only time I or Opal has come across a person, let alone a child, drinking at the wellspring of enlightenment." And he gave me his hand to shake again.

"Amen," said Opal.

There followed a drawling antiphonal recitative that related the Gerlash situation. In the winter, they lived in a town called Hoxie, Arkansas, where Evangelist Gerlash clerked in the Buttorf drugstore and preached and baptized on the side. ("Hoxie may be only a wide space in the road," said Opal, "but she don't have any homely mountains.") Mrs. Gerlash, whom Abraham had untimely gathered to his bosom the winter before, had been a hymn singer and an organ player and had done a little preaching herself. Opal, here, had got the word the day she was born, and by the time she was five and a half years old she could preach to a fare-thee-well against the Catholics and the Wets. She was also an A-1 dowser and was renowned throughout the Wonder State. In the summer, they took to the road as soon as Opal was out of school, and went camping and preaching and praying (and dowsing if there was a call for it) and spreading the truth all over the country. Last year, they had gone through the Middle West up as far as

Chicago (here Opal, somewhat to her father's impatience, digressed to tell me the story of Mrs. O'Leary's
cow), and the year before they had gone through New
England; on earlier trips they had covered Florida and
Georgia. One of these days, they were going to set up
shop in New York City, though they understood the
tourist-camp situation there was poor. Sometimes they
found hospitality and sometimes they didn't, depending
on the heathens per capita. Sometimes the Christian
citizens lent them a hall, and they put up a sign on
the front door saying, "The Bible Tabernacle." Often,
in such a receptive community, they were invited to
supper and given groceries by the believers. But sometimes they had to do their saving of souls in a public
park or in a tourist camp. ("Not much business in this
one," said Opal, gazing ruefully at their solitary tent.)
Mr. Buttorf, the druggist in Hoxie, always said he
wasn't going to keep Gerlash one more day if he didn't
quit this traipsing around three months of the year, but
the Lord saw to it that right after Labor Day Buttorf
came to his senses and hired him again. They had arrived in Adams this morning, and if they found fertile
ground, they meant to stay a week, sowing the seeds of
righteousness. Evangelist Gerlash would be much obliged
to learn from me what sort of town this was; he
said he guessed nobody could give him the lay of the
land—spiritually speaking—any better than a Bible-reading girl like me.

"But first," he said, "tell Opal and I a little something
about yourself, sister." He took a black notebook out of
the pocket of his black coat and took a stubby pencil out
of his hatband, licked it, and began to ask me questions.
All the time he was taking down my dossier, Opal

rocked gently back and forth, hugging herself and humming "Holy, Holy, Holy." I was much impressed by her, because her jaws, as she diligently chewed her gum, were moving in the opposite direction to her trunk; I was sure she would be able to pat her head and rub her stomach at the same time.

It never occurred to me that I didn't have to answer questions put to me by adults (except for the old men in the Goldmoor, who were not serious)—even strange ones who had dropped out of nowhere. Besides, I was always as cooperative as possible with clergymen, not knowing when my number might come up. The evangelist's questions were harmless enough, but some of them were exceedingly strange. In between asking my name and my age and my father's occupation, he would say, "Which do you think is the Bible Sabbath—Saturday or Sunday?" and "Do you know if the Devil is a bachelor or is he a married man?" When to these hard, interesting questions I replied that I did not know, Opal left off her humming and said, "Amen."

When he had got from me all the data he wanted, he said, "I bet you this here town is a candidate for brimstone. I bet you it's every bit as bad as that one out on the plains we were at for two weeks in a hall. Heathens they were, but *scared,* so they give us a hall. That Mangol."

"Mudhole is what I call it," said Opal.

Her father chuckled. "Opal makes jokes," he explained. Then he said, "That was the worst town we come across in all our travels, sister, and somewheres on me I've got a clipping from the Mangol daily showing what I told the folks down there. I wouldn't be surprised if the same situation was here in Adams, being in the same state with Mangol and not any too far away from Mangol and having that college that is bound to sow free-thinking. Forewarned is forearmed is what I always say. I may have a good deal of hard work to do here." He began to fish things out of his pockets, and you never saw such a mess—a knife, a plug of chewing tobacco, a thin bar of soap, envelopes with arithmetic on them, a handkerchief I am not going to describe, any number of small pamphlets and folded-up handbills. Finally, he handed me a clipping. It said,

ANOTHER SOUR, GASSY STOMACH

VICTIM SAYS GASTRO-PEP

GAVE RELIEF

There was a picture of an indignant-looking man with a pointed head and beetling brows and a clenched jaw, who testified:

"For 3 years I had been a Great Victim of stomach gas and indigestion," said Mr. Homer Wagman, prominent Oklahoma citizen of 238 Taos Street, Muskogee. "My liver was sluggish, I would get bloated up and painful and had that tired dragged out feeling all the time. Recently a friend told me about Gastro-Pep so I decided to give it a trial. After taking 3 bottles of this medicine my WHOLE SYSTEM has gone through such a change that I can hardly believe it! Now my gas and stomach discomfort are relieved and I can eat my meals without suffering. I sleep like a schoolboy." Advt.

I did not know what I was reading, but I didn't like it anyway, since it had so nasty a sound; I didn't mind hearing about broken legs or diphtheria, but I hated any mention of anyone's insides. I started to read it for the second time, trying to think of something intelligent or complimentary to say to Evangelist Gerlash, and I must have made a face, because he leaned over me, adjusting his glasses, and said, "Oops! Hold on! Wrong write-up," and snatched the clipping out of my hand. I'm not abolutely sure, but I think Opal winked at me. Her father shuffled through his trash again and finally handed me another clipping, which, this time, was not an advertisement. The headline was

GERLASH LOCATES HELL IN
HEART OF CITY OF MANGOL

and the story beneath it ran:

"Hell is located right in the heart of the city of Mangol but will not be in operation until God sets up His Kingdom here in the earth," declared Evangelist Gerlash last night to another capacity crowd in the Bible Tabernacle.

"There are some very bad trouble spots in the city of Mangol that no doubt would be subjects of Hell right now," continued the evangelist and said, "but there are so many good people and places in this city that overshadow the bad that God has decided to postpone Hell in Mangol until the time of the harvest and the harvest, God says, 'is the end of the world' (Matthew 13:39).

"Hell, when started by God with eternal fire that comes from God out of Heaven and ignites the entire world, including this city, will be an interesting place. It will be a real play of fireworks, so hot that all the elements of earth will melt; too hot all over to find a place for any human creature to live. God is not arranging this fireworks for any human creature and therefore, if you or I ever land in this place, it is because we choose to go there."

Evangelist Gerlash and his daughter, Opal Gerlash, 12, of Hoxie, Arkansas, have been preaching on alternate nights for the last week at the Bible Tabernacle, formerly the Alvarez Feed and Grain store, at 1919 Prospect Street. Tonight Opal Gerlash will lecture on the subject, "Are You Born Again by Jumping, Rolling, Shouting, or Dancing?"

I read this with a good deal more interest than I had read of Mr. Wagman's renascence, although as Evangelist Gerlash's qualifications multiplied, my emotion waned. I had assumed from the headline, which made the back of my neck prickle, that he had some hot tips on the iniquities of that flat, dull little prairie town of Mangol that now and again we drove through when we were taking a trip to the southwest; the only thing I had ever noticed about it was that I had to hold my nose as we went through it, because the smell of sugar beets was so powerfully putrid. The city of Mangol had a population of about six hundred.

Nevertheless, though the evangelist did not scare or awe me, I had to be polite, and so, handing back the clipping, I said, "When do you think the end of the world is apt to be?" Opal had stopped her humming and swaying, and both she and her father were staring at me with those fierce brown eyes.

"In the autumn of the world," said Evangelist Gerlash sepulchrally, and Opal said, as she could be counted on to do, "Amen."

"Yeah, I know," I said. "But what autumn? What year?" He and Opal simultaneously bowed their heads in silent prayer. Both of them thoughtfully chewed gum.

Then Opal made a speech. "The answer to this and many other questions will be found in Evangelist Gerlash's inspirational hundred-and-twelve-page book entitled *Gerlash on the Bible*. Each and every one of you will want to read about the seven great plagues to smite the people of the world just before the end. Upon who will they fall? Have they begun? What will it mean to the world? In this book, on sale for the nominal sum of fifty cents or a half dollar, Evangelist Gerlash lets the people in on the ground floor regarding the law of God." From one of the deep sleeves of her kimono—for that was what that grimy garment was—Opal withdrew a paper-bound book with a picture of her father on the front of it, pointing his finger at me.

"Fifty cents, a half dollar," said the author, "which is to say virtually free, gratis, and for nothing."

Up the creek a way, a bullfrog made a noise that sounded distinctly like "Ger-lash."

"What makes Mangol so much worse than anyplace else?" I asked, growing more and more suspicious now that the conversation had taken so mercantile a turn.

But the Gerlashes were not giving out information free. "You will find the answer to this and many other questions in the book," said Opal. "Such as 'Can Wall Street run God's Business?' "

"Why does the Devil go on a sit-down strike for a thousand years?" said her father.

"What?" said I.

"Who will receive the mark of the beast?" said Opal.

"Repent!" commanded Evangelist Gerlash. "Watch! Hearken!"

"Ger-lash," went the bullfrog.

"Will Hell burn forever?" cried Opal. "Be saved from

the boiling pits! Take out insurance against spending eternity on a griddle!"

"Thy days are numbered," declared her father.

Opal said, "Major Hagedorn, editor of the Markston *Standard,* in his editorial said, 'This man Gerlash is as smart as chain lightning and seems to know his Bible forwards and backwards.' " All this time, she was holding up the book, and her father, on the cover of it, was threatening to impale me on his accusing finger.

"Perhaps our sister doesn't have the wherewithal to purchase this valuable book, or in other words the means to her salvation," he said, at last, and gave me a look of profound sadness, as if he had never been so sorry for anyone in his life. I said it was true I didn't have fifty cents (who ever heard of anyone ten years old going around with that kind of money?), and I offered to trade my Bible for *Gerlash on the Bible,* since I was interested in finding out whether the Devil was a bachelor or had a wife. But he shook his head. He began to throttle his beard again, and he said, "Does a dove need a kite? Does a giraffe need a neck? Does an Eskimo need a fur coat? Does Gerlash need a Bible?"

"Gerlash is a regular walking encyclopedia on the Bible," said Opal.

"One of the biggest trouble spots in the world is Mangol, Colorado," said Evangelist Gerlash. "No reason to think for a minute the contamination won't spread up here like a plague of locusts. Don't you think you had ought to be armed, Christian soldier?"

"Yes, I do," I said, for I had grown more and more curious. "But I don't have fifty cents."

"Considering that you are a Christian girl and a Bible reader," said the man, "I think we could make a special price for you. I reckon we could let you have it for twenty-five cents. O.K., Opal?"

Opal said rapidly, "Gastro-Pep contains over thirty ingredients. So it is like taking several medicines at once. And due to the immense volume in which it sells, the price of Gastro-Pep is reasonable, so get it now. Tonight!"

Evangelist Gerlash gave his daughter a sharp look. And, flustered, she stammered, "I mean, owing to the outstanding nature of Gerlash's information, the price of this *in*valuable book is a mere nothing. The truth in this book will stick and mark you forever."

"You want this book bad, don't you, sister Emily Vanderpool?" asked her father. "You are a good girl, and good girls are entitled to have this book, which is jam-packed with answers to the questions that have troubled you for years. You can't tell me your mammy and pappy are so mean that they wouldn't give their little girl a quarter for *Gerlash on the Bible*. Why don't you skedaddle over to home and get the small sum of twenty-five cents off your Christian ma?" He opened his notebook and checked my address. "Over to 125 Belleview Avenue."

"I'm hungry," said Opal. "I could eat me a horse."

"Never mind you being hungry," said her father, with a note of asperity in his mushy voice. "Don't you doubt me, sister Vanderpool," he went on, "when I tell you your innocent life is in danger. Looky here, when I got a call to go and enlighten the children of darkness in Mangol, just down the line from here, I got that call like a clap of thunder and I knew I couldn't waste no time. I went and I studied every den of vice in the city limits and some outside the city limits. It's bad, sister.

For twenty-five cents, you and your folks can be prepared for when the Mangolites come a-swarming into
this town." He glanced again at his notebook. "While
you're getting the purchase price of my book, please ask
your pure-hearted mother if I might have the loan of
her garage to preach the word of God in. Are you folks
centrally located?"

"My brother's got his skunk skins drying in it," I said.
"You couldn't stand the smell."

"Rats!" said Evangelist Gerlash crossly, and then
sternly he said, "You better shake a leg, sister. This book
is offered for a limited time only."

"I can't get a quarter," I said. "I already owe her
twenty cents."

"What're you going to have for supper?" asked Opal
avidly. "I could eat a bushel of roasting ears. We ain't
had a meal in a dog's age—not since that old handout in
Niwot."

"Alas, too true," said her father. "Do you hear that,
my sister Emily? You look upon a hungry holy man of
God and his girl who give to the poor and save no crust
for himself. Fainting for the want of but a crumb from
the rich man's groaning board, we drive ourself on-
wards, bringing light where there is darkness and comfort where there is woe. Perhaps your good Christian
mother and father would give us an invite to their supper tonight, in exchange for which they and theirs
would gladly be given this priceless book, free of charge,
signed by hand."

"Well, gosh," I said, working my tennis shoes on over
my wet socks, "I mean . . . Well, I mean I don't know."

"Don't know what?" said that great big man, glower-
ing at me over the tops of his severe spectacles. "Don't

you go and tell me that a good Bible-reading girl like
you has got kin which are evolutionists and agnostics
and infidels who would turn two needy ministers of God
away from their door. To those who are nourished by
the Law of the Lord, a crust now and then is sufficient to
keep body and soul together. I don't suppose Opal and I
have had hot victuals for a good ten days, two weeks." A
piteous note crept into his versatile voice, and his brown
eyes and his daughter's begot a film of tears. They did
look awfully hungry, and I felt guilty the way I did
when I was eating a sandwich and Reddie was looking
up at me like a martyr of old.

"Didn't she say her daddy ran a grocery store?" asked
Opal, and her father, consulting my vital statistics,
smiled broadly.

"There's nothing the matter with *your* ears, Opie,"
he said. And then, to me, "How's about it, sister? How's
about you going down to this Safeway store and getting
Opal and I some bread and some pork chops and like
that?"

"Roasting ears," said Opal. "And a mushmelon."

It had suddenly occurred to me that if I could just get
up and run away, the incident would be finished, but
Evangelist Gerlash was clairvoyant, and, putting two
firmly restraining hands on my shoulders and glaring at
me straight in the eye, he said, "We don't have a thing
in the world tonight to do but show up at 125 Belleview
Avenue round about suppertime."

"I'd rather cook out," said Opal. "I'd rather she
brought the groceries."   Her father bent his head into
his hands, and there was a great sob in his voice when he
said, "I have suffered many a bitter disappointment in
this vale of tears, but I suppose the bitterest is right now

here in Adams, Colorado, where, thinking I had found a child of light, she turned out to be a mocker, grinding under her heel shod in gold the poor and the halt. Oh, sister, may you be forgiven on the Day of Judgment!"

"Whyn't you go get us some eats?" said Opal, cajoling. "If you get us some eats, we won't come calling. If we come calling, like as not we'll spend the night."

"Haven't slept in a bed since May," said her father, snuffling.

"We don't shake easy," said Opal, with an absolutely shameless grin.

My mother had a heart made of butter, and our spare room was forever occupied by strays, causing my father to scold her to pieces after they'd gone, and I knew that if the Gerlashes showed up at our house (and plainly they would) with their hard-luck story and their hard-luck looks and all their devices for saving souls, she would give them houseroom and urge them to stay as long as they liked, and my father would not simmer down for a month of Sundays.

So I got up and I said, "All right, I'll go get you a sack of groceries." I had a nebulous idea that my father might let me buy them on time or might give me a job as a delivery boy until I had paid for them.

To my distress, the Gerlashes got up, too, and the evangelist said, "We'll drive you down to Main Street, sister, and sit outside, so there won't be no slipup."

"It's Saturday!" I cried. "You can't find a place to park."

"Then we'll just circle round and round the block."

"But I can't get into a car with strangers," I protested.

"Strangers!" exclaimed Evangelist Gerlash. "Why, sister, we're friends now. Don't you know all about Opal and I? Didn't we lay every last one of our cards on the table right off the bat?" He took my arm in his big, bony hand and started to propel me in the direction of the Ford, and just then, like the Mounties to the rescue, up came Mr. Starbird's official car, tearing into the campgrounds and stopping, with a scream from the brakes, right in front of me and the Gerlashes. A man in a deputy's uniform was in the front seat beside him.

"Why, Emily," said Mr. Starbird as he got out of the car and pushed his hat back from his forehead. "I thought you went on home after that ruckus we had. You'll be glad to hear those scalawags are going off to the pen tomorrow, so you can come back to jail any time after 10 A.M."

Opal giggled, but her father shivered and looked as if a rabbit had just run over his grave. "We're getting outa here," he said to her under his breath, and started at a lope toward his car.

"That's them all right," said the man in the deputy's uniform. "They set up shop in the feed store, and when they wasn't passing out mumbo-jumbo about the world going up in firecrackers, they was selling that medicine. Medicine! Ninety per cent wood alcohol and ninety per cent fusel oil. Three cases of jake-leg and God knows how many workers passed out in the fields."

Mr. Starbird and the deputy had closed in on the Gerlashes. Mr. Starbird said, "I don't want any trouble with

you, Mister. I just want you to get out of Adams before I
run you out on a rail. We got plenty of our own preach-
ers and plenty of our own bootleggers, and we don't
need any extra of either one. Just kindly allow me to
impound this so-called medicine and then you shove.
What kind of a bill of goods were they trying to sell you,
Emily, kid?"

The deputy said, "That's another of their lines. We
checked on them after they left Mangol, checked all the
way back to Arkansas. They get some sucker like a kid
or an idiot and give them this spiel and promise they'll
go to Heaven if they'll just get them some grub or some
money or my Aunt Geraldine's diamond engagement
ring or whatever."

I said nothing. I was thrilled, and at the same time I
was mortally embarrassed for the Gerlashes. I was sorry
for them, too, because, in spite of their predicament,
they looked more hungry than anything else.

Opal said, "If we went to jail, we could eat," but her
father gave her a whack on the seat and told her "Hush
up, you," and the procession, including myself, clutching
my Bible and *Tom Sawyer Abroad,* moved toward the
tent and the Model T. The sheriff took two cases of
medicine out of the tent and put them in his car, and
then we stood there watching the Gerlashes strike camp
and put all their bivouac gear into the trailer. They
worked swiftly and competently, as if they were accus-

tomed to sudden removals. When they were finished, Opal got into the front seat and started to cry. "God damn it to hell," said the child preacher. "Whyn't we ever have something to eat?"

Mr. Starbird, abashed by the dirty girl's tears, took out his wallet and gave her a dollar. "Don't you spend a red cent of it in Adams," he said. "You go on and get out of town and then get some food."

Evangelist Gerlash, having cranked the car, making a noise like a collision, climbed into the driver's seat, and grinned at the sight of the dollar. "I have cast my bread upon the waters and I am repaid one hundredfold," he said. "And you, in casting your bread upon the waters, you, too, will be repaid one hundredfold."

"Amen," said Opal, herself again, no longer crying.

"Now beat it," said Mr. Starbird.

"And give Mangol a wide berth," said the deputy.

The car shook as if it were shaking itself to death, and it coughed convulsively, and then it started up with a series of jerks and detonations, and disappeared in a screen of dust and black smoke.

Mr. Starbird offered to give me a lift home, and I got into the front seat beside him while the deputy from Mangol got in back. On the way up the hill, Mr. Starbird kept glancing at me and then smiling.

"I've never known a girl quite like you, Emily," he

said. "Memorizing the books of the Bible in the hoose-gow, wearing a buck-private hat."

I blushed darkly and felt like crying, but I was pleased when Mr. Starbird went on to say, "Yes, sir, Emily, you're going to go places. What was the book you were reading down at my place when you were wearing your father's Masonic fez?" I grew prouder and prouder. "It isn't every girl of ten years of age who brushes up against some moonshiners with a record as long as your arm in the very same day that a couple of hillbilly fakers try to take her for a ride. Why, Emily, do you realize that if it hadn't of been for you, we might not have got rid of those birds till they'd set up shop and done a whole lot of mischief?"

"Really?" I said, not quite sure whether he was teasing me, and grinned, but did so looking out the window, so Mr. Starbird wouldn't see me.

Was I lucky that day! On the way home, I saw about ten people I knew, and waved and yelled at them, and when I was getting out in front of my house, Virgil Meade, with whom I had had an on-again off-again romance for some time and to whom I was not currently speaking, was passing by and he heard the sheriff say, "Come on down to jail tomorrow and we'll get some Dr. Pepper."

The sheriff's valedictory gave me great prestige in the neighborhood, but it also put an end to my use of the jail as a library, because copycats began swarming to the courthouse and making so much racket in the waiting room that Mr. Starbird couldn't hear himself think, let alone follow Fu Manchu. And after a few weeks he had to post a notice forbidding anyone in the room except on business. Privately, he told me that he would just as lief let me read in one of the cells, but he was afraid word would leak out and it might be bad for my reputation. He was as sorry, he said, as he could be.

He wasn't half as sorry as I was. The snake season was still on me in the mountain; Mrs. Looby hated me; Aunt Joey was visiting, and she and Mother were using the living room to cut out Butterick patterns in; Stella had just got on to pig Latin and never shut her mouth for a minute. All the same, I memorized the books of the Bible and I won the New Testament, and I'll tell you where I did my work—in the cemetery, under a shady tree, sitting beside the grave of an infant kinswoman of the sheriff, a late-nineteenth-century baby called Primrose Starbird.

Caveat Emptor

Malcolm and Victoria agreed that if they had not discovered each other at the beginning of the fall term at the Alma Hettrick College for Girls, where they taught, they would have lost their minds or, short of that, would have gone into silent religious orders. He was twenty-three and she was twenty-two and they were both immediately out of graduate school with brand-new Master's degrees, whose coruscations they fondly imagined illumined them and dazed the Philistine. Malcolm had studied philosophy and the title of his thesis had been *A*

Literary Evaluation of Sören Kierkegaard and a Note on His Relation to Mediaeval Christian Dialectic. Victoria, who had specialized in the sixteenth century, had written on *Some Late Borrowings from Provençal* fin amour *in Elizabethan Miscellanies and Songbooks.*

The altitude of their academic ideals had not begun to dwindle yet and they shivered and shook in the alien air that hovered over the pretty campus of this finishing school, whose frankly stated aim was "to turn out the wives and mothers of tomorrow." These nubile girls, all of them dumb and nearly all beautiful, knitted in class (that is how they would occupy themselves in their later lives when they attended lectures, said the dean when Malcolm complained of the clack of needles and the subordination of the concept of doubt to purling); they wrote term papers on the advisability of a long engagement and on the history of fingernail polish; they tap-danced or interpretive-danced their way to classes on walks between signs that read: *Don't hurt me. I'll be beautiful grass in the spring if you'll give me a chance.*

Pale from their ivory towers, myopic from reading footnotes in the oblique light of library stacks, Malcolm and Victoria had met on the day of their arrival in September. The heaviness and wetness of the day, smelling of mildew, had drawn them together first; both, being punctilious, had got to the Geneva S. Bigelow Memorial Library too early for the first convocation of the faculty and so, having introduced themselves, they had gone across the street to drink lemonade in a bake oven that called itself the Blue Rose and that smelled loathsomely of pork. Here, in a quarter of an hour, facing each other across a copse of catchup bottles and vinegar cruets and A-1 sauce, they found out that they had in common

their advanced degrees, a dread of teaching and no experience of this kind of heat, since Malcolm came from
the Rockies and Victoria came from Maine. Each di-
vined accurately that the other was penniless and that it
was this condition rather than a desire to impart what
they had learned to girls that had brought them to this
town, Victoria on a Greyhound bus and Malcolm in a
tall, archaic Buick touring car.

At the faculty meeting that morning and at all subse-
quent meetings they sat side by side. Their dismay, from
which they were never to recover, began with the opening address by President Harvey, a chubby, happy man
who liked to have the students call him Dutch—the title
was optional but the girls who could not bring themselves to use it were few and far between. He began his
immensely long speech with a brief account of his own
life: he had been born without advantages in a one-
room cabin in the Ozarks and had had, in much of his
youth, the companionship only of a blind aunt and an
exceptionally intelligent hound, both of whom, in their
different ways, had taught him values that he would not
part with for all the tea in China; from the aunt he had
learned how to smile when the sledding was tough and
from the dog he had learned how to relax. His transi-
tion from this affecting homily to the history of Alma
Hettrick was an obscure accomplishment. He described
the rise of the college from a small female seminary with
twenty students to the great plant of national impor-
tance it now was. Year by year Alma Hettrick had
grown with the times, adding something different here,
cutting out something passé there, its goal being always
that of preparing these young women for the real job
of the real woman, that is, homemaking. They had

dropped Elocution from the curriculum (the president smiled and his audience smiled back at him) and no longer taught how to use a fan, how to tat or how to communicate with a suitor in the language of flowers (the teachers laughed out loud and someone at the back of the room clapped his hands); nevertheless the emphasis was still on those articles of instruction particularly suited to the needs of a woman: Marriage and the Family, Child Care, Home Ec, Ballet for grace, French for elegance.

Beaming like Kriss Kringle, the president concluded his speech with a timely observation: "It may be novel but I don't think it's iconoclastic to liken education to business. We are here to sell our girls Shakespeare and French and Home Economics and Ballet. They're consumers in a manner of speaking. I don't mean that a student consumes Shakespeare in the sense that the supply of Shakespeare is decreased but that she can assimilate his work just as her body would assimilate meat or any other food. Let's each and every one of us sell ourselves to these girls and then sell our commodity, whether it's those grand old plays or how to run a sewing machine. Good luck!"

Two new programs had been added this year to help the consumer become a well-rounded woman and these were now briefly described by their directors. There was the Personality Clinic, headed by a stern-visaged Miss Firebaugh, who, with her staff, would counsel the girls on the hair styles and nail polish shades that would highlight their best features. And there was the Voice Clinic, where, presumably, harsh neighs and twangs and whines would be wheedled into the register of a lady. This clinic was under the direction of an ebullient Mr.

Sprackling, who was as pink as a rose and had a shock of orange hair and sideburns to match and a fierce exophthalmic green eye. He had the air of a surgeon about him: one saw him cleaving tongues that were tied, excising lisps, loosening glottal stops, skillfully curing girls from Oklahoma who tended to diphthongize their vowels.

At the back of the dais, where several deans and heads of departments sat, there was an arrangement of leaves and maidenhair ferns designed by the joint efforts of the Botany Club and the Flower Arrangement Hobby Group and made known as such by a large placard attached in a basket of sumac. It seemed to Victoria a setting more appropriate to a xylophonist or a bird imitator than to a college faculty. This, however, was less unusual than the housing of the general assembly, a week later, of the staff and the students: because of the greatly increased student body, they could not meet in the auditorium or in the gymnasium and they convened, instead, in a circus tent pitched on the quadrangle; the endorsement of its owner was printed boldly in red on the side: *Jim Sloat Carnival Shows.*

Malcolm and Victoria became inseparable. Under other circumstances they might not have known each other or they might have known each other in a more recreational way. But these singular circumstances produced an infrangible bond; they clung tottering together like unarmed travelers, lost from their party, in a trackless jungle inhabited by anthropophagists. Or they were like soldiers whose paths would never have crossed in civilian life but who stood shoulder to shoulder in profound fraternity in time of war. Their enemy, the entire faculty and all the students, down to the last instructor of cosmetics in the Personality Clinic, down to the last ambulatory patient in Mr. Sprackling's infirmary, was not aware of the hostilities that were being waged against him by these two or the plans that were being laid for sabotage: Victoria was thinking of requiring all her classes in Freshman English to read *Finnegans Wake* and Malcolm was considering delivering a series of twelve diatribes against Edward Bok, whose *Americanization of* he was obliged to teach in his course called "Philosophy of Life."

On the contrary, the enemy found the newcomers shy but cooperative and never dreamed that instead of being shy they were sulky and that they were obedient only because they had both hands tied behind their backs. So the enemy (in the persons of Rosemary Carriage, a great maudlin donkey of a senior; Miss Goss, secretary to the Dean of Extracurricular Activities; Mr. Borglund, who taught Marriage and the Family; and Sally-Daniel Gallagher, who ran the faculty coffee shop) observed with—depending on their ruling humor—complacence, with malice, with a vicarious thrill, that the fall term had started exactly as it should, with a love-at-first-sight romance between the two youngest teachers. These detectives and publicists who presented their data and then their exegesis in the dining rooms knew that each day after their last classes Miss Pinckney and Mr. Kirk went driving through the country in Mr. Kirk's car, that almost every night they dined at the Chicken-in-a-Basket at the edge of town, that they graded their papers together in a tavern on the highway to the city.

What the voyeurs did not know, because they were not close enough to be eavesdroppers as well, was that the exchange, over the drumsticks in the Chicken-in-a-

Basket, over the beer and cheese popcorn at the Red
Coach Inn, over the final cigarettes in front of Victoria's
rooming house, that this exchange, which ran the gamut
from gravity to helpless laughter, had nothing what-
soever to do with love. It might occasionally have to do
with medieval prose or with symptoms (both of them
thought they were starting ulcers), but for the most part
what they talked about were the indignities that were
being perpetrated against their principles by Butch
Harvey's pedagogical fiddlesticks. For they were far too
young and their principles were far too vernal for them
to rise above their circumstance; their laughter was not
very mirthful but was, really, reflexive: now and again
they were whacked on the crazy bone. They did not
really believe that Alma Hettrick was an actuality, although, as they often said, they couldn't possibly have
made it up. Whoever heard of anything so fictitious as
the production of *Lohengrin* that was currently under
way with an all-girl cast, directed by an Estonian diva,
Mongolian of countenance and warlike of disposition?
"An Estonian diva has no provable substance," said
Malcolm categorically. "Such a figment belongs to the
same genus as the unicorn, the gryphon and the Loch
Ness Monster."

Victoria, demure and honey-haired, and Malcolm, a
black-haired, blue-eyed Scot, muscular and six-foot-four,
were, said the vigilant campus, made for each other.
The fact was, however, that they had assigned to each
other no more of sex than the apparel. And such was the
monomania of their interlocution that they had never
happened to mention that they were engaged to be married to two other people to whom they wrote frequent
letters, often by special delivery.

Besides their fidgets of outrage and unrest, besides their fits of ferocious giggles, Malcolm and Victoria had another mood, an extemporaneous mood of melancholy that immediate time and place determined. By the languid St. Martin River, on whose banks the bracken was turning brown and on whose sallow surface gold leaves rode, they often sat in the triste dusk of autumn, talking with rue of the waste of their lucubrations. Their woe betook them too on Sunday evenings when they were driving back to the college after spending a long and private day in a little town they had discovered early in the term. On Sunday, until the sun went down, they were in a world that was separate and far and they were serene; but when the docile Buick headed home, wrath rose and set their jaws.

Built on the crest of a kind, green hill so that its inhabitants could look far up the river and far down, this town, Georges Duval's Mill, was scarcely more credible than the Estonian diva, but unlike the other chimeras of their lives it was endearing and they loved it dearly.

The twentieth century had barely touched Georges Duval's Mill and, indeed, the nineteenth had not obliterated altogether the looks and the speech of the original settlers of the region, who had been French. There was a Gallic look in the faces of the townspeople, their cuisine was peasant French and most of them were bilingual, speaking a Cajun-like patois. Some, better educated, like the mayor and the priest, spoke as befitted their station. And there were, as well, the Parisian formalities and fillips and the niceties of syntax used by two aged maiden sisters, the Mlles Geneviève and Mathilde Papin, who once, scores of years before, had gone to school in France and who now ran L'Hôtel Dauphin

and were persuaded that some time the luckless son of
Louis XVI had lived in the town.

Chickens and geese, ducks and goats and sometimes
cattle and swine roved and waddled and mooed and
quacked through the cobbled main street. The cats were
fat and were collared with smart ribbons and bows and
they sat imperiously on sunny sills, festooning themselves with their congratulatory tails. There was a public well—there was little plumbing—in the middle of a
green, and here the gawky adolescents flirted, shyer than
violets and bolder than brass. Through open windows
came the smell of bouillabaisse and coq au vin. The
children were verminous and out at the elbows; all the
women save those over seventy were pregnant. The
priest was lymphatic; the mayor was driven by cupidity
and hindered by gout; the doctor was as deaf as a post;
the town crier was also the village idiot; and the teacher
was usually drunk.

It was not the quaintness of Georges Duval's Mill that
attracted Malcolm and Victoria, for neither of them had
a drop of sight-seer's blood. In passing, to be sure, they
were pleased by the surprising survival and supremacy
of a foreign language spang in the middle of the Middle
West. And they enjoyed the rituals: the mannered
courtship by the well in which the buckets seemed to
play a part; the entourage of children that followed the
priest from the church to the rectory, led by two altar
boys who carried the chalice and the ciborium in string
shopping bags; the countless alarms and excursions of
indeterminate origin that would suddenly catapult the
whole populace into the street, still wearing their dinner napkins tucked into their collars, still holding a fork
or a mug. They liked all this and they liked it, too, that

there was a practicing witch at the edge of town who had been seen in the shape of a wolf tearing sheep by the light of the full moon.

But what made the village really precious to them, really indispensable, was that in almost every particular they could name it was the antithesis of Alma Hettrick. Looking at the candles and the gaslights in L'Hôtel Dauphin (the old ladies disapproved of electricity and spoke cattily of their neighbors who had it), seeing roosters emerge from parlors, seeing toddlers being given vin ordinaire to drink, the teachers were oblivious to modern times and modern education and modern girls. They basked in backwardness.

Apparently they were the only visitors who ever came to Georges Duval's Mill. They had not been able to find it on any map and they were sure that none of their colleagues, especially in the Social Studies Division, knew of it or they would have come armed cap-a-pie with questionnaires and Kodachrome and Binet-Simon testing equipment.

When they arrived at about noon on Sunday, Malcolm parked his car (it had a klaxon and from the front it looked like Barney Google) under a vast copper beech in a sylvan dingle behind the green, and then they walked through mud and over the cobblestones to the hotel, where Mlle Mathilde, having seen them coming, was already pouring the water into two glasses of Pernod that stood in saucers on a round marble-topped table in one of two oriels in the dining room. The other oriel was occupied by the mayor, a widower, whose poor gouty foot was propped up on a stool and was being daily worsened by piquant sauces and rich wines. After they had drunk a good deal of Pernod and could feel that they were on the mend, Malcolm and Victoria had a subtle meal. The cook's daughter, Emma, put a white cloth on their table and a Benares vase of carnations made of crinoline and wire, a pepper mill and a salt mill and a carafe of white wine. Sometimes the soup was onion and sometimes it was leek and potato and once— and they would never forget it—it was chestnuts and cress; and then they had an omelet made with mush- rooms, with delicious chanterelles that Mlle Geneviève had gathered in the summertime and had dried. With the omelet they had a salad with chervil in it, brioche, sweet butter and Brie. Their dessert was crème brûlée. And then they had coffee and with the coffee, brandy.

By now they were sleepy—the mayor was more than that, he was asleep among his chins—and they moved in a haze of contentment into the parlor, where they grad- ually woke up under the influences of the disciplinary horsehair sofa and the further coffee and the perky gos- sip of the old sisters in their nice black silk dresses trimmed with passementerie braid. While they exca- vated the doctor's secrets and explored the garden paths down which the grocer had led many a girl, the ladies worked at gros point, very fast. They were witty and spry and their eyes were clear but they were, as they ad- mitted, extremely old and after a little while they ex- cused themselves to go and take their naps. Now Vic- toria stretched out full length on the narrow sofa with a mass of round pillows at her shoulders and Malcolm es- tablished himself in a Morris chair. For several hours they read and smoked and drank the cool, strong coffee in the china pot. On Sundays Victoria liked to read *The Canterbury Tales,* while Malcolm, mindful of the Ph.D. he longed to get, worked away at the Whitehead-Russell

Principia Mathematica, sometimes sighing and at other times nodding in discernment and saying quite spontaneously to himself, "Oh, I see. Oh, of course."

At half past four the innkeepers reappeared, wearing small velvet hats, for after tea they would go to benediction. They had tea and petits fours and fruit and then in the twilight they all left the hotel and shook hands and said goodbye on the steps. The ladies went quickly downhill toward the church, whose bell was ringing, and Malcolm and Victoria made their way much more slowly back to the dell and the Buick, which loomed up in the gathering dark like a moose in a rock garden. They were so heavy-hearted that they had to stop on their way home at the Red Coach and buck themselves up with whiskey at the bar.

One Sunday early in November when the first snow was flying in great melting stars aginst the windowpanes in L'Hôtel Dauphin and the mayor was sitting with his back to Malcolm and Victoria, toasting his swollen foot before the fire in the hearth, they fell in love. Their hearts had evidently been synchronized precisely because at the same moment they both stopped eating and met each other's astonished gaze. The hands that a moment before had been spooning up crème brûlée reached across the table and clasped; Victoria quaked from head to foot and Malcolm's mouth went dry. What had led up to it? They could not remember. They were never able to recall what they had been saying just before: had they been discussing St. Augustine as a heretic? Or had they been voicing their essential indifference to the Orient? They could not say. It was like a concussion with amnesia covering all events immediately preceding the blow.

"Vicky," murmured Malcolm. The diminutive announced his state of mind. "Why, Vicky, why, my God, Victoria!"

He clapped his free hand to his forehead and in doing so he knocked over the brass vase of artificial flowers. He is very awkward, thought Victoria, how I love him! The mayor, disturbed by the noise of the vase clattering to the floor, turned around and disapproved of them with his moist, alcoholic eyes and said fretfully, "*Quel tapage.*"

"Do you know what I mean, Vicky?" said Malcolm, leaning over to pick up the scattered flowers but keeping his eyes on her. "Do you know what has happened to me . . . darling?" She nodded, scarlet.

It was difficult for them that day to follow the adventures of Mlle Mathilde's octoroon governess; they could not tell whether she had run away with a pirate or a forger and whether she had stolen a cabochon brooch or had kept a capuchin as a pet. They thought the old ladies would never leave, but at last they put their tapestry needles back into their strawberry emeries and left in a swish of silk and a zephyr of sachet, and Malcolm and Victoria began to kiss.

Of course it could not have happened like this: falling in love is not an abrupt plunge; it is a gradual descent, seldom in a straight line, rather like the floating downward of a parachute. And the expression is imperfect because while one may fall one also levitates. Nevertheless, Malcolm and Victoria enjoyed the conceit of suddenness. Forgetting all that had drawn them together, ignoring the fact that they were uncommonly attractive and intelligent (for all their schoolishness) and humorous and good-humored (for all their jeers), they pretended that at one certain moment they had been knocked galley-west by this thunderbolt out of the blue; they pretended that they had seen stars; they behaved as if there were balloons over their heads containing the word "Zowie!" And in their delirium they gave the whole credit to Georges Duval's Mill, which they personified as a matchmaker. It never in the world occurred to them that Alma Hettrick's machinations long antedated those of the town.

If they had been asked (as they might well have been if a pollster from the Alma Hettrick Social Studies Division had been around), "Which in your opinion is more important, the reading and consumption of hard books, such as *Principia Mathematica,* or the direct observation of behavior patterns in college females?" they would have replied, "Neither amounts to a hill of beans. It's love that makes the world go around."

That night they did not need to stop at the Red Coach but went directly home. A few days later a fiancée in Denver and a fiancé in Bath got air mail letters containing regretful, remorseful, ashamed, confused but positive and unconditional goodbyes.

In the next weeks the partisans of the attachment between Miss Pinckney and Mr. Kirk were worried and the critics of it said: "I told you so. That much propinquity will willy-nilly breed contempt." For Malcolm and Victoria were seldom seen together. They quit the Chicken-in-a-Basket; Victoria ate at the Faculty Club and Malcolm ate alone in the Blue Rose. The eccentric Buick now was never parked in the cinder drive of the Red Coach and those afternoon rides were apparently a thing of the past. Miss Goss, who had mothered her three motherless sisters and had got them married off and who, through habit, was doomed to mother and marry off everyone, said in the faculty coffee shop: "What *can* have happened? They were so well-suited." Sally-Daniel Gallagher, at the cashier's desk, said: "If you ask me, it's just as well. With those kind of carrying-ons day in and day out, to say nothing of night in and night out, something is bound to happen and it wouldn't do to have it happen on campus." Ray (Marriage and the Family) Borglund, saddened but ever constructive, was moved to give an open lecture on "Snags in Courtship and How to Avoid Them."

Puzzled and disappointed, or smug and malign, the campus watched the estranged couple out of the corner of its eye.

The couple, so afflicted with delight, so feverish and crazy with bliss, had agreed at the start that they did not want their treasure to be public property. On the evening they had opened their oyster and had found therein the pearl of great price, Malcolm had said to Victoria when he took her home: "This is one commodity that's not going on the market. Let's keep this luxury item under our hats." And Victoria, fingering the leather patch on his elbow as if it were the most beloved object in the world, replied: "I don't think it has any consumer value at all. I think it's sui generis."

While Alma Hettrick speculated, the Papin sisters were overjoyed that their young patrons now came to L'Hôtel Dauphin for the whole weekend. They were as sly as foxes in their departure from the college town. Victoria took a cab to the bus station and Malcolm picked her up there; and then they took a circuitous route to Georges Duval's Mill. Victoria wore dark glasses and a hat.

Alma Hettrick, however, was slyer than they were and one Saturday morning one of its agents, Miss Peppertree of the Art Department, who was catching a bus to Chicago, saw Victoria in her thin disguise get into the Buick carrying a suitcase. She just had time to call Miss Goss before her bus left. By noon the word had spread through all the college personnel who had not gone away for the weekend. Mr. Borglund frankly did not like the sneaky looks of it at all; the word "strait-laced" could never be applied to the policy at Alma Hettrick but *propriety* was mandatory. Sally-Daniel Gallagher said "Aha!" Miss Goss said "Oh, no!" But Mr. Borglund, rallying after his initial shock, said: "We'll set things straight in a jiffy."

It took longer than a jiffy even though Mr. Borglund applied himself to the problem assiduously. On telephoning the miscreants' landladies, he learned that their lodgers always went away for the weekend but had never named their destinations. Throughout the next week, although he watched them and tried to trick them out individually with leading questions, he accomplished nothing. Both of them seemed preoccupied and a little drowsy, as if they were coming down with colds. On Saturday morning he was at the bus depot at eight o'clock, hoping that like laboratory white rats they had acquired conditioned reflexes. He parked in ambush across the street in an alley; he wore a cap, a large one, and looked a good deal like Mr. Toad. He had to wait two hours in the cold and several times he wondered how reliable Amelia Peppertree was; she was inclined to be flighty and, as a Life Drawing teacher, bohemian. All the same, at ten o'clock he was rewarded for his patience. He saw what Miss Peppertree had reported she had seen and he followed the jade and her reprobate.

He followed them over roads he had never traveled or had known existed, through country so wild and forlorn that he felt he had left his own dimension and was traversing the moon; they would go along the river for a while and then they would strike out cross-country over faint lanes through the middle of tobacco fields.

Malcolm and Victoria, half-frozen, were warming their hands around glasses of mulled claret before the fire when Ray Borglund came into the dining room of the hotel. They gasped and gaped when they saw the civic-minded Swede and sotto voce Malcolm said: "I'll kill him."

"My stars!" cried the sociologist. "Of all places to run into a couple of people I *know!* I got so cold I had to stop—I was on my way to Lakeville." Since Georges Duval's Mill was off all beaten tracks and since Lakeville was in exactly the opposite direction, he made his point very clear whether he meant to or not. He rubbed his hands gleefully and came up to the fire. "Mind?" he said and, leaning down to sniff at Victoria's glass, he went on, "Mmm, that smells good. May I join you in a glass of it? That is, if I'm not interrupting something?"

He joined them in two glasses of hot wine and he joined them at lunch and, because they were in so ticklish a spot, they spilled all the beans about Georges Duval's Mill, cravenly giving him to understand that they were collaborating on a historical-ethnic-anthropological-ideological-linguistic study of this perfectly preserved fossil town. They did not need to go into so much detail (needn't, for example, have mentioned the witch) but out of embarrassment they did and, appalled, they watched Mr. Borglund's interest rise and inundate them. First of all, he was obviously persuaded of the asexual nature of their collusion and obviously relieved, and then he was drawn to their facts; next he was fascinated and finally he became so fanatic that he blew scalding coffee into his face.

"I don't know what's the matter with us vets at Alma Hettrick. I thought we were on our toes, but it takes you newcomers to show us what's been under our noses the whole time," he said. "Why, we never thought of this town as anything but a wide space in the road. Oh, maybe a little French still used but that's not uncommon along the river. But now I see it's a real find. Why, right here in this one area we've got material for a school-wide project. Why, good Lord, I can see how there could be a tie-in of all the divisions. Maybe not the Personality Clinic—but maybe so. Maybe they have some interesting native costumes. Maybe they still use old-time recipes for hand lotion." He went on in this fashion until the sun began to set, and when at last he left them he did so only because, as he said, he wanted to "contact President Harvey at once so that we won't waste a moment's time in setting up the Georges Duval's Mill Project."

The Papin sisters had not liked Mr. Borglund and the grouchy mayor had hated him. Malcolm and Victoria wanted to explain and apologize and enjoin the town crier to broadcast a warning that snoops were planning an invasion of these innocent precincts. But they did not know how to go about it. And they were so sick at heart at the threat to their bower that momentarily they forgot they were in love. After dinner, unable to speak, they started to read, but Malcolm suddenly threw his big book to the floor and said: "I don't know what they're talking about, this A. N. Whitehead and this Bertrand Russell." Later, they remembered that they were in love and they were happy, but the edge was off and that Sunday they stopped at the Red Coach and drank boilermakers and fell in with a Fuller Brush man who gave Victoria a free-sample whisk broom.

Now at Alma Hettrick a new attitude developed toward them. Their claque applauded the seriousness with which they had undertaken their investigations of this dodo of a town, while their detractors called them selfish and said that as members of the Alma Hettrick crowd they had no right to stake a claim on such a gold mine. The former were sorry that their earlier surmise had been wrong (that Malcolm and Victoria were in love) and glad that their second had been wrong (that they had had a quarrel) and proud that they had such trail blazers in their midst. The opposition said they were grinds and prudes and had no red blood in them.

On two successive Saturdays the Alma Hettrick station wagon and three other cars followed Malcolm's Buick to the hamlet on the hill and delegates from the faculty and from the student body swarmed through the streets and lanes, declaring and querying in restaurant French. Most of the residents were apathetic; some were amazed just as the unready must have been when the Visigoths arrived. Miss Firebaugh of the Personality Clinic went into raptures over the costumes of the Mlles Papin; she asked them to turn around slowly; she exclaimed over gussets and tucks; she took photographs of them using flash bulbs and the mayor winced and said,

"Allons donc! Quelle sottise!" But this was the only jewel Miss Firebaugh found; the rest of the clothes in the town had come from Sears, Roebuck.

The Child Study Group, working with Marriage and the Family representatives, made gruesome discoveries: intermarriage and rampant disease had lowered the average intelligence quotient to cretinism; incest was prevalent and was not denied. The American History people came up against a blank wall: the only thing anyone knew about Georges Duval's Mill was that a miller named Georges Duval had once owned this land but they did not know when, not even roughly when, and they did not know what had become of him or of his descendants. The only information to be had about the Dauphin was the sentimental testimony of the old sisters, who simply said that he had been there—else, they inquired, why would the hotel be named for him? There were no annals, no pictorial artifacts, nothing but oral and exceedingly uninteresting legends. There were no indigenous arts and crafts. Though urged and bribed, the villagers flatly refused to sing. One idiot child did a dance on the green but the priest explained, tapping his forehead, that she was making it up as she went along and there was no tradition behind it. The Political Scientists found an unparalleled dearth of politics. The Appreciation of Art people found that in Georges Duval's Mill there was no appreciation of art. As for the deputies from the Community Health class, they wanted to report the town to Federal authorities: the lice in the children's hair were fabulous, the barnyard filth in the streets was unspeakable, there was a public drinking cup at the well and the doctor still practiced phlebotomy.

In the end, the only one who really profited was Mr. Sprackling. He hit upon an excellent formula for his students who mumbled or slurred. "We enunciate when we are not lazy," said he, a man with a nimble tongue and an alert soft palate. "There is all the difference in the world between the way you young ladies say, 'I doan know,' and the way the poorest peasant of Georges Duval's Mill says, '*Je ne sais pas.*'" What made him think the poor peasants were not lazy Malcolm and Victoria could not guess, for in point of fact they were largely loafers and spent most of their time staring at their shoes.

In short order the project was abandoned. Mr. Borglund heartily said in the men's room to Malcolm: "Well, all is not gold that glitters and one man's meat is another man's poison. It wasn't a question of missing the boat—the boat wasn't there. Say, Kirk, are you and Miss Pinckney going on with your study of this place?"

Malcolm said that they were; he said that Victoria, who was very keen on philology, was preparing a paper for *Speculum* on "The Survival of Old French Modal Auxiliaries in One Fluviatile American Town" and that he himself was working on a monograph to be called "The Periodicity of Diabolism in Georges Duval's Mill."

Mr. Borglund gave him a searching look and blinked uneasily. "That seems a little overspecialized, if you don't mind my saying so."

The news of their true, dull nature leaked out and permeated the student body. A mature Georgia peach with a provocative scolding lock said to Malcolm, "Is it true that you and Miss Pinckney are all-out intellectuals?" and Malcolm, who had heretofore been intimidated by this girl's voracious flirtatiousness, said, "You bet your boots it's true, Miss Ryder."

Found out, they were pitied or despised. The waste! The waste to themselves and the waste to Alma Hettrick! Here they were, *so* good-looking, the pair of them, so young, so well equipped to put a sparkle into Freshman English and Philosophy, so well qualified for fun. And how did they spend their weekends? Grubbing away in that more than useless town, that ignorant, unsanitary, stupid town which wasn't even picturesque. And what for? For Victoria to browse about amongst antediluvian subjunctives and for Malcolm to concentrate on a Halloween witch.

All right: if they wanted to live in the Dark Ages, let them go ahead. But one thing was sure, their contracts would never be renewed, for Alma Hettrick was in tune with the times and that went for everyone on the staff, for every last Tom and every last Dick and every last Harry. Alma Hettrick didn't have time to fool with your reactionary and your dry-as-dust. Right now, anyhow, they were all preoccupied: *Lohengrin* was in rehearsal and the Estonian had proved to be a whiz.

Gradually Malcolm and Victoria became invisible to everyone except themselves and their aloof, accepting friends in Georges Duval's Mill.

"How I love the Dark Ages," said Victoria.

"How I love *you*," said Malcolm, and they smiled in the gloom of the shabby parlor of L'Hôtel Dauphin as, their learning forgotten, their wisdom rose to the ascendancy.

A Winter's Tale

The long French window of my bedroom frames a scene so stylized that it appears to be deliberately composed like a tasteful view from a false stage window that is meant to be looked at only out of the corner of the eye. There is a church spire toward which four slender, hatted chimneys quizzically list; there are eleven sugar maples whose winter branches seem, from a distance, to twine emotionally together; and there is a neglected clock on a tower whose hands, since Christmas, have stood at twelve. I do not know whether it is forever midnight or forever noon.

At dusk my prospect all is gray, overcast by the film of Cambridge and by the sad lackluster of February; it has an opaline, removed, Whistlerian complexion and it suits the mood that for some days now I have received like a speechless and ghostly visitor whenever I am alone, and especially at this still, personal time of day before the familial facts and courtesies of the nursery and the dining room restore me to the pleasures of my maturity. For what I address so assiduously is a winter of my youth, irrelevant to all my present situations, a half-year so sharply independent of all my later history that I read it like a fiction; or like a dream in which all action is instinctive and none of it has its genesis in a knowledge of right and wrong.

I am at peace with my beyondness and the melancholy that it implies—for these memories are a private affair and I am lonely in my egocentricity—but there do come moments when I wonder if ever again I will prefer the sun of summer to this weary light. Occasionally I am chilled as well as clouded, but I am not quite chilled enough to light a fire on the hearth, although sometimes I pour myself a glass of whiskey and drink it straight, shuddering at the sudden path of heat across my breastbone. I lie in a long chair in the cool half-light, like a convalescent too bemused to read, and perpetually smoke so that the blue vapor further blurs the chimneys and the trees. Solemnly I watch myself as I remove the winding sheets from the dead days, enlarged by time, by desuetude invested with significance and with a leitmotiv. Often I am so beguiled by my experiments, so far gone in my addiction to discovery, that it is not easy for me to come fully to life when I have left my room. It is like emerging slowly and unwillingly from some adventurous, dream-bound anesthetic into a world which, however pretty and however dear, has no magic and few amazements.

My husband, who is a lawyer and famous for his insight, and my young son and daughter, gifted with the acuity of the uninvolved, sense my vagrancy but I ignore the questions in their faces and bend, instead, to kiss the children, as surprised as they to smell the whiskey on my breath so long before the cocktail hour. Once, a few nights ago, Laurence said as he made our drinks before dinner, "You're not really *drinking*, are you, Fanny, dear?" And when I told him that I wasn't, I added, to ward off any other questions, "I'm trying to write something and I find that whiskey helps." Poor Laurence looked ashamed and terrified; writing amongst women embarrasses him, for his mother wrote godly verses and he had a maiden cousin who perpetrated several novels, long and purple. He did not even ask me what I was writing but instantly dropped the subject and told me in detail of the plane and hotel reservations he had made for our annual visit to Bermuda two weeks from now. I know that I am safe with my brown studies and my afternoon whiskey—he'll never ask again.

On one of the last days of January at about this hour, at about five o'clock in the afternoon, I was up in the attic rummaging through a trunk full of clothes that have lost their style, thinking that I might find something for my daughter Nan who is at the age of liking to parody me by dressing in my clothes. At the bottom of the trunk I found a short quilted jacket with a design of blue hunters, red horses, and yellow dogs. I have not worn it since I was twenty, seventeen years ago, when I went to spend the winter in Heidelberg, sent there by my father in my junior year at Boston College to learn the language. I put the jacket on and as I did so, that year, like a garment itself, enclothed me; and ever since I have moved in its disguising folds. From one of the shallow pockets I withdrew a small sea shell, a thin and golden scoop, and immediately I heard Max Rössler's voice saying to me, "A memento." As if it were yesterday I remember how I bitterly expanded this to myself into, *"Memento mori."* We had made an expedition to a beach near Naples and the day had been a cold fiasco. But I had taken the shell at his bidding and had thought that in later years perhaps, when I saw it again, time would have cultivated my recollection of that day into a pearl of great price. Seventeen years later, when my heart is sedate and my hair is going gray, I recall little but the discomforts of it and our dissatisfaction, so that, in order not to quarrel with each other, we had quarreled with the sea for being so gray and so interminably at low tide. There had been a muddle over the funicular tickets that had disproportionately rubbed us the wrong way; earlier at breakfast in the hotel, a menacing Dane had said in clear, frigid English to his wife, as he stared at us, that he fancied "that chap and girl" were not married. The woman was smoking a thin black cigar. Hating the Dane for the truth of what he said and hating Rössler as the sire of my cheerless, worthless guilt, I told him that I hated Europe. Momentarily it was true; I centralized my disapproval on the limp and cottony tablecloths blotchy with Chianti stains.

In my attic, on looking back, I saw that his giving me the shell—I did not forget that his doing so had made me angry as well as bitter; I thought there should have been some ritual, however small, to mark the beginning of the peremptory end—had been a valiant gesture, really, a stroke of policy as humane as it was clever, for it said, "Remember the moment of this otherwise unmemorable day when I put the sea shell into your hand as a souvenir of our love affair; and remember of it *only* that we were in love." Even so, even after all these years, I stood among the trunks and hampers with a hardened and unforgiving heart, recalling his scornfully bad Italian (he spoke it perfectly as he spoke all languages, but in Italy he was driven, by some obscure caprice, to taunt), remembering his heretofore unknown gluttony for food and drink, his waywardness when we went sailing in the Bay of Naples without a mariner and climbed Vesuvius without a guide. On the Friday of our wretched holiday he had proposed a hideous trip to Sorrento on motor bikes and I had said, "If you must kill yourself, I wish you'd do it alone." He had shrugged and slowly, insouciantly had beheaded the violets he had bought for me.

To say that I have never thought of Heidelberg or of Max Rössler in all these years is not accurate; the town has come back to me when I have smelled certain smells—oriental tobacco returns to me the interior of the Cafe Sö and the American bar at the Europaischer Hof; I see the snug Konditorein sometimes when I smell coffee in the middle of the afternoon and then I see myself, ashen and enfeebled after a day of lectures, and ravenously hungry, selecting a cake from the glass case in the front of the shop; church bells in the very early morning make me think of the monastery near my pension and of the tranquil Benedictines I sometimes encountered, reading their breviaries as they idled along the Philosophenweg. But until now I have not thought about anything except the data that my senses accped and recorded; I know that the shock of the rest of it is finished; I'm safe from injury; I can reflect and chronicle. (Surely this rage I feel at the thought of my terror in that little boat on the rabid Bay of Naples is only an echo, is no more than an involuntary reflex that continues briefly after death.) And I *must* look back. I have given myself a deadline: I'll be finished with this recapitulation before our plane takes off for the pink beaches and the southern sun.

2

My father, widowed by my birth, was an ascetic Boston Irishman, austerer and more abstinent than the descendants of Edwards or the Mathers. Wickedness engrossed him and its punishment consoled him; he looked on me, not without satisfaction, as his hair shirt, and my failure to receive a vocation pleased at the same time that it exasperated him. My junior year in college coincided with his sabbatical from the Jesuit school where he taught Latin, and he felt it would be instructive for us both to go abroad. He remained in Paris, brooding darkly on the venality of the French clergy and writing a scandalized account of his impressions of the city, while he sent me on to Germany. He had elected Germany for me instead of France or Italy because, while it was largely Protestant, he admired its thrift and discipline; and he had chosen Heidelberg be-

cause he had a friend there who would act as my sur-
rogate parent. This was Persis Galt, a Bostonian and a
convert, married to an atheist Scot who taught Anglo-
Saxon at the university. I had never seen Frau Professor
Galt—for, having been completely Teutonized, this was
how she liked to be addressed—but I had heard her legend from my aunts and from their friends who joined
them at high, protracted tea. In Boston, Persis Brooks,
born well, born rich, presented to society with care by
trusting parents, had been a singular failure, and by that
I mean she had got no proposals of marriage that had
suited her, a situation ceaselessly puzzling to these kind
Irish ladies who observed that she had had every qualifi-
cation necessary to a match with a lawyer from State
Street or a doctor from Commonwealth Avenue. They
were sorry, my aunts Patty and Eileen and the Mes-
dames O'Brien, Malloy and Killgallen, that she had
given up and gone to Europe to marry this man Galt
who was known to be acidulous and cold. Her conversion had come later on, after she had taken up permanent residence in Heidelberg, but Daddy and his sisters
and their friends had known her earlier, before her
flight, when, perhaps to spite the graduates of Episco-
palian boarding schools who had not married her, she
attended lectures given by Catholic apologists, went to
visit the co-operative society at Antigonish, made re-
treats, and became a habitual browser in the bookshop
of St. Paul's Guild at the top of the Hill. They could
never stop regretting that she had not stayed on in
Boston to set an example to her dissenting breed.

Daddy praised Frau Professor Galt to me as an ex-
emplary woman with a heavy cross to bear, her burden
being her husband who was not only an infidel but was

reported to be a scoffer as well and who had, moreover, seduced his children to his own position. On the eve of my first emancipation from Daddy these limnings of the Galt household did not engage me, and I was relieved when she wrote that she regretted she could not lodge me in her own house but that she had found a respectable pension an easy bicycle ride from the university. When Daddy and I parted at the *Gare de l'Est* with a short and manly hand shake, he said, "I am going to be in touch with Peris Galt and if I hear from her that you are drinking whiskey and are falling into the habits that go with it, I warn you I shall take steps. You will go to a Cistercian retreat house for a long, long time, and there won't be any hole-in-corner monkey business there." For, kithless except for Daddy and the spinster aunts and lonely all through childhood, I had recently been consoled and caressed by whiskey given to me by beaux, and often had come home to our flat reeling and reeking and shamelessly gay—at which times Daddy, a teetotaller, deplored the Irish in me as if he himself had not been conceived in County Clare. On the train to Germany I had a compartment to myself and half the night I drank the brandy that I had bought one day on the sly; I nestled and postured in my daydreams until I slid into dense sleep.

Frau Professor Galt met my train and drove me from the station in a miniature automobile so small that I, accustomed only to American cars, did not think at first that it would go. But it went, it went like the wind, careering up the narrow Hauptstrasse, hugging now the blue flanks of the trolley and now the curb where other baby cars like hers were parked together with bicycles and horse-drawn carts. The impetuosity that compelled

her to drive in this fashion (we narrowly missed a policeman's dog and once seemed headed for the door of a
hairdresser's shop) was nowhere evident in the calm of
her person at the helm of this wild machine, nor in her
pleasant inquiries about my father and my aunts and my
journey. She was in her middle forties and she was firm
and ripe like an autumn fruit; her heavy, lustrous hair
was sorrel and she wore it in a coronet that further
added to her stately altitude. Her pedigree was manifest; it showed forth in her well-made and canine nose,
in her high eyes, her long lip, her stalwart Massachusetts
jaw. She was plain, but she was constructed on so chivalric, so convincing a scale, she was so shapely and so evidently wrought to last that I could not begin to imagine, just as my aunts had not been able to, why she had
come a cropper in Boston; she looked to me exactly like
the purposeful matrons in black Persian lamb marching
down Beacon Street on their way to lunch at the Chilton Club.

I knew at first glance that Frau Professor Galt had
done well at field hockey at the Winsor school and I
knew, further, that ever since that time she had kept fit
in order to preserve intact the business-like organism
into which she had been born; she would be a great
walker, she probably skiied; she would rise early; she
would be intolerant of illness, idleness, or intemperance. She wore good, gloomy tweeds, a stout pair of driving gloves, lisle stockings with a lavender cast and common-sense oxfords with heavy soles. I recalled hearing
her spoken of by another of my father's friends—one of
the fashionable New York ladies with whom he associated in fashionable apostolates and retreat houses, the
ladies who displayed fine editions of Bossuet on the

tables in their libraries and rejoiced in quoting the sharp witticisms of Monsignor Ronald Knox—who said, "I'll never forget the day I met Persis Galt in the lobby of the Adlon. She was quite impossible to seize in that doubtful German costume of hers. Her hat, I declare, was an act of treason. She was quite anonymous, quite thoroughly Berlin in the worst sense. I felt I wanted to mark her with a big red crayon so that I wouldn't confuse her with someone else. And at tea, I must have taken leave of my senses for a minute because without thinking, I said, 'Aren't the women of Germany exactly like grouse in their protective coloring? You can't tell where the cobblestones end and their stockings start or find the point at which their collars leave off and their muffinish hats begin.' " The description had been accurate, but I had the feeling that Frau Professor Galt knew what she was up to and that this was not her only style; she had had her reasons for being a frump at the Adlon as she had for giving me this first impression. All the time we were exchanging trifling information we were appraising each other and doing so as if we were contemporaries. I stopped feeling like a girl and felt like a woman; an immediate antipathy between us made me wary and adult. Never before and never since have I known this sheer and feral experience of instantly disliking and being disliked by another woman for no reason more substantial than that we were both women.

I was dry and full of aches from the trip and the brandy's punishments and I was disoriented by having been obliged to change trains before dawn at the border station, so I was downhearted to learn that Frau Professor Galt was not going to take me directly to my pension, but to her house. I would have protested if I had

had the chance, but there was no breach in the soliloquy
she had begun; she touched upon a multitude of subjects: my father must be induced to come and hike
through the Schwarzwald with her; my aunts were dears
and she was glad that they were alive and well; Paris was
detestable; it was the worst sort of luck that Hitler was
not a practicing Christian since there was no denying
his qualities; now we were passing the Altesgebäude of
the university ("Just a little like S.S. Pierce, don't you
think?" I did not but replied that I did); and here was
the library on our right where at this very moment her
son August was more than likely studying one of his dry-
as-dust books on fertilizer and ensilage for he meant—
I was not to ask her why since God alone knew—to be a
scientific farmer; it was possible that her daughter Paula
was there too, reading something even worse since she
was a medical student and had a passion for acquiring
information about such things as blood.

We began to ascend a steep hill paved with brick, and
the Frau Professor told me that she lived in the house
almost at the top, one with a green gambrel roof and
iron balconies. As we drew nearer and I caught my first
glimpse of the ruined castle through tall trees and saw
in the distance the bend in the river, I exclaimed,
"What heavenly views you must have!"

Frau Professor Galt replied, "When one views
heaven, all views are heavenly," and she gave me a
quick, orderly smile.

"I'm so glad you came on the morning train instead
of the evening one," she said as we passed through her
garden gate where the snobbish legend *Cave Canem* was
posted, "for now you will be able to meet my guardian

angel at tea this afternoon. My own private monk, my Dom Paternus, my heaven on earth."

"How very nice," I said, and, appalled to think of having to stay through tea time, I added impudently, "I don't believe I've ever known a monk socially before." A cloud of reproach passed over my hostess's face, but she delivered me again that official little smile and said, "Then you have something in store for you. There's far more *mingling* in Europe than in Boston." Thus by opposing a whole continent to a single city she proclaimed herself inalienably Bostonian, however Popish her metaphysics, however Bavarian her walking shoes, however firm her resolution never again to see the swan boats and the public tulips in the Public Garden. She continued, "One of the nicest things about the pension you're going to, by the way, is that it's so near the monastery at Stift Neuburg you'll have no trouble getting to daily mass. And how those Benedictines sing! Dom Paternus's Kyrie is divine."

During this girlish speech (her vocabulary puzzled and even shocked me a little for it seemed profane to call a living monk divine; moreover, her voice altered to accommodate her extravagance in a higher key and one that was not appropriate to her stature and her general design), she had led me across a chilled, bare vestibule, up a flight of stairs carpeted in thick, grim brown and into a room familiar to my imagination; it was a room in any house on Beacon Hill where in the late afternoon a lady would celebrate the ancient rite of tea with silver and Limoges or where, being alone, she might make spills of last year's Christmas wrappings. The brilliant brass hearth accouterments were there, the fender and the Cape Cod lighter and the tools, even though the logs were counterfeit and the fuel was gas; and the *chinoiserie* was all in place, the matching Ming vases and the glass tree *sous cloche,* and Frau Professor Galt told me at once that the painting of a family group over the mantel was a doubtful Copley. But besides these plausible and predictable things (I liked them all and this was the sort of room in which I would have liked to spend *my* afternoons) there were religious objects everywhere, dreadful to the point of disrespect: figurines of St. Sebastian pierced by far too many arrows, of the Little Flower unduly dimpled and unduly vacant, of St. Francis looking like a sissy schoolboy; there was a miniature in polychrome of the grotto at Lourdes, a crucifix of bird's-eye maple with a corpus of aluminum, and a dim, bromidic print of the "Sistine Madonna."

Before the gas fire stood my breakfast table, the food kept warm by quilted cosies. Frau Professor Galt perfunctorily introduced me to my meal and then, pursuing the subject that she had not relinquished, she said, "If I lived at the Pension Haarlass, I'd begin my day with matins." She stood towering above me while I poured pale coffee into my cup and thought with gloom of the dark chapels of priories where, making a retreat, I had knelt beside Daddy at matins, shivering, sick for the sleep from which I had been wrenched. I hesitated, but I did not wish her to be misled and I said, "I'm afraid I don't even go to daily mass." This was not altogether true; I did not go to daily mass except when I was under the same roof with my father.

The Frau Professor chided me flirtatiously, "Oh, you Sabbatarian cradle Catholics! But I should think that *you* with your father and your aunts—dear Fanny, you have disconcerted me."

When I told her I was sorry I partly meant it, for there had come to me the image of my merry, plump-cheeked aunts, busier than belles with their sodalities and their novenas; their pleasure in confession and their homely use of churches as places in which to meet friends before a Wednesday matinee or in which to rest their feet during long shopping trips; their standing jokes with priests. They lived for and they lived in the church, but theirs was a natural condition; they were too secure to care a thing for polemics; they loved embroidering altar cloths, harvesting indulgences, offering prayers for the sick and the dead.

The Frau Professor rose above her disillusion. "I know you'll forgive me for treating you straight off as a member of the family," she said. "You won't think me too beastly for leaving you alone for a bit? I retire now to my chaste cell to read the noon office—for you see, I'm not like you, not born to the purple, not able to take all these riches for granted. I shan't ask you to join me because I know you're tired and you're—we don't really see eye to eye, do we? Would you like a rosary? Or will you simply meditate?"

"I'll meditate," I said, and drank disgusting coffee.

"If you would like to bathe, ring for Erika," she said. "She doesn't speak a word of English, so you must say to her *Ich möchte ein Bad, bitte.*" My German was sparse but it was serviceable and I was offended that it had been impugned. When my overseer was gone and all the doors were closed and I was left to meditate, I stuck out my tongue. And then I began to move restlessly about the room, queerly scared as if I had committed some sin graver than my mild flippancies; it was not agreeable to me to dislike Persis Galt so much after so short a time; certainly it was unreasonable of me to resent her asking me, over her shoulder as she left the room, to call her by her Christian name.

All the curtains in the room were drawn and the lamps were lighted although the sun was high in the vivid sky. One pair of heavy damask draperies, I found, covered a door to a balcony and I drew them aside and stepped out into the comely autumn. On my right rose the castle hill and for the second time I saw the sundered, rosy stronghold through the bruised leaves of the hornbeam and the lime trees that were beginning to turn; momentarily I quickened to its august antiquity and to its romantic biography of ups and downs, and realized that my reluctance to come here (I had longed to go to Florence) had been balanced by fantasies that the savory air revived. I turned from the pretty rubble and looked below at the town of gabled houses, tall and lean, that hugged the steep slopes, their chimneys raffishly askew, their leaded windows burning in the noon. I supposed that the cluster of buildings with mansard roofs would be the university, where my father had enjoined me to keep my nose to the grindstone until my declensions were letter perfect. I watched three barges pass slowly through the locks up the river, their genial flags unfurling in an easy breeze; far off, on the yonder bank, I looked on fields tilled in neat squares of violet and brown; and here and there, at their junctions, like the figures on a chessboard, stood whitewashed cottages. It was a kindly prospect, it was a tender, mothering countryside.

Suddenly, from all quarters of the town, the church

bells began to ring the Angelus; echoes loitered in the calm air to perish in a fresh shower of melody; I was charmed by this concert in recognition of high noon. For a few minutes, on the Frau Professor's balcony in Neueschloss Strasse, my senses were infatuated with foreignness and and my antic spirits rose, delighted; to confront the world of possibilities that had opened up before me (they were vague, but my confidence in them was sure) I wanted to look my best and I started to go back into the room to ring for Erika and ask for my bath. But on the threshold I was arrested by the spectacle of a young man in a uniform coming through the door with a muzzled toy Schnauzer in his arms. Simultaneously the maidservant came through another door to greet the dog with gushes, "Ah, the good Herr Rössler brought the good dog home!" She cradled the grizzled creature in her arms. "Shall I tell the Frau Professor you are here?"

Herr Rössler looked at his wrist watch and said solemnly, "By no means. She will be at her orisons. But when she gets off her knees, you can tell her she owes me two marks fifty for the damned dog's bill. He had a tooth pulled."

"Nay, nay!" cried Erika in consternation and kissed the top of the dog's head. "Be kind, Herr Rössler. Remember how you brought him when he was a puppy— oh, so sweet, so sweet," and murmuring, purling, she left the room to warm some milk for the dear good dog. The man looked at himself in an Adam mirror beside the door. "Coat carrier, dog carrier, my very obliging young friend, Herr Rössler," he said. "He flies, he's very charming, he'll be a catechumen yet." Before he left the room, he opened the other door and called, "Hello! Erika! Tell her I'll collect the two marks fifty this afternoon. And Heil Hitler!"

3

Persis Galt was going to greet the monks who stood in the doorway, and so absorbing was her salutation of the short and corpulent man in front, whom she greeted as Dom Paternus, that I got no clear picture of him until, twittering and exclaiming, the singular woman knelt on the floor to receive his blessing while her other guests busied themselves in looking elsewhere. I was as embarrassed as the others and the momentary obliquity of the monk's gaze made me think he shared our discomfort. I had expected Dom Paternus to be a thin and pallid hull for the ascetic spirit of which I had heard so many dithyrambs in the few hours I had been under this roof; far from that, Dom Paternus, by twenty years older than I had imagined, was round and red. His head was perfectly spherical and perfectly bald and his small, winsome ears stood out straight. He had a bright double chin and jocose eyes and a pink nose. He was something like Friar Tuck and something like Father Lynch from St. Anne's parish who often played two-handed pinochle with my Aunt Patty.

I had not been at all surprised that Persis had changed from her tweeds and brogans into a less workaday costume. At lunch time she had emerged from her chaste cell in a black velvet dress with a long skirt and a tight bodice that cherished her small waist; her long arms moved beautifully in narrow sleeves that terminated in pointed cuffs extending halfway down her splendid hands; at her throat (the neck of her dress was low) she wore an ebony cross on a velvet ribbon. I was sure that her intention had been pious, but the result was provocative; her chic and her decolletage at sunny midday had unsettled me; and they unsettled me even more now in her gathering of monks, of shabby students from her husband's Beowulf class, and of bulky Stormtroopers and Blackshirts. After lunch she had invited me to have a look at the room where she prayed and I did not fail to be impressed at the sight of her kneeling at her cherry *prie-dieu;* she was the only decoration in the room; indeed it was chaste and more than chaste, it was sterilized.

Now she got to her feet, warmly clasped the hand of the other monk, and turning to me with her arm outstretched to Dom Paternus as if to a dumb beast, she said, "Here is a pretty American who has come to be your neighbor at the Haarlass. You must take her in hand at once because she says she doesn't go to daily mass." The monk forebore to judge me on these grounds and did no more than affably acknowledge the introduction. The Frau Professor told me—and told the whole room—that I would find my pension absolute heaven. In the beginning, she explained, it had been the house where the oblates had been shorn before they entered the monastery, hence its name. Herr Pirsch, the landlord, was a devout man and the cook, Gerstner, despite a somewhat cretinous look, had the soul of a saint and often took surprises to the monks, surprises, that is, that did not interfere with their laws of fast and abstinence.

Dom Paternus and the younger brother, Dom Agatho, listened gravely and with infinite patience like the indulgent husbands of women addicted to telling twice-told tales. She went on to say that I must not get the impression that there was anything worldly about her brothers; on the contrary, they could not be more pious, but there was a heartening liaison between them and a certain section of the Heidelberg laity of which, it was clear to me without being told, Frau Professor Galt was the leader.

There were other conversations in the room and there were, as well, the sounds of spoons on teacups and the gush of fizz water into glasses and a drift of street noise, but these were only a blurred background for the cascade of speeches from the leading lady's lips. She had returned to her tea table and had assumed a presidential posture, erect and magnanimous; she seemed to be bowing to the applause of her constituents when she said, "I should have been born in the middle ages." This was evidently meant for me since the declaration seemed new to no one else. She went on to say that her husband (he was late as usual, the wretch) and her children (late, too; how like *him* they were!) could have lived at no time in history but these very days. "I love them, the darlings," she said, "but alas, alas, they've missed the whole point of life. My poor abandoned Paula and her awful preoccupation with the pancreas! I'm sure St. Francis never knew about his enzymes—what's the good of all these new acquisitions of the body, I should like to know. August is a little less absurd with his agriculture—one should love the land, but I know that you, Dom Paternus and Dom Agatho, didn't learn your farming in laboratories."

"Speaking of the land," said Dom Paternus, a merciful man, "that gorgeous Spanish chestnut on the Kuehruhweg has begun to turn. I went up this morning to look at it."

"After lauds or before?" She was indefatigable; I thought the Benedictine sighed. He did not answer; he picked up a tea caddy and said, "Your tea is so good." But Frau Galt was not to be put off and she repeated her question. The younger monk answered for Dom Paternus, "Why, afterward. It's too cold and dark nowadays at the hour we get up to go for a botanical ramble. It was bitter this morning. Dom Placid came to breakfast wearing a red sweater—I dared not look below his waist to see if he had decided his rheumatism had entitled him to any other dispensations." Persis frowned, not liking this frivolity—the intramural humor left her out of things—but the monks and I smiled at the mild joke. And she took the conversation back, repeating what she had told me at lunch (an abominable meal of steamed eel and unsalted dumplings), that she and I would bicycle to see the cathedral at Speyer, a building that had always induced in her great peace of mind; since my birthday came on the Dedication of St. Michael the Archangel she would give a lunch party in my honor after the last mass; we would possibly make a pilgrimage on foot to some shrine or other. Then, addressing me, she said, "I forgot to tell you that we play bridge every Tuesday at the Europaischer Hof. I hope you'll join us there as often as you have the inclination."

Having been chilled to the bone by her other plans I accepted this invitation with relief, and even with enthusiasm, although I was afraid that "we" would be the monks (armed with pastoral dispensations to accom-

modate their secular sister) or members of that top
flight laity into which I felt I was being drawn willy-
nilly.

Abruptly she stopped talking; I followed her sidelong
glance to the door and saw entering it the young man
who had been here earlier with the dog; now, though,
he was in civilian clothes and he was through with his
sulks, smiling agreeably. Persis Galt said, "I am monop-
olizing my guest of honor. Didn't I introduce you to
Mellie Anderson, Fanny? She's that sweet little thing
over there by the Schnaaps; August's girls always seem
to be near the Schnaaps. Speak to her, won't you?"

I left her side and so did the friars, we were replaced
by Herr Rössler and the Frau Professor's voice ceased to
be audible. At the same time the tension in the room
relaxed and there was even laughter. On my way to
Mellie Anderson I was several times detained, once by a
sad, grubby girl in octagonal glasses whose eyes all afternoon had followed Persis worshipfully and who told me
that in another year she was going into an order of Ger-
man-speaking nuns in the Rocky Mountains. "Persis is
wonderful," she said reverently. "If I didn't have a vocation, I'd like to be exactly like her." Poor soul! Emotion
leaked from her strained eyes; she was the dismalest
sight on earth. Again I was halted by a heavily decorated
army officer who told me irrefutably that he had met me
in Berlin at the Olympics when I was staying with the
Gaisenströcks and when I denied this, saying that I had
arrived in Europe only ten days before, he asked me if
Giselle Gaisenströck had had her baby yet. And Dom
Agatho with an ingratiating grin told me that his uncle
had been born in Cincinnati.

Mellie Anderson and I had everything in common;

she, too, had been sent to Persis Galt, but by a zealous
mother instead of father, and she, too, was lodged in the
Pension Haarlass. She had been here for a month, the
longest month of her life, she said, eyed constantly and
chided constantly by Persis Galt, who had spies everywhere, among the servants at the Haarlass and at the
Europaischer Hof. Mellie felt sometimes that she was
going nutty the way her slightest aberration from the
straight and narrow boomeranged; Persis wrote volumi-
nous letters to her mother and her mother wrote back
threats—Mrs. Anderson was evidently much like Daddy.
Mellie had taken up with August Galt, though she de-
tested him for the rowdy and rambunctious Nazi he was,
in the hope that Persis would ease up on her vigilance;
the hope was dashed, for Persis openly and even ostenta-
tiously disliked her son and now Mellie was stuck with
him. The fact was, she said, that Persis loathed all her
family and they all loathed her. Then why didn't they
leave one another? I asked.

"She has the money," said Mellie. "She has money
enough to buy something better to drink than this peasant slop. Have some?" The smell of the Schnaaps was
worse than the taste; we drank from wineglasses. Mellie
went on, "It all has to do with money. Even in my case
it does—and it will in yours too probably. If my mother
stopped my allowance, what would I do? So I go to mass
at seven every morning no matter what I've been doing
the night before—I am sure the chambermaid keeps a
report card for me—and come here to let her explain the
Epistle of the day and refrain from making irreligious
jokes and show up on bridge night—and when I think of
how I looked forward to this year! I was naïve enough to

think that Mother was giving me a lot of fun and games."

Mellie's grievances were manifold and justified; I liked her and I was listening to her, but at the same time I was watching Persis and Herr Rössler. At the beginning of lunch, Erika had spoken of the two marks fifty that her mistress owed the aviator and Persis said tartly, half to herself, "What an ungraceful thing to speak of. One would think he'd have some affection for the animal he gave me." It occurred to me to ask Mellie to explain Rössler's role in the house, but on second thought, I decided to puzzle it out myself. The man had risen but he lingered beside the tea table as if he were receiving some final instructions and then he made his way towards us. Persis Galt resumed her earlier role; she summoned the monks to return to her; her voice became a carillon: "You must teach me to love Monica's son as much as I love Monica!" she cried. "I've prayed, I've prayed with utmost contrition and my heart is still hard toward St. Augustine."

Softly Mellie said, "Listen, I can't stand another minute of it. I'm going to tell her I'm going to Benediction. Watch out for Max Rössler—he's her Number One spy." She returned her glass to the tray and then she groaned, "Oh, Jesus, here come the atheists." August Galt, so blond and broad and Aryan that he looked more German than any German in the room, and Godfrey Galt, black-haired, beak-nosed, looking clever and cantankerous, saluted Persis as if she were a chance acquaintance, and came to meet me.

My host, casting hard looks everywhere, rubbing his hands together, made me think of a hangman. "My wife knew your father," he said. "In Boston. She has reproduced a Boston drawing room with considerable fidelity, don't you think?" I agreed with him and started to elaborate but he interrupted me. "I live in a hideous house. My wife cannot bear the light of day. She is fond of darkness, inconvenience, bad ventilation, gorgon-headed waste. I myself am by way of being a Bauhaus man." He was building a modern house in the hills above Heidelberg, he told me, and his son said, "There will be nothing for Mutt to do in Vat's house."

"In my house," said the professor, "there will be nothing for a woman to do but sit and stare," and with this he began to stare at his wife's back. He accepted the glass of Schnaaps August poured for him, drank it like medicine and took leave of us, saying, "I'll just say hello to the Blackfriars and Blackshirts. Grüss Gott, Heil Hitler, what's the difference?"

Mellie said to August, "I have been waiting for you for an hour. I am leaving *now,* this instant. You meet me and I mean it."

I had never seen so much ill-humor displayed simultaneously by so many people. August, who had not spoken to me at all, snarled like a dog and followed Mellie, who paused beside Persis and curtsied. "I've had a divine time," she said in cheeky burlesque, "but I must run to Benediction. I haven't said a rosary since morning."

"*Aufwiedersehen,* my darling," said Persis. "In Christ!"

"In Christ! Heil Hitler! *Guten Abend! Aufwieder-sehen! Danke schön!*"

I had no time to see the effect of this on Persis Galt or on the monks because Max Rössler was at my side and had taken my elbow and was guiding me to the dining room. "I'm to give you a real drink and then I'm to take you to the Haarlass," he said. "My name is Max Rössler, I know yours. Persis apologizes but as you see she can't leave her guests."

Until we had gone into the cold, quiet dining room I had not realized that I was tired to death, and tired in a way that I enjoyed; it was a merited fatigue and it claimed my bones and my blood as well as my muscles. It was a condition in which I was vulnerable to everything, to liquor, to joy, to despair, to love, to quarreling; I might cry or I might be crippled with giggles. I cared nothing at all for Mellie Anderson's warning; I was too grateful for the delicious drink the spy had given me, too happy to be out of earshot of the Frau Professor Galt.

This dark young man was well turned-out; his manners were a second nature and he spoke his perfectly idiomatic English without any accent at all; his laugh was easy and somewhat professional and gave me the feeling that he was peering into the darkness over footlights which at once blinded and reassured him. The smell of his tobacco was as unusual as incense and when he offered me a cigarette I found the taste of it entirely new. He smoked through an amber holder which he bit between his good white teeth. He was very handsome and he looked like the Devil. His forehead was high and his nose was sculptural and all the surfaces of his face were fine; his eyes and his mouth expressed nothing. His upper lip was long and the lower one was full but its fullness did not suggest intemperance or even pleasure; it was the mouth of a child who had been pampered in his sulks which, in adulthood, had become selfish desires, desires for power, perhaps, or for a feudal preservation of the *status quo*. And his eyes, polished and dark like some hard wood, copied and clinched the self-love of the mouth. His face was less a face than a representation of a kind of conduct and it had, therefore, a certain antiquity which made his American slang anachronistic. I, used to simple, noisy boys, not much younger than Max Rössler, was flurried by his sophistication, which I distrusted and admired. We covered some customary topics; we exchanged compliments on each other's countries although I had seen nothing of his and he had never been to mine. We were sure that I would enjoy my winter here although my study of philology depressed us both. I would find the veranda cafe of the Haarlass agreeable, he told me; he often went there on sunny afternoons at this time of year, when it was especially nice to look at the autumn leaves on the Jettenbühel across the river.

"Is there a bar there?" I asked him.

"A bar? You mean do they sell drinks? My God, of course! You are in Europe, Fräulein."

"Then I would rather drink there than here," I said. "I want to go there now."

"At your service," he said and bowed and gave me an ambiguous smile, half seducing and half warning; I felt mocked and as green as grass and needlessly I added, "I don't mean you have to stay. I halfway promised to meet Mellie Anderson."

"Well, they *don't* have a bar at Stift Neuburg where presumably Mellie is telling her beads like a good girl." He smiled warmly, really amused and surely on our side, and he took my hand; the touch of his warm fingers on my cold ones was exciting; he bent toward me as if I were much shorter than I was, as if I were some small woman whom he loved. "We won't go to the Haarlass yet," he said. "We'll go to the Cafe Sö. There won't be anyone there."

4

Persis Galt, a Blackwood specialist, played bridge ferociously on Tuesdays. The salon at the Europaischer Hof which she dominated was a sumptuous room, brightly lighted, thickly carpeted, and full of artificial roses and counterfeit Louis Quatorze. Technically this room could be used by any guest of the hotel or even by a nonresident pleasure seeker who was willing to buy enough drinks at the bar to make his visit worth-while. But Persis had some power over the lackeys so that, at a word from her, anyone could be denied admission. If her bridge nucleus, which numbered twelve with an occasional peripatetic thirteenth, was annoyed by outsiders, they were treated with such snubs and outright discourtesies by the waiters and the bartender that they departed in humiliated silence.

It was my misfortune almost always to draw as partner a Hungarian dipsomaniac called Countess Tisza who for many years had been working on a life of Walther von der Vogelweide. Her bridge, as she steadily drank (her capacity had been likened to that of the Great Tun in the castle which held forty-seven thousand gallons) became so disengaged from any kind of method that I often thought it would be possible to bring legal action against her. The Countess was sometimes in and sometimes out of favor with Persis, but in or out, she was always at the Europaischer Hof on Tuesday evening and each time without fail she asked Max Rössler and she asked me why we were not interested in each other. The question embarrassed me and Rössler seemed not to hear it. It was sometimes for this reason that the Countess fell from our leader's favor, but more often she was sent to Coventry for making a scene with the bartender, whom she suspected of watering her Scotch, or for accusing someone of being homosexual. Whenever she took a false step Persis Galt and her cohorts not only commented devastatingly on her drinking but, as well, attacked her friend von Ribbentrop, who they said was a man no one would want to know, a sycophant and, worse, a bore; although at other times it was because of this friendship that the Countess was looked on respectfully as someone who got about in the most amusing and important places. When she was "in" her boozing was called an eccentricity.

The other players, for the most part, were residents of this hotel; if they had had the money they would have lived at the Ritz in Paris or in London or in New York or Boston. They were chic, uneducated, indolent and discontented; they lived in Heidelberg because this was a good hotel and it was cheap in Germany and they were not far from the casino at Baden-Baden. They were so entirely cosmopolitan that there was no way of telling their nationality save by their surnames.

As I looked back, I realized that I had imagined a much more pastoral way of life in Germany; I had thought of waltzing, wine festivals and pleasure steamers on the Rhine. I had thought of seidels of dark beer and evenings of fraternal song, of Mosel in stemmed glasses for quiet trysts. At the Europaischer Hof the drinks were expensive (we paid for our own), the conversation was tedious, the anecdotes were provincial and obscure, and the evenings ended invariably in a squabble over the score. Frau Galt, an adroit Yankee, generally managed to extort an undue sum from me which I paid without protest when she casually remarked, "I *must* remember to write to your dear father tomorrow."

Sometimes Persis and Max Rössler played against the Countess and me. The combination of the Countess's irresponsibility and my preoccupation with Rössler's hands and with his gentle leaning toward that hypothetical *petite* caused me to play so badly that the Frau Professor caustically observed, "I am sadly enlightened. I thought in America these days one took in bridge with one's mother's milk."

Rössler had never come to the Haarlass. I knew that I had frightened him away from me when we had gone that first afternoon to the Cafe Sö, but still I did not know why. Twice I had terribly disrupted his stagy calm, once when I asked him where he was to be stationed after his three-months' leave was over and again when invasively I told him I had seen him look at himself in the mirror in Persis Galt's drawing room that morning. He did not answer my question and he chose to ignore my other tactlessness by calling for the check.

On the train from Paris I had made no bones to myself about my intention to have a love affair in Heidelberg, and I was not in the least ashamed that the images of my daydreams were largely derived from scenes in *The Student Prince.* I did not mean to love. I meant to be "in love" and to be sorry when it was all over; but because I was a levelheaded girl (my rebellion against

Daddy was little more than a convention) I did not wish to be a spendthrift: I expected some time to marry. But my plans had gone amiss, for I was in love with Max Rössler and I loved him. I had neither eyes nor ears for any of the German or American youths from the university with whom I drank beer and danced occasionally, who were accessible, who would gladly have helped me carry out my lighthearted project. Daily I expected Max to come to the Haarlass and daily I waited, watching the road from Heidelberg as I sat on a rock on the hillside behind the inn. In my disappointment I gazed through tears that did not fall at the fields where the Benedictines were swinging scythes or sowing the winter wheat. From the paths in the hills behind me I heard fagot gatherers greeting one another and heard the Hitler Jugend singing on their way home from a hike. Sometimes I waited until the light began to fade, the red softening to the smoky flush of a peach which was then overtaken, at evensong, by a green light that lay over the monks' paradisus. And then when all the light and all my hope were gone, I would return forlornly to the cafe and if I found no one there I knew, I would play a game of solitaire. I did not understand his delay; the days of his furlough were going fast.

It was delay rather than neglect, I thought, for he was not unconscious of me. I could tell that by the way he sometimes looked at me when I cut the cards for his deal, or implied a toast to me as he lifted his glass. Now and again at the end of an evening he saw Mellie Anderson and me into a cab. Dissatisfied, I looked at him standing there on the steps of the hotel, his carnation as white as his starched shirt, and said to myself that I might as well give up, that anyhow he was not worth it, that he looked like the sort who would come a dime a dozen on the Riviera.

One night late in October as we all left the Europaischer Hof Persis observed that the night was much too fine for a cab and she suggested that Max and Mellie and I walk home with her to the Neueschloss Strasse and come back then to the town for a cab to the Haarlass. Mellie, as she often did, pleaded a headache and disappeared, making a beeline for the Roter Ochsen where she would spend the rest of the evening wrangling with August Galt and his Nazi friends who refused, laughing like peasants, to believe that she had been a member of the Young Communist League.

It was a bewitched night, balmy, misty, muting. As we stood chatting a moment before the door of the Galts' house I looked up at the castle, dematerialized by the river mist, and felt stopped dead by the timelessness not only of Heidelberg but also of this false and enigmatic man, the deathless archetype that figured in the dreams of all masochistic schoolgirls. Tonight he was dressed as a man of action, the lieutenant in uniform, and when, after seeing Persis into her vestibule, he proposed that we walk up to the castle I agreed too readily and gaspingly, sounding like Persis or like Mellie's parody of Persis, "Oh, an absolutely heavenly idea!" We climbed the steep street in silence; in the stubbornness of his ideals, Max bent his head downward as if I were three inches shorter than I was.

He asked me if I liked Heidelberg by now and I replied that I did; we brutally ridiculed the Countess; we talked about the weather. When we passed Charlemagne's dry fountain just inside the castle gate it occurred to me that there were probably ghosts here; I earnestly wanted there to be for I wanted an emotion, and terror would be better than none. And all the same in direct denial of my wants and of my intentions, I said, "I can't stay long. I have a lecture in the morning at nine."

"So?" Was he bored or was he a bore? Both, I concluded, and I agreed now with Mellie, who said he was depthless and stupid.

We stood on the parapet of Ottosthur looking down on the roof tops dimmed by the mist and I found the Haarlass, its veranda cafe a blurred scar of lights. Rössler said, "Schenck will be marking the Americans' beer coasters double." It was true; the head waiter was a thief and a panhandler.

"I thought you often came to the Haarlass," I said.

"I do. I was there last night."

I was quite beside myself, as if I had an intolerable pain but could not describe it to the doctor. I did not know whether to be angry that he had come to my pension and had not told me (last night I had spent the evening in my room writing to Daddy and translating my *Beowulf*) or to be frenzied with the suspicion that he had been there with a girl, or to be insulted that he had so casually told me he had been there at all.

I finally said, "It is often rather fun in the veranda."

He made no reply. He did not speak and he did not look at me; I found him unforgivable. I wondered whether his privacy came from shrewdness or if there was not something else besides, an old confusion or uncertainty. His retirement was not always the same kind and now, standing beside me on the parapet, staring down like a general from a reviewing stand, he withdrew almost perceptibly into some private speculation;

he would not have noticed if I had walked away. Em
barrassed by our silence, even though he had dictated it,
I snatched at straws and caught the memory of having
read somewhere of an English princess named Elizabeth
who had married into the Palatinate and had spent her
entire life here in homesickness. She had had her gar-
deners plant daphne and hedges of yew to make her
think of England.

I said, "Tell me, do you know anything about the
English princess, Elizabeth, who took being here so
hard?"

Instead of answering, he repeated the name Elizabeth
with a loving prolongation of the vowels and in a voice
of the greatest tenderness. I had taken off my gloves and
had laid my hands flat on the chilled stones. He said the
name again with as much affectionate direction as if it
belonged to me and he embraced me, not suddenly but
with so sure an art that it was not until he was about to
kiss me that I found my voice, crying out one of those
commonplaces that spring to the lips of a girl taken by
surprise. My gloves fell to the paving. Max dropped his
hands. Indeed, I had been so surprised that I had not
realized until I saw the patience of his smile that the
whole sequence of these trivial events was based on the
coldest cynicism. For he had not thought of conquest
any more than now he thought of defeat. He was
neither bewildered nor disappointed, neither humiliated nor angry. He restored my fallen gloves—I fancied
that he clicked his heels as he handed them to me—and
as if this hiatus had not come he said, "I have no information about the English princess at all. I suggest you
try a history of the Heidelbergerschloss."

I put on my gloves and turned to go. "Wait a minute,

Fanny," he said. A sixth sense prompted me to move a little farther down the parapet. But he stood absolutely still, wearing a look of grief for which I had no preparation. "Listen," he said, "have you any idea how much I hate Persis Galt?"

"Hate her? Why *hate* her? She's only a goose."

"She is also my mistress," he said. "She has been for five years. For four of them I have hated her."

I was smashed. I put my gloved hands to my cheeks and stretched the skin tight over the bones. Max sat down on the floor of the balcony and leaned his back against the breastwork. This was so out of character, it was a gesture so unmilitary, so pitiful and weak that I could not hold back my tears for him and for myself, but I made no sound and I listened to his stale, sad tale.

At eighteen, five years ago, he had studied under Herr Professor Galt and several times had been to the house on Neueschloss Strasse where he had been charmed by Persis in her medieval costumes, surrounded by her monks and her priests and bishops from Munich and Berlin. She had had an altogether different style in those days, as bogus as her present one but far less foolish. She had seemed the soul of sympathy and of serenity; Rössler, together with half a dozen other students, was in love with her. He sent her flowers with no card, "certain, of course, that she would know who had sent them. I thought so incessantly of her that it seemed impossible for her not to know." He lurked in the doorways of houses and shops next to those he had seen her enter, but he had not the courage to speak to her when she came out. "Anyhow, she would not have recognized me. Even then she and Galt made a point of not knowing each other's friends. I was only one of many supernumeraries who could be told to ring for Erika for more hot water on one of her days." Then one night he had gone to the Europaischer Hof with Liselotte Schmetzer because her husband was ill and she needed a partner and there, to his astonishment, was Persis Galt in a role he had never dreamed. Earlier he had thought of her as unapproachable; it was her piety and her inviolable position as the wife of his professor that had appealed to his romantic nature and he had never had any intention of making an actual overture to her: the hopelessness of his case was the poetry of it. He had known, he thought, exactly how Dante felt when he watched Beatrice at her prayers. But at the Europaischer Hof, he had discovered that she was an accomplished flirt, less shy than the commonest slut on Semmelstrasse. They had left early when she said she felt faint and could not drive herself home, and they went to his rooms straight off.

For the first year Max was unable to see, because he was too enraptured, any discrepancy between Frau Galt's life of devotion and her transgression of the Sixth Commandment. But through growing a year older and through taking Persis for granted as his personal property—of which he began to tire; she was voracious of his time—he saw what she had done, what he had done, what they had done together, and from that time forward the principle of his nature was self-disgust. But he had continued with the affair because he was so deeply enmeshed in it; she had made him grow old too fast; he lived in a kind of connubial sluggishness, convincing himself that by not breaking off he was punishing her in her own terms. He had concluded that she had taken a lover to make up for a lack of talent, a lack of talent which she had deceived herself into thinking was a talent for writing poetry or painting water colors or marrying a Bostonian but was really a lack of talent for being good. In the absence of goodness, she had to have power, and who could be better controlled than an eighteen-year-old weakling? "Because I *am* a weakling," he said urgently as if I must believe in the justification for his self-excoriation. "In every way I am the worst possible coward. I am afraid of the sky so I am an aviator; I am afraid of the sight of blood so I am a soldier. I cancel out a phobia with a mania. I am afraid of Persis so I go on with her, on and on and on—"

"You could leave her," I said. "You don't depend on her for money the way her family does. She can't get your parents to punish you for what she knows about *you*."

"Let me tell you something, Fanny. Sooner or later everyone who crosses that threshold gets blackmailed unless they're too disabled, in one way or another, for her to bother with."

"What's her hold over you?" I said with terrible spontaneous anxiety.

"It doesn't matter. She has one but it doesn't matter. Let's go down to the Roter Ochsen."

At the foot of the stone steps that took us down the castle hill into the Kornmarkt, Max took my face in his hands, "What are you crying for, for God's sake?" he said unkindly. "Didn't you ever hear of adultery before?"

"I wasn't thinking about you."

"You *were* thinking about me. You've thought about me from the beginning. You'd better not, Fanny, I'm a swindler from being swindled. I am sick, I must die, may the Lord have mercy on my soul."

Under the cold searchlight of his eyes I felt like a frangible object that he could take apart or could break or could sell or could take home with him to be used for something or other, altered perhaps, to go with the furniture of his rooms. He took the will out of me as neatly as if he had removed the stone from an apricot, and I received his plausible caresses as gratefully, as obsessively, as if I received the man himself. "I've warned you," he said.

5

It was an intolerable love affair, raddled and strangled with our knowledge of its end. If I had a lecture we met at the Stadtgarten in the town where Persis never went; hurrying from the university, I thought only of the small round table at which I would meet him, and it was as if this meeting were the aspiration toward which my whole existence bent and which receded from me to an incommensurable distance once I had recognized it: I ran in dreadful fear that he would not be there.

Often he went away from Heidelberg for a few days at a time, never saying where nor for what reason or whether he would ever come back, and at these times I went to confession at the monastery, where I chattered like a goose through the wicket to an ancient monk who did not listen because I spoke in English. Hearing the sandaled feet of the friars on the stone stairs somewhere above, I hysterically reiterated *Deus te amo* to myself as if this were a charm to dispel the effluvium of my own grave. Once after this I went across the river in the ferry and climbed the castle hill, and while I stood debating with my soul in the English garden, I allowed my blue rosary to fall from my hand. Some child would find it, although as it slipped from my fingers, its gilt gauds glittering, I wished it would not be found except by the feet of a salamander running across a lichened rock.

Almost immediately Max and I had become inseparable, forcing ourselves through our obsessiveness to ignore all the admonitions we heard and saw. Often I was naïve enough to think it was unsafe only because he was an aviator and there might be a war, but most of the time I knew better than that, I knew that it would have ended with a smash at any time and for any woman. There was no pleasure in it, I suffered perpetually, it was monstrous to live through, but I could not have escaped it, not possibly. We were restive, continually seeking diversion, hiding continually from Persis. We went walking for hours through the blue mist of the forests or we took the tram to Neckar-Gemünd and went on from there into the hills. We sought out shabby Bierstuben in Handschusheim. On Persis Galt's days at home and on bridge nights at the Europaischer Hof we were wild with impatience and frantic with deceit but we stayed until the end. Moving, or when we were surrounded by others, our stubborn hope stayed alive until Max's misery suddenly rose between us and nothing was any more of any use. There was something in him, some prehistoric wound, that made me walk within this love (but it was not love; it was another thing, I don't know what) on tiptoe, thinking only of the split second next to come. I dared not disturb the sleeper whom I often saw in his large, cold eyes, for I did not know his identity although I sometimes thought I almost knew.

The week in Naples had been almost like a week any other two lovers might have spent together and once, as we drank rank Italian beer at a quayside bar, he even asked me to marry him, but the quixotic idéa could not be entertained even in fun and he laughed in his thorough and bitter knowledge of himself—*his* knowledge, not mine, for he would not share it with me. This had been the last week of his leave and he got off the train at Karlsruhe, where he was to be on maneuvers.

The day I got back August Galt and Mellie Anderson and I walked up to Ziegelhausen. On the way August told us he had a bad hang-over acquired the night before at a farewell party for two aviators who were leaving for maneuvers. He was burdened with photographic gear and he asked us, when we got to the village, to pose for a picture. His reason had behind it a lengthy and fuzzy logic; he had no photograph of the aviators, Rüdiger and Barth, but he would remember whenever he looked at our picture why we had been in Ziegelhausen on that particular day. "Why should you care," Mellie asked him, "if they're only going on maneuvers?" He pretended not to hear her, for she was suggesting that perhaps they were on their way to the war in Spain. Just as August snapped the shutter the town crier wheeled slowly by on his bicycle. As if it were a lamentation, this archaic man with his silver bell intoned the announcement that cards for the potato ration would be issued on the next day. Mellie and I, breaking our pose, turned to each other in astonishment. The butter ration, inaugurated a month or so before with fanfare and a slogan, had not seemed extraordinary—but potatoes—that *sine qua non* of every German table!

"I know what you're thinking," said August as if he had only now heard Mellie. "How many times do I have to tell you that Franco is in this thing alone? Are you deaf?"

At this time Persis Galt was blessedly preoccupied with a new project. She was gathering about herself a group who were to prepare themselves for becoming Benedictine oblates, the idea having come to her when Mellie's mother wrote that she was becoming one. Once every two weeks she summoned them all to dine with her at the Europaischer Hof and after the consommé and the pheasant, the artichokes, the Nesselrode and the Mosel and the brandy, they all recited compline. Mellie and I were obliged to attend these dinner parties because Persis, busy as she was, never forgot that she was our proprietor and gave us to understand that she and our parents were in close, indeed it might be said, in quotidian correspondence. She took us to the high mass at Stift Neuburg where none of us received; she brought us books of sermons and lives of saints and meditations, mawkish verses by ungifted nuns; and she behaved, in general, as if the house were on fire and there was no time to waste. At the same time Daddy was writing me endless letters of instruction and questions. He told me that he planned to come to Heidelberg in January; he expected me to come to Paris at Christmas.

A few days before Christmas there was a Day of Recollection at Stift Neuburg. At an interlude between services the ladies and several of the monks went across the road to the Wirtschaft to have tea before an open fire. Dom Paternus offered me a yellow apple, saying, "May I tempt you?" and everyone laughed but Persis, who turned blue with horror. A chair was drawn into the circle for Countess Tisza, who had just come in from the chapel, and when everyone had made a few minor adjustments and the Countess had declined tea (it was almost possible to hear her thinking, If I can't have whiskey, I don't want anything), the Prior, thinking that we had worn out the conversation we had been having about the spiders and reptiles of the Philippines from which Dom Bardo had recently returned, charmingly inquired of the Countess whether she had liked the new statue of St. Benedict in the entry.

The Countess, fixing him with sincere eyes (one could not help admiring her for the way she carried it off) replied, "Father Prior, explain it to me! Will you forgive me if I say it seems to me the sculptor hasn't captured Benedict at all?"

Dom Bardo, a white-haired urbane old man, chuckled cosily. "Good for you! I have an ally, Dom Prior. The Countess doesn't like it either." The grave face of the little noblewoman did not alter as she reproached the monk. "You are unkind, Father. I have only asked for an explanation."

I had seen the statue; it was roughhewn of quartz, an oddity in itself distracting, and what had struck me at first was that all the saint's appurtenances—the vase from which emerged the dragon's head, the raven at his feet clutching the loaf of bread, the crosier and the halo— were unconnected with the figure as if they had been put there as an afterthought; it was as though St. Benedict had annexed these things but their sponsorship remained that of the sculptor. It had occurred to Dom Prior too who, smiling at Dom Bardo, said, "I find it hideous. It's not only a travesty of Benedict, it's bad art. Michelangelo said that a really good piece of sculpture could be rolled down hill and not be broken in any part."

Persis Galt flushed and swallowed angrily. "The same could be applied to a barrel, Father." She went on to argue that the subject was so sacred that even the worst treatment of it could not be harming, that displeasing as the statue might be, they were bound in conscience to admire and revere it because it represented a saint. Poor Persis! In their own bailiwick the monks defied her and not even Dom Paternus came to her rescue, for it was she who had commissioned the statue and she who had paid its exorbitant price. But he took pity on her presently when it was time to go back to the monastery. "What are your Christmas plans? I hope you will make your duty with us."

She paled a little. "I am so sorry," she cried. "I've contracted to go to Strasbourg."

The monk turned then to me. "And what will you do? Will you go to your father in Paris?"

"I'm going to Freiburg," I said.

"To Freiburg?" demanded Persis. "I heard only yesterday from your father that he was expecting you in Paris."

"I've written him that I don't want to come to Paris until spring."

As we were leaving, and as Mellie and I refused the offer of a lift in Persis' car, she plucked me by the sleeve and said, "If I didn't know you so well, I'd think you were going off to be compromised." And she looked at me sharply, believing the opposite of what she said. "Who do you know in Freiburg?"

I wanted to say, "The same man you think will be in Strasbourg." For I knew that Strasbourg, just over the border from Karlsruhe, was where she and Max had often met in the past. But I said, "Friends from the boat."

6

I saw him for the last time in Freiburg. It began to snow in Baden-Baden, and as the train paused there a well-tailored Englishman passing through the corridor said over his shoulder to his companion, "God, what a beastly country! Have a look-see at that muck out there!" The snow drifting through the rafters of the train shed in the wintry light looked unclean as if it would smudge whatever it fell upon, and for a moment I wished that, like the Englishmen, I were leaving Germany, were leaving all this murkiness for some brilliant southern sky. In a disabling ennui I stared at two lovers who sat opposite me in the carriage, fingering each other's hands and exchanging bashful grins of rapture. I was displeased with the spectacle of them for I felt no rapture myself, and I closed my eyes to the dreary village and to the sweethearts and thought not of Max but of unimportant matters: the error in my week's bath bill, a fish stew at the Haarlass that had poisoned Mellie, a blouse I had seen and liked in a shop on the Hauptstrasse. I had been awake for years and years, I thought; this morning my eyes had opened wildly long before the sun was up when the bells were ringing for prime and, confused, I had thought it was Sunday. Adjusting the eiderdown, I had closed my eyes again and had said to myself, "God does not know I am awake."

A pall of grime hung over the bleak platform in Freiburg as it had hung over Baden-Baden, and because I moved through the station slowly I was too late to get a cab when finally I emerged through the storm doors. The Platz was deserted except for an old policeman who stood with his dog at the main entrance of the station. I advanced through the bountiful snowflakes and asked him the way to the Hotel Salmen.

"Heil Hitler!" he saluted me. "Straight ahead." He pointed down the wide avenue that began at the station yard and when he raised his white-gloved hand once more and we said in unison, "Heil Hitler!" he smiled at me out of some spontaneous happiness, and though I was surprised I smiled back. "The snow!" he exclaimed to me. "So beautiful!"

The air, with this gentle, mothlike snow, was sweet after the close compartment, which had been blue with the smoke of all the cigarettes and sour with the reek of red wine that a sullen soldier had steadily drunk out of his canteen. A little canal ran at the side of the street; but for its soft sound there was an immense quiet in the avenue and nothing seemed to stir within the timbered houses through whose closed shutters came bent shafts of light.

Max was waiting for me in the public bar, sitting at a table drinking a brandy and looking, in his civilian clothes, like all the tall lean sanitary Englishmen sitting at other tables alone or in pairs, also drinking brandy. I had not been prepared for so immediate a meeting in so great a throng and I was upset to see that there was a

second glass on the table and that he meant our rendez-
vous to be begun in this crowded, brightly lighted place
full of skiers loquaciously recounting their day's adventures. He did not see me at first. He was fitting a cigarette into his holder and only when he snapped open his
lighter did he look up. He rose then and waited for me
to cross the room: I thought, he would never come to
meet me. He drew out a chair for me and he could not
help touching my shoulder, lightly and in a way no one
could see; and leaning over the table he said, "Ah, I am
so eager." Someone was somewhere inexpertly playing
Chopin on a piano with a crackly tone, but there was
delicacy in the playing, and in the moment between our
greeting and our conversation, I listened pleased. Our
conversation, when it began at last, was as urgent and
shapeless as that of any other lovers who, but for their
love, would have remained strangers. There was no
point in which we lost ourselves in interest of what we
were saying, and the talk around us was as pertinent to
us as anything we might whisper to each other.

A very old man with a thick mustache and spectacles
sat drinking Glühwein with his wife. He said in a high,
peckish voice, "That young woman was unmannerly
about my eggs."

His wife tenderly touched his hand. "All the same,
Franz, the sun was lovely. You said so yourself."

"Yes, yes, all right," he said irritably. "The sun *was*
lovely. I said so then and I say so now. But I repeat, that
girl was rude about my eggs."

"Persis knows I'm here," I said to Max. "I told her I
was coming."

"It's all right," he said. "She thinks I'm meeting her
in Strasbourg tomorrow."

"Is there—" I decided I did not want to ask him a question about the war in Spain just then.

At the table on our left an Englishman and a Frenchman sat together. The Frenchman said, "I have been refreshing my memory of Florence," and withdrew a map from his coat pocket. He added with humble woe, "For I shall not ever see it again."

"What are you talking about?" said his companion.

Max and I waited for the Frenchman's answer as if it had something close to do with us.

"I'm afraid I haven't made myself clear to you, Montgomery," said the Frenchman. "I'm not what you think I am at all. I am no intellectual although at one time in my life it was said by a number of my teachers that I didn't have a half bad brain. My plan to seek culture in the culture centers of Italy was just my little joke, poor as it was. The fact is that I am about to be married to a widow of great respectability who owns a pension in Passy. We met on a bus last summer to Fontainebleau. She is one okay dame."

"Is that the end of the American lesson for today?" asked the bored Englishman. "You ought to take better care of yourself."

"You mean I'm nuts?" The Frenchman laughed. "What a wag I am. Good lord, yes."

The smell of evergreens was as strong as mint in the warm room. Skiers warmed their feet at the fireplace and bragged of the jumps they had made and the climbs so steep they had had to use bearskins on their skis. A heavily pregnant cat sat on the stool beside the fire. If I had not been taught better, I would have thought that all of this belonged to the real world and that we were present in it. But I was not so fooled; what we saw and what we heard, though we received and though we acted with absorption, came adventitiously, did not last, meant nothing.

All my selves but one spoke falsely when I said, "I have never been happier."

Max said, "I shall never be this happy again."

Everyone in the bar was enjoying himself, everyone, that is, but the cross old man, who smoothed the bristles of the goatbeard in his green hat and continued to mope over his eggs. Two pretty blond American girls sat smiling like dummies with two men who were perhaps their fathers or perhaps their sugar-daddies. The men observed mildly that the mark was up, that it was a pleasure to travel in Germany with the present rate of exchange, that there had been a scientist fellow in Cologne who had had some interesting things to say about the pressure at the bottom of the hotel swimming pool.

"If you had come earlier," said Max, "we could have taken the *Bergbahn* to the Schauinsland and had drinks there. I would have managed the *Bergbahn* better than I did the funicular."

"I wish I had. I wish everything bad could be canceled out by something good."

"That's wishing for the moon."

He told me that he had lived three years in Freiburg when he was a child and that he had learned to ski in the mountains that surrounded the town. It was in keeping with the piecemeal nature of our relationship that I knew nothing of his background and that he knew nothing of mine; indeed, it had hardly occurred to me that he had been a child. "I was told that a sort of witch called the Budelfrau lived on the top of the Schlossberg and had marvelous eyes that could see mischief but not good. I thought she lived beside a path-marker and whenever I went up to ski, I was certain I was going to crash into it and break all my bones. I can't imagine why. I was far too good a child for the Budel-frau to bother with."

"I am sure you were," and I had never been more sure of anything. I could see him, as silent and forbear-ing as a saint, walking unmolested through all the ter-rors of childhood, never knowing the need for armor until he was eighteen and it was too late.

We killed another half an hour with another brandy. And then lightly, as if he were offering me another piece of information as casual as that about the Budelfrau, he said, "Did I tell you I am off to Spain?"

"To Spain?" I said, mimicking his grace and calm. "To the war?"

"What else? Would I go to look at pictures at this time of this particular year?"

"I'm sorry," I said.

"I imagine you really are," said Max. "And the pity of it is that I can know and that even so I can't really wish I weren't going. I don't believe in the damned war, but I don't care. I haven't any politics and I haven't any ideals."

I was sure he really did not mind going; in a sense, he had gone already, already he was dead and buried in an unimaginable land, and already he was no more than a memory to me; but a memory indispensable and im-prisoning.

"It's too bad you don't care," I said. "I think I would."

"It *is* a waste," he said. "It would be wonderful to be

a Christian or entirely to love one's country. Entirely loving oneself would be the best of all."

"Do you have to go? I don't want you to go, Max." In spite of my resolutions, I was dying hard.

"I'm grateful, Fanny, I really am. But, yes, of course I have to go, and I have no intention of coming back. You understand, it is not I do not *hope* to come back but I don't *intend*."

"Oh, think of me! Think for a moment of me!" I really was angry now and I cried, "You're vain and sentimental!"

"Certainly," he said crisply. "I am a German."

"For God's sake tell the waiter to bring us some glasses of a sensible *size*," I said. "And before I forget it, who is Elizabeth?"

He smiled, "My sister. Only my poor sister."

We had dinner in our rooms. As the waiter arranged the table with lobster from Hamburg, figs and oranges from Italy, wine from Alsace, I intently studied a map of the mountains that lay under a glass slab on the desk, making a note of the names: Güntersthal, Schauinsland, Feldberg, as if I were getting them by heart for an examination. I would take with me nothing new except these names. If Max died in Spain, and now I felt sure he would for he had willed himself to die, I thought I would not mourn him very long. It was not at all that I did not love him (Oh, but did I? Oh, it was a dismembering confusion!), was not sunk into this love as permanently as into stone, but that in willing himself to die, he forbade me to interfere with his plans. Turning as the waiter closed the door and Max opened a bottle of champagne, I went to take my glass and across the room, as if from across a field of flowers, I called, "I love you," as if they were the last words I was ever to utter in my life.

It was a long night and this was the only one, for orders had come for the bootleg troops; they were to be sent out on the day after Christmas and all leaves had been curtailed. When it was daylight we went to the windows and looked out at the stiff vineyards on their zigzagged arbors. The bells began to ring for Lord Jesus, their tones commingled and cadenced against one another like a madrigal. I had put on the quilted jacket he had brought for my Christmas present: its design was of blue hunters on red horses with yellow dogs running at their feet. And I had taken the sea shell from Naples out of my coin purse and put it into one of the pockets. We stood listening to the bells and to the wind's wings beating the branches of the cedar trees against the window-panes.

"Will Persis go mad at losing you?" I asked.

"She'll find another paschal youth," he said. "But I doubt if she'll find another Jew. There aren't many of us left."

"Max! Oh, Max! Oh, my God!"

"Hush, Fanny. Listen, my sister is taking my rooms for a few weeks until she can get to England, but she won't be there for a day or so. Here is the key. If you want anything, take it." Dressed in his slate blue uniform, his cape loose at his shoulders, he was at the door.

"Persis knows? Is that her blackmail?"

"Hush, Fanny." He opened the door.

"*Aufwiedersehen,* Max," I said.

"*Lebewohl.*"

7

Elizabeth Rössler never came to Heidelberg and I never could bring myself to go to his rooms. I had a letter from her, though, sent from Berlin. It said, coldly and dutifully in perfect English, that Max had been killed "on maneuvers near Karlsruhe" and that he had directed in his last letter that I be notified if anything happened to him. The day I got it I bicycled to Heilbronn with Mellie and two rowdy American boys. We played poker all night long and got drunk on atrocious champagne, I had a wonderful time.

There was a day when Persis Galt came to my room at the Haarlass to say that a friend of Godfrey's had seen Max and me in Freiburg. I was too woebegone to fear her; she was too afraid of me to scold me. She had come, craven, to drive a bargain with me: we would keep each other's secrets. I agreed although I did not give a damn. She was in her masquerade of tweeds and I pitied her immensely.

My father died that May in Paris and I came back to Boston and my aunts.

Soon the scene from my window will begin gradually to change; I find myself reluctant to think that the leaves will presently be coming out. Similarly, I remember, Heidelberg was intolerable to me when the wild plum began to bloom. I hardly dared go into the hills for fear of meeting pairs of sweethearts; I scarcely dared look out the windows of the veranda for fear they would be rowing on the river to Neckar-Gemünd. There had always been the danger that I would mourn

Max, that I would miss him, would become inward about him. It had been necessary to get back to America to return to the exterior. And so, until I was summoned to Paris to Daddy dying of a thrombosis, I hid in my Gothic grammar, in the confessional boxes and in my room, half hallucinated by the Haarlass homemade red wine. I never thought of the future and I never thought of the immediate past. I lived in a heavy stupefaction.

It is warm today and the window is open. At half past five I throw the sea shell out and see it caught in the tall privet before my house. I am exalted; I believe that I am altogether purged. I look at the clock that still reads twelve and I say, "Goodbye, then, *lebewohl.*"

When *did* that clock stop? Midnight or noon? Someone has come into my room and I wheel to face my husband. He sees the decanter beside the long chair and he sees the glass in my hand and he sounds like Daddy when he says, "Fanny, I don't like this at all."

"Do like it," I say and laugh and hold out both hands to him. "I've decided to give up trying to write poetry." He really should not look so pleased.

"Well, in that case—" he says and pours a glass for himself. "Isn't that jacket new?"

"No, it's old. It's as old as the hills."

"It's hideous," he says. He is right; perhaps seventeen years ago it was not so coy as it is now. I turn back to the stuck clock for a split second and during it I think, my God, Jew or not he was a Nazi; and then I think, what did Nazi mean when I was twenty? So, finding no reason for preserving my guilt, I watch it give up the ghost. Tomorrow at this time we will be in Bermuda.

"I know it's hideous," I say. "But Nan won't know it is."